FRIED BY JURY

CLAUDIA BISHOP

BERKLEY PRIME CRIME, NEW YORK

This is a work of fiction. Names, characters, places, and incidents either are the product of the author's imagination or are used fictitiously, and any resemblance to actual persons, living or dead, business establishments, events, or locales is entirely coincidental.

FRIED BY JURY

A Berkley Prime Crime Book / published by arrangement with the author

PRINTING HISTORY
Berkley Prime Crime mass-market edition / May 2003

ISBN: 0-425-18994-5

Berkley Prime Crime Books are published
by The Berkley Publishing Group,
a division of Penguin Group (USA) Inc.,
375 Hudson Street, New York, New York 10014.
The name BERKLEY PRIME CRIME and the
BERKLEY PRIME CRIME design
are trademarks belonging to Penguin Group (USA) Inc.

PRINTED IN THE UNITED STATES OF AMERICA

10 9 8 7 6 5 4 3 2 1

CHARLES SHEFFIELD
1935–2002

Acknowledgment

Many thanks to Jean Drake—who named Captain Cluck. And the warmest regards to Pam Wissore—who contributed to this title.

CHAPTER 1

"Judge a deep-fat frying contest? Here? In Hemlock Falls? I'd rather eat a rat!" Margaret Quilliam held her sauté pan over the flames on the gas stove and poured a few drops of extra virgin olive oil into it. Perhaps finding her preference for rodent a little too direct, she added politely, "I mean, no, thank you."

Meg's addendum didn't fool any of the three people sitting in the kitchen at the Inn at Hemlock Falls—not Mayor Elmer Henry, not Marge Schmidt, and especially not Meg's older sister, Quill, who'd been against asking Meg to judge the Fry Away Home deep-fat fried cooking contest in the first place.

Quill occupied the rocker by the cobblestone fireplace, which was at right angles to the main work area in the kitchen. Marge and the mayor sat at the prep table directly across from the stove. Not the safest spot if Meg decided to throw something.

Meg scattered chopped scallions into the pan and shook it gently over the burner. Meg was short, and so was her hair. She looked like a raffish elf. She wore cotton sweatpants, beat-up running shoes with the laces untied, and as a concession to the unusual warmth of the day (it was May in upstate New York), a skimpy halter-top. Her socks were the best indicator of the state of her temper. Quill had already checked them out: Vesuvius-red. Not a good sign at all.

The scent of sautéed scallions, garlic, olive oil, and butter rose into the air and collided with the smell of lilacs drifting through the open windows. Outside, the lawns and grounds of the Inn at Hemlock Falls lay gentle with the tender green of spring. Inside, the old beamed kitchen was just as pleasant, with its well-scrubbed birch countertops, hanging copper pans, dried herbs, and flagstone floors.

Quill rocked and tugged pensively at her hair.

"Now, Meg, just settle down and think about why you should judge." Elmer Henry—a stout and balding man who became stouter and balder every year—ran one finger nervously around his shirt collar. He'd dressed for weather usual to Hemlock Falls in May (damp and cold), but his thick wool sports jacket was already slung over one shoulder in an attempt to escape the heat. From his surreptitious scratching, it looked as if he wanted to get rid of his Husky Man's gray wool trousers, too.

"We might as well pack it in," Marge Schmidt said. Her lower lip jutted out like a cowcatcher on a small locomotive. "She's not gonna do it."

Elmer turned pink with earnest effort. "Some of the greatest chefs in the country have judged the Fry Away Home contest. Last year it was in New Orleans. Year before that it was San Francisco. And this year Harry Holcomb picks Hemlock Falls, New York, for Pete's sake. We're asking you to judge this world-famous national contest and you're turning us down?"

"Yep."

Marge grunted. "Told ya. You know why? She's a food snob." Marge, the richest citizen in Tompkins County, had achieved a lot in life by favoring the direct approach. "And Harry Holcomb's offering twenty-five thousand bucks to whoever judges the contest, to boot. So you're goin' to be a poverty-stricken food snob."

"I'm not a food snob," Meg said indignantly. "And I don't care about the money."

"Everybody should care about money," Marge said, affronted. "Everybody does, except you. You really turn down that TV show and that expensive job cookin' in New York? That's what I heard down to the diner. I couldn't b'lieve it. I could *not* believe it."

Quill could believe it. Meg *had* quit her three-day-a-week star turn at La Strazza. And she'd backed out of Lally Preston's TV show, too.

"I care about money," Meg said indignantly once more. "I just don't care that much. I care more about food. And I'm not a food snob, Marge. I love food. I respect food. I'll try anything once. But deep-fat frying? Ugh. You might just as well use Kleenex as flour. Double ugh. Or wrap the food in Michael Jordan's sweatsocks and fry *that*. Triple ugh. Or . . ."

"Fine," Marge said shortly. "We get the message. Forget it. We don't want you messing around with this contest anyway. Like as not, with you *and* your sister in on it, we'd end up with half the folks who signed up deader than door-nails, and who needs that kind of publicity? We've had more than enough of that already."

This candid, if unfortunately phrased reference to the number of murder cases Meg and Quill had solved in the past didn't seem to bother anyone but Quill, who made an apologetic face to no one in particular.

"There's no *taste* to fat-fried food," Meg continued in her best runaway tractor-trailer style. She ran her free hand through her short dark hair. "It all tastes like Crisco! And who wants to eat Crisco?! Just look at what people fry and eat. Anything. Ants. Rattlesnake. Elvis Presley fried dill pickles. And does any of it taste like ant, rattlesnake, or dill pickle? It does not! It tastes like Crisco. Deep-fat frying is anti-food. Nullified food. Null food. There ought," Meg added darkly, "to be some kind of law against it." She banged the sauté pan on the prep counter and scowled. She didn't look like an elf anymore, Quill thought. More like a rabid pug.

"Well, jeez," Elmer said feebly. "Tell us what you really think. Har-har."

Nobody else laughed.

Meg waved a wooden spoon menacingly. "Those bodies you mentioned, Marge? You're right. Corpses will litter the contest tent. You betcha. But from heart attacks, Marge. Not because Quill and I attract murder. No siree. People will drop dead from all the clogged arteries. Boom!" She thwacked the wooden spoon. "Boom!" She thwacked it again. "Bo—"

"Stop," Quill said.

"Fine." Meg tossed the wooden spoon on the floor. "That stuff's not a killer? Look at what happened to Elvis, for Pete's sake."

"You lay off of Elvis," Elmer interrupted heatedly. "That man could sing."

"Fine. But he's dead, isn't he?"

Marge looked as if she was about to take issue with this. Meg held up her hand in warning. "No. I will not judge the Fry Away Home contest. Period. I am amazed," she said loftily, "that you even asked."

"Who else could we ask?" Elmer said with transparent guile. "The best chef in the whole of the Eastern U.S. of A., that's who."

Meg shrugged in supreme indifference.

Like Tennyson's Six Hundred, the mayor persevered in the face of defeat, mostly, Quill thought, because the rival chef who had tentatively agreed to judge the contest wanted a lot more than the twenty-five thousand Mr. Holcomb had agreed to pay. And it was all Elmer's fault. The mayor was going to have to find more money if Meg bugged out. And the Hemlock Falls Chamber of Commerce was not in charity with Elmer at the moment. Not at all.

Quill pulled her sketchpad from her skirt pocket and tried to concentrate on drawing a weeping willow in new bud in the hemlock grove next to the Inn. Elmer's hectoring intruded on her like a fly buzzing around a freshly painted room. Reluctantly, she dragged her attention back to the conversation.

The mayor was in full persuasive swing, like an over-stocked Chevy dealer trying to get rid of a used Hyundai. "Meg, the three of us here feel privileged to be appointed as the Special Fry Away Home Task Force." He paused impressively and repeated, "Privileged."

Quill found this dubious. She didn't feel privileged to be part of the task force. She felt harassed. But she hadn't the backbone to say no when Elmer had dragooned her into being on the committee. She and Meg were co-owners of the twenty-seven-room Inn. And as the mayor pointed out, there was no tactful way the Inn could avoid some involvement in the Fry Away Home cooking competition. Not in a village the size of Hemlock Falls—whose population was currently four thousand five hundred and thirty-six, excluding tourists. The Inn was the village's third largest employer. And Meg was the only chef with a national reputation for three hundred miles in any direction. She didn't see him, Elmer Henry, shirking his duty, did she? He hadda do it. Because the office of mayor was well, the mayor. And Marge knew her duty, too, even though she was the richest person in Tompkins County and could retire to Florida any time she wanted. In a million-dollar RV, if she wanted to.

That was what the mayor had said.

Quill sighed, gently.

Elmer persisted. "Yes, we're privileged. Aren't we, girls?"

Marge shot him a look as girlish as an alligator. Quill herself let the comment pass. She'd just finished a course at the nearby Cornell School for Hotel Management called *Dealing with Sexism in the Workplace*. The most effective response to demeaning, politically incorrect hoo-ha-ism from the mayor was cheerful obliviousness. Which was nice, because Quill had always found obliviousness easier than most people did.

The mayor charged on as if stumping for office, which, in a way he was. The town wasn't about to reelect a mayor who'd cost them a ton of money in chef's fees. "I mean to say, Quill, Marge and me, we're in charge of this whole danged festival, practically. We have the full political confidence of the Hemlock Falls Chamber of Commerce behind us. All twenty-four of 'em. The Fry Away Home festival's going to be one of the most important celebrations of the whole calendar year."

"So? Why hassle me to judge the stupid thing?" Meg asked in a sensible way. "You guys don't need me."

Quill watched the mayor's reaction with interest. Elmer scratched furiously at his trousers, rubbed his nose, and started to bluster.

This was a sensitive point in the meeting, and she and Marge had anticipated it. Harry Holcomb wanted celebrity chef Banion O'Haggerty to judge the contest. O'Haggerty's standard fee was twenty-five thousand. That was the price of having the world-famous chef, and Holcomb was willing to pay.

"Didn't he, Quill?" the mayor demanded.

"Yes," Quill said, who'd missed most of the harangue.

"You see, Meg? Quill was right there in the office, too. Mr. Holcomb himself insisted I take charge. Me. Personally. And when he asked me how come he should choose Hemlock Falls for this important event, all I had to do was lean over and whisper one name: Margaret Quilliam. That's what I told him, right there in the boardroom of Holcomb's Wholesome Fried Chicken, Inc. In Detroit City. Chef Quilliam? Holcomb says to me. Well, Elmer. If you can get *her* you got me. And Holcomb's Wholesome Fried Chicken, too. That's what he said."

Actually, it hadn't gone that way at all. Which was why Quill would rather be doing something really safe right now—like roller-blading down Route 96 into Ithaca at rush hour—rather than explain to Meg the consequences of her refusal to judge the contest. In reality, Holcomb had dismissed Meg's credentials with a wave of one elegantly manicured hand and demanded that they get a judge whose reputation rivaled Emeril's, that is, Banion O'Haggerty. The field of three or four chefs with world-famous reputations was small. Meg got along with all of them—sort of—but she hated Banion O'Haggerty. Which was beside the point, because O'Haggerty could stay at the Marriott, and the contest was going to be held at the high school athletic field and Meg didn't have to meet him at all.

All that was okay. Not fine, but okay. So Marge asked O'Haggerty to judge the contest—to keep Quill out of it, and to keep the mayor well out of it.

O'Haggerty had temporized. He'd hedged. He'd asked for thirty thousand dollars. Elmer had jumped into the negotiations. And somehow, some way, (Elmer wasn't talking) O'Haggerty had increased his asking price to fifty thousand dollars, because, O'Haggerty said, he always added a pain in the ass charge if he ran into a pain in the ass.

Holcomb refused to come up with the extra money, so the mayor had to make up the shortage.

O'Haggerty was due to give the mayor his final answer within seventy-two hours. Quill didn't know what they were going to do if Meg accepted and the other guy did too, but the mayor had waved this possibility away with cheerful insouciance. Leave the politics to him, he'd said. Ya had ta go with the flow when you were playin' with the big boys, he'd said. He personally could skim these rapids like a champ.

In Quill's opinion, the mayor's canoe was about to sink. She rubbed her nose and contributed an opinion. "There are worse sponsors than Holcomb, Meggie. Holcomb's Wholesome Chicken isn't all that bad, as fast food goes. They use canola oil, and they offer a whole line of heart-healthy chicken as well as the fried stuff. I mean, we could be talking Captain Cluck here, instead of Holcomb's Wholesome."

"Cluck!" Marge said with a derisive snort. "That fathead."

The Captain Cluck chicken franchise—Holcomb's chief and most-hated rival—had been cited by the FDA for so many violations of the Safe Foods Act that the stock had dropped 30 percent in the boom economy of the year 2000. (There was a persistent rumor that the American Heart Association was considering a series of wrongful death litigation, but Quill herself put that into the urban myth category. She didn't think that Captain Cluck used mouse parts in its infamous Chicken Nibblers, either. Or at least, not enough mouse parts to justify a real health threat.)

"I don't see what's so wrong with Captain Cluck," the mayor said a little defensively. "That stuff's not so bad."

Quill made a face. Captain Cluck (Charlie Kluckenpacker to his few friends and the editors of *Fortune* magazine) was sole owner of Captain Cluck's Crispy Chicken, and a folk hero to those Republicans who believed that the federal government had no business interfering with a guy who was just trying to make a buck.

Marge blew her nose into a red bandanna she'd pulled from her pocket, and then said forcefully, "Let's get back to the main point, here. Meg, as you're the only official three-star gourmet chef in these parts, we had to ask you to judge this contest before we confirmed anybody else. I knew what the answer'd be, and I dunno why the heck we're wasting our time with you." She swung her machine gun turret eyes to Quill. "But we got to have somebody famous. Holcomb deserves a break, here. He's setting up a Holcomb's Wholesome out on Route 15, which is going to help bring a few more folks down to Hemlock Falls, and this contest of his is going to pull a lot of national media attention."

"How nice," Meg said. "I wish you and Mr. Holcomb all the best. But I just don't have the time."

"So. You turned us down." Elmer shot a desperate look at Quill, which upset her considerably, because she'd told him so, and she couldn't do anything about it. Then with a disingenuous air that wouldn't have fooled a poodle, he said, "Who else we got down to judge, Quill?"

Quill jumped a little at this frontal assault. They'd agreed that the best way to ease Meg into things was to encourage her to offer to find a substitute. Meg being Meg, she'd get busy and forget about it, and then the mayor would act surprised and delighted that Holcomb's own celebrity candidate had accepted the job. That was the plan, anyway.

"You must have *somebody* in mind, Quill," Elmer said with a spuriously innocent air.

Quill gave him an indignant look. She hadn't liked this elaborate deception in the first place. But at least Elmer had volunteered to drop the bomb himself. And now Elmer was off script.

"Quill hasn't heard a word you've said," Meg said kindly, though inaccurately. "She's thinking about something else altogether." Meg squinted at Quill. "What *are* you waiting for, Quill? You guys knew before you asked me I'd say no. So what's up?"

There was another short silence. Marge looked at Quill and raised her ginger-colored eyebrows in an inquiring expression. Quill looked at Meg's socks. They were a very violent red. "Um," she temporized. Then, "We do have to find someone, Meg. Who would you suggest?"

The mayor opened his mouth, and then shut it with a yelp when Marge kicked him in the ankle.

Meg frowned suspiciously at all of them, added a splash of vermouth, a pinch of dill, and a handful of peeled shrimp to the mixture in the pan, tasted it with a wooden spoon and made a face. She handed the wooden spoon to Marge.

Marge sipped, chewed, smacked her lips thoughtfully, and shook her head.

Meg dumped the pan's contents into the prep sink.

"Hey!" Elmer protested. "That looked pretty good to me!"

"It was okay," Marge said, "but just okay. Not much of

a snap to it. You gotta be better with shrimp than that."

"This is why we need you to judge," Elmer said, peering wistfully at the shrimp in the sink. "You got standards, Meg. And they're priced right, too."

"Marge has standards," Meg said, which was true. Marge and her partner had owned several diners in Hemlock Falls—all of them successful. "She and Betty would be great judges. They do some of the best American home cooking in upstate New York—"

"Further away than that," Marge interrupted with a truculent air.

"Including deep-frying perfectly acceptable things like potatoes. But I. I am philosophically opposed to the practice of deep-frying itself. So forget it. And what do you mean, my standards are priced right?"

Elmer shrugged innocently. "You ain't cheap," he admitted. "But you aren't demanding any fifty thousand dollars, either."

"Fifty thousand dollars?" Meg said. "Who the heck is worth fifty thousand dollars for a one-day show?"

"You make Monsieur Croque," Quill said in an attempt at a diversion. "You said you don't deep-fat fry food, but you do. You've had fried food on the menu before." She responded to the Mayor's bemused expression: "Monsieur Croque is a French version of ham and cheese sandwiches, deep-fried. And tempura, too, Meg. You make a terrific tempura. And Artichokes French."

Meg nodded. Anyone else would have said the expression on her face was that of a reasonable woman. Quill knew better. "True. True," Meg said. *"But it's not the same!"*

"So I don't get it," the mayor said. "You fry that stuff pretty good, from all accounts. So what's the problem?"

"Commercial deep-fat frying's hot, sticky, smelly, dangerous stuff." Meg picked up her boning knife and regarded it with a thoughtful expression. "And the commercial fryers soak the fat into the food." She slid her whetstone from a drawer in the prep table and dropped a bit of oil on the surface. "The fat takes over. And I won't do it." She began to sharpen the knife with complete absorption.

Marge and the mayor exchanged meaningful glances.

"Thing is, we need a celebrity chef," the mayor said with a sigh. "We don't get you, we're gonna have to ask somebody else."

"Go right ahead," Meg said cordially. "Quill knows who's available. Get some suggestions from her."

Marge and the mayor grinned in triumph.

"Quill?" the mayor asked. "You got a suggestion, don't you?"

Quill fought down a cowardly desire to run out of the kitchen to somewhere safe—like Myles McHale's sheriff's office on Main Street. Meg couldn't commit too much mayhem if she, Quill, were safely locked in the slammer. Although at some point, she would have to come out.

Quill funked it. If Meg's socks had been pink, even, rather than red, she might have plunged in and put the chef's name right out in front of her sister. Instead, she said, "Well, you know the guys better than I do, Meg."

"Sure I do. And as long as it isn't Banion O'Haggerty, I'm cool with whomever you want." Meg drew the boning knife along the edge of the sharpener, and then tested the edge with her thumb. "I hate," Meg said calmly, "Banion O'Haggerty. If Banion O'Haggerty sets one foot in this town, he's toast."

This silence was a lot longer than the first one.

Quill did not shout, "I told you so!" Instead, she flipped to a fresh page in her sketchbook and made a rapid drawing of Meg with her eyes bugged out in rage, whirling her sharpest chef's knife over her head and pursuing a panicked little Quill.

Marge prodded on, "So it's not the whole idea of Quill getting a celebrity cook in for a couple of days that bugs you? Just this guy Banion O'Haggerty?"

"Me!" Quill said indignantly. "It's not just me who's in

charge of judge recruitment! We're on this committee together!"

There was an infinitesimal pause in Meg's knife sharpening. "I said I don't mind and I mean I don't mind." Meg set the knife aside, wiped out the sauté pan with a fresh kitchen towel, and grabbed the olive oil. "What I *do* mind is the three of you goggling in my kitchen while I've got forty pounds of fresh shrimp on hand, and no interesting way to prepare it. What I *do* mind is a lot of mindless palaver when I Am Trying To Cook! What I *wouldn't* mind is if you all got out of here and left me in peace! The editor of *L'Aperitif* is coming to eat in *my* dining room in *three days* and I promised her a new way of preparing shrimp!"

"Fine," Marge said.

"We'll leave you alone," Quill said.

"Thank goodness," the mayor said. "Thing is, Meg, we already asked—"

Marge grabbed the mayor by the left arm; Quill tugged on his right. They pulled him through the swinging doors to the dining room.

The mayor shook himself free of their clutching arms with an assumption of dignity. "I knew what I was doing," he said. "As mayor of this town I pretty much always know what I'm doing."

Neither Marge nor Quill rose to this tempting bait.

"You should have let me tell her," the mayor complained.

"O'Haggerty hasn't said yes, yet," Quill pointed out. "What if he turns us down? There's no reason not to wait to tell her until we know for certain."

Marge tugged at her bowling jacket. "We're making progress at least. We asked, she said no. Now she's got the idea we have to get somebody else. Fine. We give her a while to get used to it. We'll tell her who it is soon enough."

"We haven't got all that much time," Elmer pointed out. "Mr. Holcomb's media campaign's movin' full throttle day after tomorrow, according to Harvey Bozzel. And Holcomb wants Banion O'Haggerty."

"You better start gettin' creative, Elmer. You're gonna have to come up with that extra twenty-five k."

Elmer took out his handkerchief, mopped his face with it, and said with false heartiness, "I told you guys. No problem. I screwed up, sure, but we're gonna make enough on our part of the ticket sales to cover it."

Marge pursed her mouth. "Oh, yeah? And what if we don't?"

"We'll cross that bridge when we come to it. I'm just as glad Meg said no. He's a lot better than Meg, as a matter of fact, 'cause he's got that TV show. More people know who he is. And she hates him. So what? How bad can it get?"

"Maybe O'Haggerty will say no," Quill said feebly. "And Meg will reconsider."

"He won't say no to fifty thousand smackers," the mayor said with all the conviction of a true Rotarian.

"Meg did," Marge said. "Well, to half of it. And if O'Haggerty says no, we got to try maybe Julia Child or the Iron Chef. Or that kid from England. Who knows what kind of money they'll ask for at the last minute? Time's running out, here."

Elmer's washed-out blue eyes widened at the thought of spending even more money. "You're right, Margie. We got to sit down and plan this out right here, right now. And I wouldn't mind a little something for my stomach while we're deciding, either." He looked around the dining room with an air of mild surprise at the lack of something to eat.

Quill loved her dining room. The carpet this year was a deep French blue. The tables were laid with heavy cream cloths. Cutlery and glassware shone in the flood of sunshine coming through the floor to ceiling windows. The mahogany-paneled walls gleamed with polish. Outside the floor-to-ceiling windows, the waterfall unrolled over the lip of the Gorge like a bolt of gray-green silk. It was ten o'clock in the morning—too late for breakfast and too early for lunch.

"Lots of places to sit and eat," the mayor said eagerly.

"The kitchen can come up with something," Quill said, her hospitality automatic.

"Not here. It's not far enough from the kitchen." Marge clapped her hands together briskly. "Meg'd be in here like a shot wanting to know what's going on. And I agree with Quill, we don't want to borrow trouble when trouble'll come soon enough. We could go to the Tavern Lounge, maybe."

"Then all we'll have to eat is brioche or rolls," Quill said firmly. "The wait staff won't be here for another hour and Meg will be furious if we ask one of the kitchen staff to run all the way out to the lounge with a full breakfast."

Elmer sighed wistfully. "But she said it'd be okay to invite somebody else to judge. She said—"

Marge poked him in the back. "Start walkin'. I don't care what she said. You watch what she was doing with that knife? Sharpening it. Sheesh. I don't want her coming after me."

Quill led them through the dining room, past the foyer where Dina Muir sat behind the reception desk, head buried in a textbook on freshwater pond ecology, and through the flagstone passage to the Lounge. There were a few coffee drinkers and brioche eaters here—most of them tourists on their way through Hemlock Falls to somewhere else. By common, unspoken consent, the three of them chose a table farthest from the small crowd.

Marge sat down with a grunt. Quill signaled Nate, who was polishing wine glasses behind the long curved mahogany bar, for three coffees then sank into a chair next to the mayor with a sigh. "I don't like it," she said. "I'm a Quisling. A Benedict Arnold. A Robert Hansen."

Marge chuckled. The mayor looked bewildered.

Quill stuck both hands in her hair and tugged at it. "I hate keeping this from Meg."

"We'll know soon enough," the mayor said importantly. "I got a call into Harry's office and he's going to get back to me as soon as he hears from O'Haggerty's agent." He seemed surprisingly sanguine for a mayor who was going to have to come up with twenty-five thousand dollars in an election year.

"Harry?" Marge said. "You call him Harry, now? You on a first name basis with Holcomb? Since when?"

"You aren't the only businessman in this town, Marge Schmidt. Harry needed a lot of advice from me on the zoning for the franchise store he's putting up on Route 15. Put the whole thing in my hands. Elmer, he says to me, I'm counting on you to have the way clear the minute those backhoes roll into town to start the foundation work."

"You think you're gonna talk Holcomb into that twenty-five grand, don't you. You're a damn fool, Elmer," Marge said flatly.

Elmer inflated like an affronted gander. "Because Harry didn't come to you first, Ms. High and Mighty Financier? There's other people in this town that know just as much as you do about getting business done with the backroom boys."

"No. One thing you've never learned, Elmer, is that there're no such things as buddies in business. Guy that's your best friend one week is the guy who's taking over your business the next. Business," said Marge with a fond expression, "is a lot like war."

Elmer's woebegone expression got to Quill. "It doesn't mean he doesn't like you, Elmer. And it doesn't mean he doesn't want you to call him Harry. It's just . . . Marge is right. I don't think Mr. Holcomb is going to give you the extra money, either."

"I got it covered." His pocket beeped the first notes of "For He's a Jolly Good Fellow." "Hang on, hang on," Elmer said importantly. He pulled his cell phone out and snapped it open. A bright raspberry phone, Quill noted, a really bilious color. "His Honor, here," he barked.

Marge folded her arms under her considerable bosom, leaned back in her chair and chewed her gum with a thoughtful air. Quill herself was uncertain about the niceties of cell phone etiquette. When a member of your party started blabbering away about private stuff in a public place, what did you do? Stare at the ceiling? Pretend you were deaf? Start another conversation so it wouldn't appear you were listening in?

"Okay, Charlie," Elmer said. Then, "You got it, Charlie. You're one of the big boys." He chuckled. Then he chuckled again. Then he said "Bye, Charlie" and hung up.

Quill and Marge stared at him.

"Tell me that wasn't who I think it was," Marge said, ominously.

"You weren't talking to Charles Kluckenpacker, were you?" Quill asked.

To her astonishment, Elmer turned beet-red and yelled, "*So* what if it was?! What d'ya mean, Quill! If you're accusing me of some kind of deal to cheat this town! Well, you can't, that's all!" Elmer twisted his large red hands back and forth in agitation. Quill laid her own hand on his wrist and said, "Of course not, Elmer! Why would you think that?"

"What I think is that you two gals don't know a thing about the way things get done in this town . . ."

Quill thought that she was going to get very tired of the phrase "this town."

"And you know what? I'm goin' to tell you how much I think of this tow—"

"Stop," Quill said.

"One of the finest businessmen in these United States, yes, I mean Charles Andrew Kluckenpacker, the man who just made a personal call himself to me, right now? Well, Charlie has a lot of confidence in Elmer Carrington Henry."

Marge snickered. "You gonna handle him like you handled O'Haggerty? End up owin' him out of your own pocket?"

Elmer's face got redder. "Charlie and me, we've been on the horn, back and forth like, for quite a while."

Marge frowned, suddenly. "When did this buddy-buddy stuff with Kluckenpacker start, Elmer? And how come you never mentioned it before?"

"A while ago." Elmer pinched his nose, scratched the back of his neck, and jiggled his knee up and down.

"A while ago," Marge said reflectively. "About the time Holcomb showed up to get zoning for his fast-food place?"

"Maybe. So what? Co-incidence, that's all. Charlie called me to see about setting up a Captain Cluck chicken franchise on that piece of land I own out to Trumansburg. I said nossir. Nossir. We already have a Holcomb Wholesome Chicken store being set up on Route 15, and in the interests of fair play, I just couldn't see it. Now he calls me off and on, out of respect, and you tell me I haven't got the interests of this-here town at heart. You tell me that I didn't screw myself in my own backside by not selling that piece of land to him."

"Oh, dear," Quill said.

"You're more of a damn fool than I thought, Elmer." Marge sucked her lower lip hard and released it with a pop.

"What're you talking about?!" Elmer demanded. "You're just jealous because I can deal with the big boys."

"Kluckenpacker knows dam' well he doesn't need your piece of land or your permission to put up a Captain Cluck's. If he's been cozying up to you, it's because he wants a spy."

"I am *not* a spy!"

"Sure you are. Guy wants to find out what was going on. And you tell him. I hope you had enough brains not to call up your pal Harry and tell him about Kluckenpacker's call." Elmer's face changed. Marge shook her head. "You did. Right. Well, now they both know each other's business. And that can't be good for Hemlock Falls."

"I'm brokering, like," he said feebly. "And why can't it be good for Hemlock Falls?"

Marge snorted. "They hate each other's guts. And now that you've made yourself out to be—"

Quill kicked Marge's ankle. Gently. Elmer was about to cry.

"A bit of a boob," Marge amended. "They're going to think they can run right over us like they run right over you." She relented a little. "But maybe you're not all that big of a boob. If it hadn't been you a-spying, it would have been someone else."

"It can't be that bad, Marge," Quill said.

"Yeah? Maybe not. I've heard the feud between Kluck and Holcomb goes quite a bit beyond from what we read in the papers, though. And the one thing this place don't need is to land smack in the middle of a fight between those two."

Quill, with every intention of staying out of it, couldn't help her question: "Why not?"

Marge's forehead furrowed, but her expression didn't change. "Kluck plays dirty. Or so I've heard."

"Well it sounds as if he wasn't interested, anyway," Quill said. "I mean, the mayor didn't sell him that piece of property and that seems to be that. No Captain Cluck Chicken shack in Hemlock Falls."

Marge nodded reluctantly. "Maybe. I should have heard about it. I mean, Holcomb's Wholesome is the first fast-food place to be built in our area, and the news was all over before Holcomb sent out the first survey team. Maybe you're right. I'm getting worked up over nothing."

Quill, whose private opinion for months had been that Hemlock Falls had gotten along just fine without a fried chicken franchise, and who had even less interest in the possibility of a second, greeted Nate and the arrival of the coffee with relief. "Okay, guys. Here's the coffee. Let's just plan this contest peacefully and quietly."

"Oh, my god!" Elmer jumped out of his chair. His face was bright red. He stared at something behind Quill's chair. "Oh no. Oh holy heck. Oh, *durn it!*"

"There you all are!" a voice shouted behind her

Quill and Marge turned around at the same time. Quill took a deep breath. Marge shook her head grimly. "It's Doreen."

"Yes," Quill said faintly. "It is Doreen. Oh, dear."

"So much for peace and quiet." Marge raised her voice to a bellow. "Over here, Doreen!"

Elmer smacked the table with one large hand. "Don't you ask her over here, Marge Schmidt!"

Quill turned in her chair to get a full look at her most reliable (if testiest) employee. Doreen had been head of housekeeping at the Inn almost as long as they'd been open. Quill knew her as well as she knew Meg. And she really really didn't want to believe what she was seeing now.

"Just look at her!" Elmer said furiously. "Just look at her! You know what she's done?"

Marge shrugged. Quill, still staring at Doreen, didn't answer. It was all too obvious what her chief housekeeper had done.

Doreen was dressed like a chicken. Normally, Doreen dressed in comfortable trousers or a no-nonsense denim skirt and cotton shirt. Today the pants had been replaced by black leggings, topped by a thigh-high skirt of yellow feathers. She wore a yellow vest of feathers above that. A baseball cap with a long black beak nested in the middle of her hair and shadowed her beady black eyes. Above the cap, attached to a bobbling wire, was a glittery halo.

All the Captain Cluck employees dressed like that.

Quill watched her housekeeper thread her way through the tables. Doreen was skinny, with wild gray hair that rose around her face in a thicket, and the Captain Cluck chicken outfit made her look even more like a chicken than it would Marge or Quill or anybody else that Quill could think of except maybe Shelley Duvall.

"You never said a word!" Elmer hissed in rage.

"I had no idea!" Quill protested. "But it's Doreen, Elmer. I mean . . ." She waved her hands rather helplessly. Doreen's entrepreneurial efforts, from Nu Skin to recruiting souls for the Church of the Rolling Moses, were as well known as Quill's futile objections to them.

"I thought I did." Elmer breathed loudly through his nose. "I thought I knew her! But I never thought she'd turn into a traitor!" he muttered. "A traitor!"

"B-wok, wok wok *wok!*" Doreen said, flapping her elbows. She sat down in the fourth chair at the table, grinning hugely.

"What the heck are you doing?" roared the Mayor. *"That's a Captain Cluck outfit!"*

"Sure is," Doreen said.

"You better not be doin' what I think you're doin'," Elmer said with a futile attempt at menace.

"Don't be a damn fool, Elmer." Marge's expression as she gazed at Doreen was thoughtful, in the way that a pterodactyl might have looked when something unwelcome showed up in its nest.

"I just don't b'lieve you sold out this town," Elmer muttered. "I just don't b'lieve it. I don't b'lieve Charlie went behind my back like this. And what am I going to tell Mr. Holcomb?"

"It's Holcomb, now, is it, Mayor, not my old pal Harry?" Marge dismissed the mayor with a glance and turned her basilisk gaze on Doreen. "You sure you're not in over your head, here, Doreen?"

"And why should I be?" Doreen demanded with immediate belligerence. "You're not the only four-star businesswoman in Hemlock Falls."

"Okay, guys." Quill put both hands firmly on the table. Since this coincided with the arrival of more coffee, there was a brief flurry of activity. Coffee splashed on Doreen's chicken suit and splattered the mayor's tie. Nate muttered a few choice words. This gave Quill a moment to think, and by the time the table was dry, the mayor placated, and Doreen's feathers smoothed, she had her temper in hand.

"That's a Captain Cluck's Chicken suit," Quill said, just to clarify matters.

"You betcha." Doreen fluffed her vest and straightened her beak with pride.

"You're opening a Captain Cluck's franchise." Quill knew she was stating the obvious, but she said it anyway. Just to be sure.

Doreen smirked. Quill hated it when Doreen smirked, since it invariably accompanied one of the housekeeper's riskier entrepreneurial efforts. Not riskier to Doreen's personal finances—she rarely got in over her head—but somehow, always, inevitably, Doreen's forays into business resulted in an exodus of guests from the Inn. And with this particular venture, there was the distinct possibility it might lead to the exodus of citizens from Hemlock Falls. Just how nasty was Captain Cluck, anyway? And how lethal was his food?

"I know what you're thinkin'." Doreen held up an admonitory hand. "And it's got nuthin' to do with my job here."

"Stoke know about this?" Marge interrupted.

Axminister Stoker—Doreen's third or fourth husband (Quill wasn't entirely sure)—was the owner and publisher of the *Hemlock Falls Gazette.*

"Stoke and me, we're partners," Doreen said proudly. "I'm in charge of publicity. He's puttin' up the cash for the building and the equipment."

"Two fast-food franchises in Hemlock Falls," Quill said. "My word. Oh, my word."

"Just *where* is this chicken shack goin' up?!" Elmer shouted. All three women ignored him.

"It was only a matter of time," Marge said. "We're growin', so fast-food competition had to come sooner or later. I took a look at McDonald's and Burger King myself, but the buggers want too much off the top." As the wealthiest citizen in Tompkins County, Marge had a flat rule that if any bugger were going to get too much off the top, it would be Marge Elizabeth Schmidt. "Thing is, didn't expect it to be fried chicken. The town can't handle two fried chicken places. Not enough volume. What I am sure of is that Holcomb and Kluckenpacker know that, too." She punched Doreen lightly in the arm. "Where's it at?"

"We're lookin' at space down by the Paramount Paint Factory. Haven't decided yet."

"Right off Route 15," Marge said.

It took Elmer a little longer. "Wha . . . you can't! That's right across from where Holcomb's Wholesome is at. That's illegal activity, Doreen Muxworthy-Stoker, and well you know it."

Marge laughed pitilessly. "Nothing illegal about it. But if you're kicking yourself because you didn't get good old Charlie to buy your parcel, I got some sympathy for you."

"Elmer refused to sell his land!" Quill said in indignant defense of the mayor. "And I think it was a noble thing to do."

"Ahuh." Marge put a piece of gum in her mouth and chewed on it skeptically. "Elmer just didn't get his price, that's all. Am I right, Elmer?"

The mayor scowled like a balked baby. Quill sighed. So much for honor among politicians.

"Well, Doreen, that's good. Good spot. What about the Zoning Committee? You haven't got permission to build— I woulda heard about it."

"Well, we're workin' on it," Doreen admitted. "And things ain't finalized yet, like I said. Duane Peterson hasn't got back to us on our counteroffer for the property. But the Captain sent the chicken suit, and said it'd be a fine thing to show it off around town. Let people know he's serious."

"Ahuh. I'll just bet he did. Well, the Fry Away Home contest is heating up nicely, I'll say that for it." Marge rubbed her chin in a considering way. "You talk to the Captain about our—" she paused, considered her words carefully, then said, "—zoning issues?"

Nobody said anything, but Quill breathed a silent sigh of relief. Maybe she didn't have to worry about Doreen counting linen dressed like a chicken after all. There was a 140-pound obstacle between Doreen and the erection of a Captain Cluck's Chicken shack. (Not to mention the permanent addition of the chicken suit to Doreen's wardrobe.) And that obstacle was Carol Ann Spinoza, the meanest person in Tompkins County.

Zoning Committee members were appointed each year by the town council. For as many years as Quill could recall, the members were exactly the same as they had been the year before: Harland Peterson (president of the local Agway, and a dairy farmer of some substance), Freddie Bellini (Bellini's Fine Funerals), and Norm Pasquale, coach of the high school football team. But a month ago, Norm had retired and moved to Des Moines (for the weather, he'd said) and somehow, some way, Carol Ann Spinoza had wriggled her snaky way into the vacant seat.

"It wasn't *my* fault," Elmer said after a long moment, although no one had mentioned Carol Ann's name aloud. "That woman . . ." he trailed off. A sigh went around the table. Carol Ann looked like a cheerleader: blonde, bouncy, and clean. But she was sneaky as a snake and as mean as a tarantula. And just like a snake, she never seemed to age. (Quill herself suspected that somewhere in Carol Ann's attic, a portrait of Carol Ann was getting hideously old and ugly.) Carol Ann had been fired from her job as tax assessor, to everyone's relief, but she hadn't remained down and out for long. Quill had suspected that some way, some how, Carol Ann had engineered Norm Pasquale's departure and the subsequent vacancy on the Zoning Committee.

"We'll cross the zoning bridge when we come to it," Doreen said pragmatically. "In the meantime, the folks at Captain Cluck sent ahead the publicity kit, and this," she looked down at her costume with a pleased air, "was in it."

"You aren't," Quill asked carefully, "going to wear it to work, are you?"

"Good PR," Doreen said, her feathers rustling defensively. "And the Captain Cluck publicity kit says you should take every chance you git to make folks aware of the mouthwaterin', fingersuckin', purely heavenly (she adjusted her halo), *awe*-inspirin'—"

"Stop," Quill said. The latter string of adjectives and adverbs provided the introduction to the notoriously tuneful Captain Cluck's Crispy Chicken theme song, which Quill absolutely did not want to hear sung in the Tavern Lounge—or the entire village of Hemlock Falls for that matter. It stuck to one's brain like Velcro on Velcro. Once you heard it, you couldn't get rid of it. And she hated the chicken it advertised, anyway. "Your feathers will get matted," she said. "You'll wear out the suit if you wear it to work."

"They'll send me another one," Doreen said. "Said so, right in the kit."

"Let's put it this way then. No. You are not coming to work in the chicken suit."

Doreen bristled, which gave Quill a new appreciation of the chicken suit, since the feathers did plump up just like an angry hen's. "Now, look here, missy—"

"No, *you* look here, Doreen. No. And when I say no, I mean—"

"You can't wear the durn thing around town, either," Elmer said flatly. "I won't allow it."

"*You* won't allow it?" Quill said.

"You're durn right."

"Somebody die and leave you king?" Marge inquired. "No law against wearing a chicken suit."

"I'll make one!" the mayor said. "See if I don't. Harry Holcomb is the main sponsor of the Fry Away Home festival—"

"So?" Quill said dangerously.

"And they've been very good to this town. Very. So Doreen can't wear the chicken suit. It's against town policy to incite . . . ah . . . incite?"

"They haven't been very good to this town yet," Quill said, in automatic, if counterproductive defense of her housekeeper's civil rights. "And even if they had . . ." She clutched her hair with both hands and tugged at it, hard. "I can't believe I'm having this conversation. I cannot. Doreen, please remove the chicken suit and set up a time where we can go over the linen inventory."

"I kin do that just as well in feathers as not." Doreen's chin jutted out.

"Not," Quill said. "And I mean no. What about tomorrow for the linen inventory?"

"I'm off on Tuesdays."

"Doreen!" Elmer patted Doreen on the arm in a fraternal way. "You go on ahead. Go. You take that suit right off."

"Elmer," Quill began, "I *really* would appreciate it if you'd leave this to me and Doreen. Doreen? Off with the suit. Please. And back to work. *Please*."

"Huh!" Doreen said. "You tellin' me to beat it? You *orderin'* me to take off this suit?!"

"No! I mean, not exactly." Quill clutched her hair again, which was suffering a lot this morning. She'd have to remember to brush it before she got on with the rest of her day. If she ever *did* get on with the rest of her day. Maybe she would be stuck here forever with Marge and the mayor and Doreen in a chicken suit. Maybe she was dead, and this was hell.

"Quill?" Doreen repeated. "Are you ordering me?"

Maybe she should retake that course in managerial assertiveness. "Please take off the suit, Doreen. Please, please, please."

"Well, *I'm* ordering you to take it off," Elmer added, with an infuriating disregard for Quill's authority as manager of the Inn, "and I'm telling you to beat feet, too, because we got stuff to discuss. So you scoot on off now, Doreen."

"Discuss what stuff?" Doreen asked, her nose twitching.

The mayor got huffy. "Never you mind. It's official business and I got decisions to make for this town. Go on, Doreen, go."

Doreen went. A few yellow feathers trailed behind her.

"Shoot," the mayor said, turning to Marge and Quill. "*Now* what are we going to do?"

CHAPTER 2

"What are we going to do now?" Marge asked rhetorically. "You tell me. You're the mayor. Go ahead. Make some mayoral decisions."

The cyber-notes of "For He's a Jolly Good Fellow" chirped once more from the mayor's shirt pocket. He snapped it open and said huskily into it, "Yeah? Oh. Howdy. Sure. Sure thing."

Quill sighed. It was probably Adela, the mayor's formidable wife. The mayor continued his side of the conversation. Quill sipped her coffee. Marge chewed her gum with a thoughtful air. Quill looked at her finally, and whispered, "What do you think?"

"About what?"

"The chicken mess."

Marge grinned. "It's war. Holcomb and Kluckenpacker hate each other."

Quill groaned. "I'd better talk to Doreen."

"What about? You gonna tell her she can't open a Captain Cluck Chicken shack?"

"Well, I . . ."

"It's the God-given right of every thinking American to open their own chicken shack, if they want to," Marge said seriously.

"That's true, but—"

"You want to interfere with her rights as a citizen, well, all I can say is I thought the better of you."

"You think I should do *nothing*?"

Marge nodded. "Best way. Tell you what, Quill. It'll never get past the Zoning Committee. That's one thing about Carol Ann Spinoza. She'll tie that application up six ways from Sunday asking really stupid questions so she can throw her weight around. If she'd been on the committee when Holcomb made his application, we'd all be at the Shady Grove Rest Home before we had one piece of Holcomb's Wholesome. You can bet on it."

Quill didn't bet on anything as far as Carol Ann Spinoza was concerned. She made a mental note to talk to Doreen.

Elmer concluded his phone call, put the phone away and said, "Next order of business."

"Who was that?" Marge inquired. "George? Dick? Colin, maybe, asking some advice about Pakistan?"

"Now, Marge," Elmer said in a futile way.

"Huh! It was Adela, that's who. Telling you to pull up your socks, as usual."

Elmer couldn't resist a look at his socks. "I'll tell you when I'm ready," he said crossly. "What were we talking about before Doreen messed us up?"

"Doreen did not mess us up," Quill said firmly.

"Oh, yeah. Meg. Now about Meg . . ."

Quill greeted this as a less incendiary topic than Colonel Cluck, although it probably wasn't. "Okay. As far as Meg goes—I thought the whole discussion with her went pretty well. Tomorrow I'll tell her we're considering a couple of people and then a few days after that I'll tell her about Banion O'Haggerty. I'll wait until after the *L'Aperitif* editor leaves."

"You might want to talk to her sooner than that." Elmer hunched confidentially over the table and said into Quill's ear, "Banion O'Haggerty's comin' in this afternoon."

For a long moment, it didn't sink in. Then Quill said, "He's accepted the job as judge for the Fry Away Home contest?!" She tugged at her hair. "He couldn't have!" She tugged harder. "He's supposed to be making up his mind!

He has another seventy-two hours to make up his mind! And he's going to say no and we're going to get the Iron Chef. Or at least somebody that Meg doesn't hate. And you didn't tell me?!"

"I just took the call," Elmer said with wounded dignity.

"You did, did you!?" Quill said. "Well, why didn't you stop him? You could have said we couldn't find the extra twenty-five thousand dollars he wants."

"If we could have saved the extra twenty-five thousand that O'Haggerty's going to cost us, I would have been just as happy," the mayor said. "But we got the discretionary fund and we'll make it back selling tickets anyhow."

"You . . . you . . . politician," Quill said in exasperation. "Darn it. Well, you can just tell Meg for me, Elmer."

"At the very end, I tried to tell Meg that right in the kitchen," Elmer said with a long-suffering air. "But no. You ladies just horned right in and dragged me out of there without a proper respect for the mayor's office *at all*. I tried. You wouldn't let me. You do it. Fair's fair."

"Elmer. Shut up." Marge said.

"I will *not* shut up!"

"If you don't shut up right this minute," Quill said between her teeth, "I will scream. Right here. At this table. And not only will I scream, but I'll stand up and point at you when I do it. I mean it, Elmer. Just. Go. Home."

The mayor stood up, wounded dignity in every inch. He scratched once at the itchy waistband of his gray wool trousers, and retreated without another word.

Quill waited until he'd disappeared into the hall to the front of the Inn, and then buried her head in her hands.

"Doesn't make that much difference," Marge said. "O'Haggerty accepts now, two days from now, who cares?"

"I care," Quill said crossly. "It's more of a lie this way. It's the timing!" She took a deep breath. "Nuts. If he's accepted, I'll have to tell Meg. And if I have to tell Meg, she'll know that we knew she wasn't going to take the judge's job and that we were just asking her as a matter of form. And she'll yell at me. And she'll refuse to cook. Oh, *man!* Marge, there'll be hell to pay and you *know* the *L'Aperitif* people are coming the day after tomorrow."

"Now, Quill," Marge said. "Meg ever actually meet O'Haggerty?"

"I don't think so," Quill said. "She hates his TV show. She says he's a phony. And he wrote that book *A Knife in the Back* or whatever it was, and she hated that, too." She closed her eyes briefly. "We should have gotten Emeril. Meg likes Emeril."

"Holcomb wanted O'Haggerty and anyways, Emeril couldn't fit it in," Marge reminded her. "You want Emeril, you gotta book a coupla years in advance. Besides, if Meg likes Emeril, there's no reason why she won't like Banion, too. She's seen him on TV, like the rest of us. And he hasn't accepted the judge job yet, not officially. I know because I'm in charge of the contracts, and he hasn't signed the contracts. Well, it's not a contract, as such. It's a letter of agreement." Quill sighed. Marge could be annoyingly persnickety. "If he hasn't signed the contracts, then that's a verbal acceptance and it don't count here. Now look. When I talked to that agent of his first time out, he did say that Banion's just wrapped up a whole mess of shoots for next season. And if he did accept, it'd mostly be because he wants a little rest before he starts writing his new cook-book. He's just coming here for a fat check and an easy time of it at the Inn, Quill. And he wants to meet Meg, of course."

Quill felt a stir of hope. "He does?"

"According to his agent." Marge patted Quill's hand. "He admires her cooking. I got Dina to book him a nice room, just in case. I better tell her he's takin' it."

"Here?"

"Of course, here." Marge sat back indignantly. "Why not here! This is a three-star inn, Quill, or so that brochure of yours says, and for Pete's sake, you want I should book him into the Marriott?"

"We decided he'd stay at the Marriott!" Quill shouted. "And if he stays here, he'll eat here!"

"Maybe not," Marge said with a competitive smirk. "You got Banion O'Haggerty coming into town, I want to remind you there's other places to eat in Hemlock Falls. He knows about my diners, you can bet on that."

"This is awful. Meg told all three of us she hates him. And you think she's going to agree to cook for someone she hates?"

Marge said, "Baloney!" Then, "Get a little sense, Quill. How could Meg hate him? She's never met the guy. Now, I grant you, it might be a case of a little professional jealousy. If so, Meg'll give that up soon enough. I mean, if it's just that he's more famous than she is, then you don't have to worry about it. Meg's a pretty reasonable person, underneath. She'll come around."

"I have no idea why she hates him. I do know that I have to tell her. Right now." Quill, distracted, drained her coffee and got to her feet with purpose. At least she hoped it was with the right kind of purpose and that she'd head back to the kitchen and not out the front door to the safety of the open road. "You should have warned me, Marge."

"I didn't know, did I?" Marge said indignantly. "It's that dam' fool . . . well, speak of the devil." Elmer came trundling back into the room, with all the skittishness of a maid in a bad French farce.

"What do you want?" Quill asked coldly.

"We got a problem. You can't actually *tell* Meg Banion's here," Elmer said in an urgent under-voice. He sat heavily at the table and wiped his sweaty brow with a handkerchief. "His agent asked me himself. Just got another call. On the . . ." He patted his shirt pocket importantly.

"Oh, for Pete's sake," Quill said. "You and that stupid cell phone."

"Couldn't do business without it."

Quill could think of a lot of things the mayor could do without. Like his teeth. She took a deep breath and counted backwards from one hundred.

"Anyhow, Mr. O'Haggerty doesn't want any notice of his visit here today. Wants a rest, he said." Elmer nodded decisively. "So. Don't say a word."

"Don't be stupid, Elmer." Marge narrowed her eyes at him. "Know what? You been acting peculiar over this whole thing. First you booted O'Haggerty's price up into the stratosphere. Then you started kissin' up to Captain Cluck. Now, you've never been the brightest bulb in the chandelier, Elmer, but you've never gone peculiar on me. What's up?"

"Nothing's up. I'm just trying to execute the duties of my office. Part of which means respecting the wishes of the dignitaries who come to visit this town. And if Banion O'Haggerty wants to slip in unnoticed-like, well, we have a civic duty to keep our lips buttoned."

"How can he slip in unnoticed?" Quill asked. "His cable show runs five days a week. Anyone who has a TV knows him on sight."

"Come to think of it," Marge said. "Why's he coming here today? The contest doesn't start 'til Friday. This is Monday. His agent said he wanted a little time off, but that's a *lot* of time off for a guy as busy as he is."

"It's not our place to ask questions," Elmer said. "Thing is, Banion needs a bit of a rest. Wants to be incognito for a while. Doesn't want any special treatment. He's a regular guy. We gotta respect that. He wants to stay up in his room and get his food sent in on a tray, who's to care? He wants to wear those big dark glasses and a hat maybe and walk around with no one knowing who he is, we gotta accept that."

Marge chuckled. "You're a fathead, Elmer. I always meant to tell you that. You're a fathead."

Elmer bristled. "Who you calling a fathead?"

"You act like a fathead, I'm going to call you a fathead."

Quill laid her hand on Marge's arm. "Easy, guys." She turned to Elmer. His face was pink. He looked like an indignant baby. "It's not fair not to tell Meg. It's just like politics, Elmer."

"What's just like politics?! You don't elect chefs to public office! Chefs don't campaign! Chefs don't—"

"Fathead," Marge said.

Elmer swelled. "I'm asking again. Who you calling . . ."

"This is all beside the point," Quill interrupted hastily. "It's Meg not knowing who she's cooking for, Mayor. I mean, how would you feel if the current governor came to hear one of your campaign speeches, and you didn't know he was in the audience?"

"Guy's not a member of my party," Elmer said stiffly. "Why'n the heck would he come to one of my speeches?"

"That's it exactly," Quill said, although as usual Elmer had missed the point. "You're from opposite parties, and if you didn't know he was there, you might say something you'd regret a bit, later on—"

"You know something I don't?" the mayor demanded. "He coming to that speech I'm giving over to the Kiwanis next Wednesday?"

"What? Of course not! I was just—"

The mayor rose to his full five feet seven inches, his face a mask of injured dignity. "You should have told me, Quill. I'll tell you something." He threw his napkin on the table with bitter relish. "You can't trust those guys in Albany. Not for a New York minute."

"Maybe you oughta give his office a call," Marge said snidely. "Tell him not to come." She rocked back in her chair, muttered "fathead" then gathered her patience with an obvious effort. "All right, all right. Don't get your knickers in a twist, Elmer. The governor doesn't have time to get to every penny-ante politician's speech given in New York State. Quill was just saying that so you'd see that this isn't fair on Meg."

Elmer hesitated, about to make an issue of the "penny-

ante" shot, then gave up and sat back. He thought hard for
a minute. "I see your point, Quill. Okay. You go and tell
Meg Mr. O'Haggerty's dropping by. But you leave me out
of it, you hear? And you tell her it's like, just an impulse
stop. Not that we knew about it in advance, or anything.
And you tell her to pretend she doesn't know who he is."

"I will not," Quill said. "I never should have agreed to
these deceptions in the first place." She straightened her
shoulders determinedly. "I'm going to make a full confession."

"I've come," Quill said a few moments later as she pushed
the swinging doors open into the kitchen, "to make a full
confession."

Bjarne Bjarnson, recently promoted to head chef, looked
up from the vegetable sink in reproof. He was tall, thin,
and melancholy, a Finn who'd recently graduated from the
Cornell School for Hotel Management.

He was also alone.

Quill loved their kitchen, from the cobblestone fireplace
that occupied the south wall to the long mullioned windows
looking out over the vegetable gardens on the east, to the
flagstone floors, re-laid and repaired the year before after
an unfortunate incident involving one of Meg and Quill's
investigations into murder. But except for the appliances
and Bjarne splashing at the sink, it was missing its most
important figure.

"Hey, Bjarne," Quill said. "Meg was here just a moment
ago. Did she step out?"

Bjarne stuck his lower lip out thoughtfully. "Meg," he
said, "is not here."

"I can see that," Quill said agreeably. "Where is she?"

"I have heard it said that confession is the better part of
valor."

"What?" Quill said. Then, "Did Meg go somewhere?"

"This is, perhaps, an American expression with which
you, Quill, should be more familiar."

"Anyway, it's discretion," Quill said. "Discretion is the better part of . . ." She stopped herself. "Oh, never *mind*. She found out, didn't she? About Banion O'Haggerty."

"That, too," Bjarne said mysteriously. He picked up a sheaf of red-leafed lettuce and shook it gently under the running water.

"So," Quill said. She sank into the rocker by the fireplace and set it into motion. "How did she find out?"

"That you, her sister, older by a few years, and therefore wiser, that you, her sister, the only member of her blood family living on this earth, sold her down the ocean?"

"River," Quill corrected, mildly. And Finns obviously placed a high premium on blood relationships. She hadn't known that before. "Who told her?"

"Miss Dina Muir." Bjarne began to separate the lettuce leaves onto white toweling with finicky deliberation.

"She did, huh?" Quill pushed the rocking chair a little faster. Good. Old. Dina. It's not every day that your trusted receptionist stabbed you in the back right in front of your face. Or something like that.

"Dina said that he—"

"He's not God, Bjarne. Nor the devil, for that matter. He's a chef."

"Maitre O'Haggerty would be here in time for dinner. And that she felt Meg Ought To Know."

"I just found out myself," Quill said lamely. "That's why I'm here. To let her know."

Bjarne shut off the taps in a way that reminded Quill of his stories about wringing chicken's necks in the old country.

"And I didn't sell her anywhere, Bjarne. I was just trying to make the best of a difficult situation." She sighed. "But you're right. You're absolutely right. About Banion O'Haggerty. About the Chamber inviting her to judge this contest. About not revealing all the plans up front. But it all came up so fast! I mean, that's not a defense, but these Harry Holcomb Wholesome Chicken characters just suddenly decided out of the blue that Hemlock Falls was where the Fry Away Home contest was going to be held this year, and the Chamber of Commerce was anxious that nothing jeopardize the decision, because Holcomb pulled out of New Orleans the year before at the last minute, and they wanted everything to go smoothly and I love Meg, Bjarne, you know I do. But she's not..." Quill hesitated. "Smooth," she said, finally.

"She is an artist," Bjarne said loftily. "As," he added with a significant look, "am I." He began snapping celery stalks with quick twists of his powerful fingers. "Finns," he added, seemingly apropos of nothing, "have long had an interest in deep-fat frying."

Quill stopped rocking.

"I, myself, am considered to be ..." Bjarne spread both hands deprecatingly, "a master of the deep-fry. Not to put too find a point on it."

"Fine point," Quill said automatically, "not to put too fine a point ... Bjarne? Did *you* want to judge the Fry Away Home contest?"

He laughed bitterly.

"I mean, um ..." Quill did a rapid mental review of the second-to-last course she'd taken at the Cornell School for Hotel Management, the one before the one on how to deal with sexual harassment. "Incenting the Creative Employee," that had been the topic. And there'd been a paper due, on "Issues Surrounding Competitive Issues." Or something like that. She hadn't gotten around to turning it in. Or writing it, for that matter. She did remember the part of the course about crawling apologies. Although it hadn't been called crawling apologies, it'd been called Being Accountable for Management Error.

"I am really, really sorry about the oversight, Bjarne. Of course we should have thought of you. I can't imagine why we didn't think of you, Bjarne," she said earnestly. "You know that you are one of our finest employees. You're one of the best chefs we've ever had in the kitchen—"

"Was," Bjarne said, with true Finnish tact. "I, like Miss Meg, no longer work here."

He tossed the snapped celery into the disposal, turned it on, and walked out the back door.

Quill sat rocking by the stone cold fireplace and pulled thoughtfully at her lower lip. The kitchen was very quiet. She glanced at her watch. Twenty minutes until the lunch staff arrived. Three under-chefs. Two dishwashers. Five waiters. The valiant small army of the Inn at Hemlock Falls. Waiting for their general. And their assistant general, or whatever junior generals were actually called. Both of whom were MIA.

She pulled her cell phone from her skirt pocket and regarded it with distaste. Their business manager John Raintree had insisted on cell phones, an innovation of dubious merit, as far as Quill was concerned. She had enough trouble focusing on the dailiness of life. How much more would she have if her neurons were zapped by a cell phone-engendered brain tumor?

She speed-dialed Meg's cell phone number, and listened to the breep-breep-breep with no expectation whatsoever that her sister would pick up.

The back door to the kitchen banged, and Quill snapped the phone shut. She half-rose from the rocking chair, then sank back as Max the dog trotted hopefully into the room. Quill had agreed to the cell phones. John had agreed to the dog door.

"You," she said to Max.

Max sat down with a thump and scratched one long floppy ear. Max was the world's ugliest dog. His shaggy coat was a muddy mixture of grays, ochre, and brown. His ears flopped forward in an Afghan-y kind of way, except when he regarded Quill, as he was now, with loving affection. Then they made a half-hearted effort to stand up. "Trouble in River City, Max," Quill said. "At least you haven't deserted me. Have you seen Meg? Find Meg!"

Max yawned, scratched the other ear, then trotted past

Quill and out the swinging doors to the dining room. A muffled yell and a smothered curse told Quill that the dog had made his way past Kathleen Kiddermeister, head of the wait staff, who must have arrived early. Quill got up and followed him.

Kathleen, her face red with annoyance, was picking up a pile of freshly laundered tablecloths scattered over the plush carpeting. "That damn dog," she muttered as Quill came into the room. "Honestly, Quill."

"He's on a search mission," Quill said by way of apology.

"The only thing that hound searches for is dumpsters." Kathleen set the reassembled tablecloths down on a chair. "The only thing he can *find* is dumpsters. The only thing he *likes* is dumpsters."

Max's bedraggled tail disappeared into the foyer. "Excuse me, Kath." Quill speeded up just in case Max was headed out the front door, which was always kept open as soon as the weather turned mild. Max wasn't headed out the front door. He was sitting next to Dina, regarding her slow consumption of a fruit wrap with thoughtful interest.

"You," Quill said, not meaning the dog this time.

"Me," Dina agreed cheerfully. She sat behind the fine mahogany reception desk, textbook open before her, her glossy brown hair twisted carelessly on top of her head. Dina's pursuit of a doctorate in limnology from Cornell had lasted her entire tenure as Quill's receptionist. The extreme slowness of her studies had to do with the life cycle of copepods. Quill didn't want to know any more than that.

"Okay, Dina. Where's Meg?"

Dina's nice brown eyes peered at Quill over her big round glasses. "In the kitchen?" she suggested.

"Not. Not in the kitchen. And not answering her cell phone, either."

"In her room, maybe?"

Quill deflated a little. She hadn't thought of that. "Did you see her go up?"

Dina shook her head. The shortest way to Meg's quarters from the kitchen was up the winding staircase in the foyer. She could have stomped out of the rear door and around to the Tavern Lounge side of the Inn, but Quill didn't think so. Her sister tended to take the shortest line between two points. "Ring her there, would you?"

Dina punched in Meg's extension. No answer. "Maybe she's with Andy?"

"Andy's away for a three-day conference. Something to do with new methods of treating pediatric fractures." Andy Bishop, Hemlock Falls' best (and only) internist, had a specialty interest in pediatrics. He had a specialty interest in Meg, too, but his and Meg's marriage plans had a lot in common with the excruciatingly prolonged life cycle of the copepod.

"Then it beats me." Dina gave the last third of her fruit wrap to Max, who mouthed it, then dropped it on the Oriental carpet that covered most of the oak floor in the reception area. It appeared to be raspberry.

Quill put a fast slam on her rising temper, and said mildly, "When you told her about Banion O'Haggerty— and you did tell her about Banion O'Haggerty, Dina—did she seem upset? At all?"

Dina blinked. "She was very upset," Dina said in a kind way. "Very very. Words of reproach simply flew about the room. I won't," Dina added with conscious rectitude, "repeat them."

"Other than the words of reproach—"

"About you, mostly. And come to think of it, opprobrium might be closer to it than reproach—"

"Did she say what she was going to do about it?"

"She was too mad," Dina said simply. "Did you look at her socks today? You know how you can tell how the day's going to go by the color. Red. Red socks. You should have known."

"*I* should have known!" Quill shrieked. "*You* were the one that blew me in, Dina."

"Well someone had to tell her. I mean jeez-Louise, Quill, this incredibly good-looking, incredibly sexy fellow chef is showing up right here in Hemlock Falls . . . I mean, have you seen that TV show of his, Quill? The guy's a dish. The guy's a hottie. The guy's—"

"Here," said Banion O'Haggerty, walking in the front door. He set his Louis Vuitton carryall onto the floor with a thump. He grinned at them both, dark hair falling attractively over one intensely blue eye. "And I love a good entrance line."

Quill's hands went automatically to her hair, which was red, wildly springy, and prone to fall all over the place at inopportune moments. Dina slid quietly under the fine mahogany desk. Max barked.

"Welcome," Quill said. She abandoned any hope of fixing her hair. "I'm Sarah Quilliam."

Banion's cerulean gaze switched to Dina. "Are you okay?" he asked. He bent sideways and peered under the desk. "What's your name, dear?"

"Dina," Quill said. She decided that Dina had been punished more than sufficiently. "Her name's Dina and I knocked over a big box of rubber bands and . . . *Dina*?"

"What?"

"Don't come out until you pick *all* of them up, okay?"

"Okay."

"Tough boss," Banion O'Haggerty said in admiration.

"Not too tough, I hope. It's nice to meet you, Mr. O'Haggerty. And we're very glad to have you at the Inn. Can I offer you something from the Tavern Lounge? Dina will take care of checking you in and getting your luggage up to your room. If you don't mind waiting of course."

"If the offer for refreshments includes you, Miss Quilliam, you don't have to ask twice."

"Ah. Um," Quill said, with her usual witty response to badinage from attractive men. "This way. Oh, and you can leave that second case. Dina will take it up for you."

Banion hefted the leather case he was carrying with a

grimace. "Nope. Never let it out of my sight."

"Your recipes?"

"My knives."

"Of course." Banion walked companionably beside her as she led the way down the hall to the Tavern Lounge. "My sister feels the same way about her set."

"Your sister. I am really anxious to see your sister. She's quite the hot topic on the circuit."

Quill glanced curiously at him. Everybody with a television knew about Banion O'Haggerty. It was startling to think of her very own sister (if Meg wasn't at the courthouse this minute, filing a writ to break the familial bond, if that were possible) as a matter of interest to somebody so famous.

Banion was an Irish expatriate, and had landed on the cooking scene with a splash several years ago with the publication of a tell-all book about what professional cooking was *really* like behind the scenes. Like everyone else who'd read the book, Quill was amazed that the restaurant business hadn't collapsed completely once patrons knew what a really pissed-off chef could do to food out of revenge or bad temper. The book had been followed by Banion's engaging cooking show *Leftovers*. (Banion was notoriously divorced. At least twice.) The combination of his self-deprecating charm (just a lonely bachelor, seeing what I can do with what's left in the fridge) along with his rangy sexiness, moved *Leftovers* off the Food Channel and into prime time in nothing flat.

"This," he said, as they walked into the Tavern Lounge, "is *Mar*-velous."

Marvelous, Quill thought. Oh, yes. Banion's catchphrase, like Emeril's "*Bam!*" only much, much more libidinous.

The Tavern Lounge had a long, curved mahogany bar, walls of a deep, unnamable blue-green that Quill had mixed herself (that everyone else called, for lack of a better noun, teal), and extremely comfortable chairs at each of the small round tables. Banion stopped in front of one of Quill's more recent paintings. "Oh, yes," he said. "You're *that* Quilliam."

"Um," Quill said. She wondered, fleetingly, if she could buy a book on suitable repartee. She didn't have any. Not an ounce.

"I heard that you don't display your work anywhere else but this room?" Banion's raven-dark eyebrows quirked upward.

"You did?" Quill waited for the bout of nonplussedness to subside, which bothered her almost as much as her internal Gothic descriptions of Banion's good looks. "There's one or two at MOMA. But I don't really show."

"Well, you should. You should. But you've heard that before, and from better critics than I, I'm sure. So!" He drew an expansive breath. "Where shall we settle? Why not at the bar?"

Quill trailed him to the barstools. Nate the bartender, who'd picked up a polished cloth the moment they'd entered, was briskly setting the bottles and glasses to rights.

"Help you?" Nate said.

"Grey Goose. Rocks. Lemon peel."

"*Mah*-velous," Nate said, and grinned.

Banion cocked his forefinger like a gun and said, "Pow."

Nate's grin widened to canyon-like proportions and he pointed his own forefinger back. "*Pow!*" Nate responded pleasurably. "Quill? What would you like?"

She glanced at her watch. Eleven o'clock, and as far as she knew, there wasn't anybody in charge in the kitchen. Surely Meg wouldn't just walk off and leave chaos in her wake. And of course Bjarne would see reason and come back. And even if neither Meg nor Bjarne was there, the sous chefs could cope.

"Aaagh," she said. She slid off the barstool. "If you guys would excuse me for just a minute, I've something to attend to."

Dina was on the phone as Quill passed through the foyer, Max sprawled at her feet. The dining room looked wonderful, as it always did just before it opened. The day's menu was posted on the chalkboard at the entrance. The table arrangements were early Dutch iris and miniature daffodils. The wait staff was gathered near the coffee bar, uniforms crisp. The air held that hush of expectancy that always gave Quill a small, excited jump of the heart.

And then there was the kitchen, and Quill's heart gave a lurch of a different kind altogether.

"Well," she said briskly. "How *is* everybody?"

Three sous chefs, two dishwashers, and an errant waiter looked back at her. There wasn't anyone else there.

Maybe Meg was in the storeroom. And Bjarne might have stepped out for a forbidden cigarette.

"Where's Meg? Where's Bjarne?" That from Elizabeth Chu, like all of the sous chefs, a Cornell student on co-op.

"I'm not even sure if I should be prepping these radicchio." Emir Sulaiman, another Cornell student. "And nobody's paid any attention to the soup stock, Quill. It's boiled away to almost nothing. And the meat delivery's out on the back porch. Should I bring it in, or what? Meg likes to see to that herself. It should have been sorted and the stuff set to marinate by now."

Kathleen stuck her head in the door and waved an ominous little green slip. "Two potato leek soups. A chicken French. A salmon Q." She frowned. "Where's Meg?"

"Salmon Q?" Quill said.

"Salmon Quilliam. Where's Bjarne?"

"Um. Hospital," Quill said. "Nothing serious, they're visiting a friend. But it's serious. The friend I mean."

Kathleen snorted. "Bjarne and Meg visiting a sick friend at lunch time with two turns booked? Right."

Elizabeth blinked at Quill. "I mean, who's in charge today?"

Quill took a deep breath. How hard could it be, really? She knew most of Meg's recipes. She'd watched her sister cook from the time they were both in high school. Who's in charge?

"I am."

It was hard. It was impossible. For one thing, Quill couldn't cook professionally. And somebody who can't cook professionally can't supervise somebody who's learning how to cook, even if the recipe's known by heart. By twelve-thirty, with the one o'clock crunch looming, Quill was ready to shave herself bald and retreat as fast as possible to a monastery in Tibet. She remembered—as she chopped, sliced, diced, braised a filet with the left hand, and sautéed a chicken breast with the right—how snappish the wait staff became when the food was late. Or undercooked. Or overcooked. Or when the chef sent out Chicken Marengo to a vegetarian guest. She remembered the more gruesome stories from Banion O'Haggerty's book, *A Stab in the Back*. She forgot completely all sense of decorum and screamed as loudly at the sous chefs as Meg ever had. She even contemplated taking every single ounce of butter in a three county area and pushing it all down the disposal because nobody can cook gourmet food without butter and then they could all quit and go home.

"Hey, beautiful."

Quill, snarling, turned from wrapping pastry around a fiendishly slippery slice of filet (what kind of idiot eats Beef Wellington at lunch, anyway?), her filleting knife held aloft in an unintentionally threatening manner. "Hey *Beautiful!?*" she shrieked. "Don't you 'hey beautiful' *me!*"

Banion O'Haggerty flung both hands up in a mock-defensive gesture. "Just thought I'd come back and see if I could lend a hand. I hope you don't mind."

Quill wiped the back of her hand across her forehead, leaving, she could tell, a long streak of slimy greasy horrible butter behind. "Sorry," she said. "I'm truly sorry. It's just that Meg is, um . . ." She stopped herself. "Did you say lend a hand?" Then, "How did you know?" Then, "We're coping just *fine*."

Banion untied her apron and drew it gently over her head. He took the filleting knife out her hand and laid it carefully on the prep table. "Now," he said. "Stand back, beautiful. This is going to be *Mar*-velous."

CHAPTER 3

"And how does this all make you feel?" Dr. Benziger sat relaxed against the comfortable back of his high leather chair. But then, Dr. Benziger was always relaxed. Quill had yet to see him a. startled, b. distressed, or c. discomposed. He did furrow his brow on occasion, a signal that he was listening intently.

Quill herself perched on the very edge of the comfortable leather couch placed directly across from her therapist. Her elbows were on her knees and she held her chin in her cupped hands. She'd spent the last month, three times a week in this position and her co-pay insurance was running out today.

Quill knew that psychiatrists weren't supposed to be startled, distressed, or discomposed no matter what their patients told them, but she was in a constant state of anxiety that he would be, d. bored, since she didn't have any interesting mental illness at all, as far as she could tell. Except for the anxiety about boring him to death. She tried to think of a psychologically interesting reply to the question of how she felt; it was the twelfth time in twelve visits and she still hadn't come up with a snappy answer.

"Confused," she said finally.

Dr. Benziger furrowed his brow. He was an inoffensive-looking man with thick black glasses, a brush cut, and a neat mustache. "Let me recap for a moment. Currently, you have two deadly enemies—both among the richest men in the United States—due to check into your Inn at the same time. Your housekeeper has elected to invest in a business notorious for Food and Drug Administration violations, a business, not unincidentally run by one of the aforementioned hostile businessmen." He paused. "Furthermore, one of the most notorious celebrity chefs in the culinary world has taken over your kitchen—"

"He did a sensational job," Quill said wistfully.

"And your sister has abandoned you because this man is her deadly enemy. In addition to this, in a week's time, your Inn will be the focal point of a national contest with reporters from both print and television media occupying the grounds." He paused again, and then asked, "Just what is it that you're confused about?"

"Do you think I have the right to tell Doreen not to dress like a chicken?"

"I don't know. What do you think?"

"Well, that's the whole point, isn't it?" Quill had learned very quickly not to be exasperated when her therapist refused to give her advice. "What right do I have to tell other people what to do? Meg and I run an inn. We agree on some basic rules. You know that great line Nero Wolfe has?"

Dr. Benziger did not read detective stories. He'd mentioned it before.

"A guest is a jewel on the bosom of hospitality," Quill said. "That's what Nero Wolfe says. I mean, we've added a couple of rules because you have to, these days, and because Doreen—well I've already told you about Doreen. Rule One: Don't belt the guests. Rule Two: If you have to throw them out make sure they have some other hotel to go to. Rule Three: If they send food back to the kitchen make sure the door to the dining room is guarded so Meg can't get out and yell at them. But other than that, I'm not sure where my responsibilities for other people's behavior ends."

"You are not responsible for anyone else's behavior," Dr.

Benziger said. "Remember our letter of agreement."

Quill remembered it very well. Dr. Benziger had brought up the letter of agreement on her very first visit. It was the cornerstone of the therapeutic process: when he gave her advice, she agreed to listen to it.

Quill tugged at her nose, then sighed deeply. "But I *am* responsible." She sighed again. "I feel horribly guilty about Meg. She's been gone for almost four hours, now." Quill bit her lip. "Although I have an idea where she might be. I should have thought of it before."

"You are not responsible for Meg's behavior, Quill." Dr. Benziger looked at his watch. "Our time's about up for today. But you might think about this: you are not responsible for Meg abandoning you. And don't allow anyone to talk you into doing what you don't want to do. Trust yourself. And Quill?"

Quill turned, her hand on door.

"Stand up for yourself," he said kindly. "Don't let other people push you around. Remember. You know what you know."

Quill had tied Max to the wrought iron lamppost that stood directly in front of the newly constructed Hemlock Falls Medical Center Building. Dr. Benziger, who came into Hemlock Falls three afternoons a week from his larger practice in Rochester, had joined the group a month ago.

She let the glass door to Dr. Benziger's office close behind her and went to retrieve her dog. Max lay curled in a shaggy heap, his head between his paws. He regarded her sourly for a long moment, then rose to his feet, head down, tail drooping, a study in the Abused and Abandoned. It was sheer dog dramatics; she'd left his portable water bowl filled with spring water within easy reach; his collar was padded with sheepskin; and she'd folded her spring coat underneath him so he wouldn't have to lie directly on the concrete sidewalk. The water bowl lay upside down several feet away where Max had flung it in disgust. And he'd slipped out of his collar again. Quill was touched to see that he'd stuck his head inside her coat sleeves while waiting for her; she could tell from the mass of shaggy hair that lined the arm holes.

He forgave her for leaving him almost instantly, as he always did, and she had an aggravating few moments getting his collar and leash back on while he leaped at her in joy. She stood up, finally, leash in hand and said "Home, Max" and tried not to feel put out when he pulled hard in the opposite direction.

It was a mile and a half walk from this spot in the village to the Inn. Walking to and from her appointment three times a week was part of her new self-improvement program. The other part was, of course, Getting a Grip with the help of Dr. B. What with the brand new medical center and the resort being constructed at the lower end of Hemlock Gorge, Hemlock Falls was in the middle of a self-improvement program, too, so Quill felt happily in synch with the village as she and Max walked briskly down to Main Street.

Most of the buildings on Main were cobblestone, dating from the mid-nineteenth century when Hemlock Falls had enjoyed its first real expansion, and almost all of them had been turned into shops of one kind or another. Everybody on Main seemed to be celebrating the early spring warmth. The white flower urns at the base of the wrought iron lampposts had been cleared of winter debris, and the earth in them freshly turned. Nickerson's Hardware had a sidewalk display of brightly colored wheelbarrows, pitchforks, and rakes. Quill and Max swung by the Croh Bar, where a few umbrella tables had been set out in front. Esther West's Best Dress Shoppe had bunches of artificial daffodils stuck inside the plate glass window. The Fork in the Road, Marge Schmidt's and Betty Hall's all-American diner, had its doors open to the spring breeze.

Quill reached Peterson Park. Beyond the little brick pillars that marked the entrance, the small meadow and thick woods were glowing with the pale-yellowy-green of young spring. "It's a beautiful day, Max," Quill said, breathing deeply. "Let's go look for Meg."

Max barked, wagged his tail furiously, and sat down.

"Meg, Max. Look for Meg."

Max barged ahead to the end of the lead as they turned onto the well-kept gravel trail that led through the park. Quill was under no illusion that Max was tracking her sister; old candy wrappers, discarded Coke cans, and wadded trash of the sort Quill didn't care to think about were of much more interest to him. But when they reached the center of the park with the statue of General C. C. Hemlock on his oddly formed horse, he barked victoriously at the sight of her sister on the park bench beneath, even though Quill knew darn well she'd seen Meg first.

"I don't know why you even bother with the leash," Meg said as Quill sat down next to her. "He can slip his collar any time he wants to."

"It gives me an illusion of control."

Meg looked at her watch. "You're back from Dr. B."

"Yep."

"Did you tell him about this morning?"

"Yep."

"What'd he say?"

"I said I felt guilty. He said I'm not responsible for your behavior."

Meg sat up indignantly. "He said *what*?! What kind of rat therapist tells you it's okay to lie to your sister?"

"He didn't say it was okay to lie to you. He said I wasn't responsible for how you took it."

"If you hadn't lied to me, I would be in the kitchen right this minute. And you're as responsible for the kitchen as I am. We both own the damn place."

Quill sighed. The logic of this was inarguable. "I don't think this was such a hot idea."

"Seeing the shrink? Or lying to me?"

"Don't call him a shrink, Meg. He's a therapist."

"Fine. A rat therapist who encourages his patients to duck major character issues. Like lying."

"I'm not ducking the issues. I'm confronting the issues. I'm in therapy, for goodness' sake. That ought to count for something."

"You lied to me. You never lied to me before you went into therapy."

"That's not true," Quill scoffed.

"Oh? Oh! You've made a practice of lying to me all these years and you're just now getting around to admitting it?"

"Of course not. But our relationship as sisters is an important part of my emotional life, and of course I talk about you."

"I'm the last person in the world to stand in the way of your getting help, Quill," Meg said with infuriating condescension. "Just leave me out of it, okay? I'm not in therapy. *You* are."

"You asked me what happened in my session!" Quill shrieked. "I don't talk about you. I mean I do, but I don't complain about you, which is what you seem to think. You know me better than anyone else, Meg."

"I don't see why you're spending all that money. You can always come to me with your problems."

Meg in a pious mood was the last straw. Quill gritted her teeth and strove for tolerance. "I'm not a particularly religious woman, you know. When a person's confused, you either go to a priest or a shr—I mean a therapist. I'm going to a therapist."

"So you've said."

"Everybody we know in New York goes to a therapist." Quill tugged absently at her hair. "But everybody we know in New York is clinically depressed or chronically anxious or bipolar or dysthymic and I'm not any of those things."

"What are you, then?"

"I've told you. I've told Dr. Benziger. I've told Myles. *I'm confused!*"

"Does Blue Cross cover that? I mean, is confusion a what d'ya call it, a psychological impairment?"

"So far," Quill said darkly. "But the co-pay ran out today."

Meg shifted restlessly on the bench. Quill was relieved. Meg had been sitting quietly. Far too quietly. Her sister was almost always in motion, even when the two of them had a chance to sit and relax over a glass of wine. Quill took her hand and squeezed it lightly. "I am really sorry about this business with Banion O'Haggerty."

"S'all right," Meg muttered.

"I thought you'd pitch a fit over having a rival around. I took the cowardly way out."

"I do not pitch fits," Meg said, her voice rising. Max, who'd flopped flat out on the grass as soon as Quill had taken her seat on the bench, sat up and cocked his head in an interested way at the prospect of loud noise from Meg. Loud noise from Meg was frequently accompanied by airborne objects—a lot of them food related.

"Well, no." Quill retreated hastily, having just spent one hundred and twenty dollars learning to stand up for herself. "You don't pitch fits, Meggie."

"I express myself fluently over legitimate concerns."

"Yep, you do."

"I admit that sometimes, once in a great while, fluency gets the better of me."

Quill kept a prudent silence.

"And occasionally. Very occasionally, I get a little more athletic than I should."

John Raintree, their business manager, had a standing order with the cookware company to replace the eight-inch sauté pan that was Meg's favorite missile.

"So I suppose I shouldn't have actually walked out this morning. But Bjarne was there, and he's run the kitchen alone before."

"Bjarne walked out, too."

Meg's eyes widened. "Wow." Then, "Jeez. Who cooked? Not Margaret. She's not ready."

"I did."

"*You* did!" Meg started to laugh. "Oh, poor Quill!"

"I managed," Quill said a little stiffly, then, because Meg was going to hear it from the staff anyway, and besides, she wasn't going to lie to her sister anymore, "and Banion helped."

Meg bit her lip. "Banion, huh. Well, he would. He's a sucker for the limelight."

"There's more to this um . . . disaffection . . . for Banion O'Haggerty than meets the eye," Quill said. "Isn't there?"

"Um."

"You've run into him before?"

"I've *slept* with him before. Not," Meg added hastily, "that I intend to do it again."

"Wow," Quill said. Then, "Can't say as I blame you. He's really cute." Then, "Hey! When?! You never told me! I thought we told each other everything."

"In New York," Meg said sulkily. "You know. While I was cooking at La Strazza."

"You've stopped cooking at La Strazza. You said it was interfering with your relationship with Andy too much . . ." Quill clapped her hand over her mouth. "You slept with Banion O'Haggerty while you were engaged to Andy?" Another insight struck. "*That's* why you quit La Strazza! And the TV show!"

"I'm still engaged to Andy," Meg said. "And I don't want to talk about it. And besides, you slept with John Raintree while you were still in love with Myles."

"*I never in this life slept with John Raintree.*"

"You thought about it."

"That doesn't count."

"Well, I thought about it and I did it and that's it. End of story." Meg's face was pink.

Quill, thinking of how Banion had whirled around the kitchen like an exceptionally handsome pirate boarding a frigate wasn't sure if she was jealous or admiring. "He does," she admitted finally, "carry a load of testosterone."

Meg made a face compounded equally of smug, chagrin, and embarrassment.

"Well," Quill said. "There's a monkey wrench in the machinery for you. Did he . . . I mean is he here . . . did he show up because . . . ?

"I don't know." Meg wriggled. "It didn't end well, as these things go."

"What do you mean 'as these things go'? Are there other guys you've slept with that I don't know about?"

"Not really." Meg held up her hand in an I'm-not-going-to-talk-about-this gesture. "He wasn't really ready to have the relationship end, and I was, but he's the kind of guy, Quill, that always *does* end a relationship. He just didn't like it that I ended it first."

"Maybe he's in love with you."

"Banion's in love with himself," Meg said briskly. She bounced to her feet. "Come on, let's get back. It's way after four and I've got to get back to the kitchen."

Quill grabbed at Meg's coat. "Wait a second. What about Andy?"

Meg bit her lip. "He's away at the conference."

"Meg, this passive avoidance is very bad for you, psychologically speaking."

"Cut it out," Meg said. "You know what? You spout stuff like that every time you come back from Dr. Benziger. It's getting worse."

"I'm just trying to establish the right degree of your inner responsibility here."

"I'm going to establish a clod of mud in your hair if you don't cut it out."

"Andy may never meet Banion in the flesh, Meg. But he's already met the emotional consequences of Banion, in your behavior."

Meg headed up the slope that led to the Inn at a brisk

trot and yelled over her shoulder, "I'll think about it to-morrow."

"That's what Scarlett O'Hara said," Quill yelled back. "And look what happened to her!" She ran up the slope after Meg, not because she wanted the exercise but because Max pulled so hard at the leash she had to either run or let him loose. Meg slowed down as soon as Quill reached her and they marched more or less amicably side by side.

"Nothing all that awful happened to Scarlett O'Hara," Meg said. "She's one of the few liberated women of pre-World War II fiction."

"It's a horrible book," Quill said reprovingly. "It's racist, historically inaccurate, and sexist."

"Well, you brought her up, not me. I mean I. Anyway, she's lost Rhett Butler but so what? She's got a great business, she's rich, she's only twenty-seven years old, and she's beautiful."

" 'Scarlett O'Hara was not beautiful, but men seldom re-alized it when caught by her charm as the Tarleton twins were,' " Quill quoted.

Meg went very still. "I'm not beautiful either, and as for charm . . ." She whirled and trudged along, her head down. Max whined and tried to lick her hand. "Ugh, dog spit," Meg said, and sniffed.

"Oh, Meg." Quill stopped under a weeping willow and tried not to think of the trite symbolism. She gave her sister a brief, comforting hug. "It'll be fine."

"What'll be fine? That if Banion hangs around until Andy gets back it'll be fine if Andy finds out *that I slept with him*?"

Quill glanced nervously around. They were almost at the lip of the Gorge, and the Inn was only a few hundred yards beyond that. "Well, gee, Meg. Andy's a grown man. You're an adult woman. And you're *loaded* with charm, Meg, and you're beautiful, too."

"I've got it!" Meg's face, a little damp from weeping, flushed with satisfaction. "I should have thought of this before. I'll judge the stupid Fry Away Home contest. And then Banion will have to leave. Plus, I'll have twenty-five thousand dollars. I should have agreed to judge the contest anyway—I was just being charmless. What do you think?"

Quill didn't know what to think. Harry Holcomb had made it pretty clear that Banion O'Haggerty was his first choice. On the other hand, Harry Holcomb had refused to come up with more than twenty-five thousand dollars for the judge's fee, and the mayor would greet Meg's decision with unalloyed relief. And what about the contracts? If Banion had signed the contracts, wouldn't they have to pay him anyway? "I'll fix it," Quill said. "Don't worry. But Meg, shouldn't you tell Andy about this anyway? I mean, isn't it better that he knows?"

Meg cast a skeptical look at her as she clambered over the lip of the Gorge. "What do *you* think?"

Quill scrambled up the slight rise after her and stopped at the top. Meg, jogging, was already halfway across the lawn toward the Inn. She didn't know what to think. She'd just accepted her sister's relationship with Andy. It was a given. They'd been together forever, it seemed. He was the first man in Meg's life after her first husband's death more than ten years ago.

But what did she know about Andy, really? That he treated her sister well. That everyone in Hemlock Falls seemed to like him. Quill stood uncertainly in the twilight.

Max tugged impatiently at his leash. "I'll talk to Marge about the judging!" Quill called out. "It's going to be fine!"

Meg raised one hand without turning around, ran across the flagstone terrace, and disappeared into the Tavern Lounge.

Quill resisted the strong temptation to wander along the Gorge instead of returning to her duties at the Inn. But she stood there for a moment, watching the change of colors in the sky as the sun drifted below the hills. The wind stirred her hair. The air was redolent with the exuberant scent of the water. And the sound of the water from the falls itself was incredibly soothing, a serene sound, better, she'd told Dr. Benziger, than any antidepressant ever made. Okay. She'd talk to Marge, and fix that. She'd have a very stern talk with Doreen about the chicken suit and fix that. And she'd placate Bjarne, too, and make sure that Banion's exit from the contest was as considerate and tactful as possible.

And there was Myles to look forward to, later in the evening. She could tell him everything, and it would all drop into the proper perspective.

She ambled toward the Inn in one of those pleasantly settled states of mind that had been all too unusual in the last year. She became only half-aware of the distant shouts. She was totally unaware that Max had slipped his leash until his barks jerked her attention to the activity at the front door of the Inn.

Three figures—no, four—seemed to be trying to jam through the front door all at the same time. There was a lot of shoving, more shouts, a couple of "whacks," and then they all seemed to fall through to the lobby at once.

Quill made a sound like "urk." What was it Dr. Benziger said? Don't let anyone make you do things you don't want to do. Which obviously didn't apply to career obligations like settling fistfights.

Maybe it wasn't a fistfight.

Quill walked into her lobby, chin up.

It was a fistfight.

She noticed three things all at once: Dina stood on top of the beautiful old mahogany reception desk, well out of the way of the melee; Max ran in circles around the small foyer; and two women were backed against the old fireplace, one thin and elegant with crisp gray hair, the other young, blonde, and with a lot of midriff showing between her Versace jeans and her halter-top. The blonde was screaming "Hit 'im again, Harry!" in between sneezes.

And then there were the two guys socking each other on the cream-colored Oriental rug. Actually, they were *trying* to sock each other. Quill's not-so-secret guilty pleasure was action movies, especially those that starred Arnold Schwarzenegger in dishabille. So she considered herself something of a fight expert and she was mildly surprised to see how clumsy a real fight was. A short, chubby bald guy had his arms wrapped around Harry Holcomb. Harry Holcomb flailed away ineffectually with one hand and tried to land open-handed smacks on the bald guy's head with the other. Quill looked up at Dina, who looked back at her in a bemused sort of way.

Quill stepped around the struggling men. Two Oriental vases always stood in front of the reception desk, filled with seasonal flowers. Right now, they held sprays of purple, pink, and white lilacs. Quill hefted the nearest vase to her waist, and dumped the contents on Harry Holcomb and his opponent.

"That always works in the movies," she said to Dina after a moment.

"Well it isn't working now," Dina said. "Quill, *do* something."

Quill backed up to the leather couch and rubbed the back of her neck. "Maybe you'd better call Myles."

"Call the sheriff?" Dina shouted heatedly. "You mean you need a man to handle this? Come on, Quill . . ." She took an involuntary step backward as the thrashing figures rolled closer to her perch. "Well . . . okay." She swung herself carefully down to her chair and reached for the phone. "Maybe I'd better call Andy, too. That looks like blood on the tall guy."

"Andy's not here," Quill said, raising her voice over the grunts and shrieks.

"Sure he is."

"What?!"

"I said 'sure he is!' He came back from the *convention early*."

"You ladies need a hand here?"

Oh, my, Quill thought. For just as in the better class of Arnold Schwarzenegger movies, Banion O'Haggerty had come to the rescue. There he was, amused eyes bright blue, lounging against the archway to the dining room. Meg, Bjarne, Kathleen Kiddermeister, and a few early patrons of the dining room peered around Banion with horrified interest.

Quill gestured rather helplessly at Banion, and then she wished she hadn't. He took two strides over to the struggling men, kicked the bald one hard in the ribs, and then kicked Harry Holcomb hard under the chin.

The two men broke apart and crouched panting on the carpet.

Silence reigned, except for the shrieking blonde, who quieted instantly at a look from O'Haggerty. She sneezed violently and said in a small apologetic voice, "Allergies." Then, "Charlie, you are a miserable son of a bitch." Her blue eyes narrowed with hatred so sudden and malign that Quill was taken aback.

"Did you have to kick them, Mr. O'Haggerty?" Quill asked coldly. A siren wail rose in the distance, signaling the imminent arrival of the Hemlock Falls Volunteer Ambulance. "It seems excessive."

"Effective, though," Banion grinned.

Quill exchanged a brief glance with Meg (*You slept with this jerk?*) then knelt by the side of the bald man, who lay slumped against the reception desk. He was breathing heavily and there was a long scratch on one cheek that bled a little. Quill lifted his head gently and looked into his eyes. They were a watery green (and somewhat baleful) but not, thankfully, dilated. He squinted up at her. He looked familiar, and Quill, who was very good at remembering faces, mentally added a beaky hat and a feathery halo. "Captain Clu . . . I mean, Mr. Kluckenpacker. Are you feeling dizzy? Can you see clearly?"

"Uh," Charlie Kluckenpacker said. Then, "Did I knock his block off?"

"Not quite."

"Is he bleedin'?"

Quill correctly assumed that Charlie was not expressing concern for Harry Holcomb's well-being. "Buckets," she said cheerfully, without looking around to check.

"Uh." Charlie slumped back with a satisfied grin.

Quill moved aside to let Dina pat his face with a damp cloth. The sneezing blonde dabbed at Harry's nose with a fistful of used Kleenex. (Quill had bet wrong on that one—she'd matched the elegant gray-haired woman with Harry Holcomb.) Holcomb was standing up, nose bleeding, furious, but clearly not in danger of a concussion. He shoved the blonde aside and glared at Captain Cluck. "You stupid s.o.b. What the hell did you think you were doing?"

"Harry, you're bleeding!" the blonde said. She dabbed ineffectually at his nose. "Charlie, you're a beast."

"Beast yourself, Charlene. Takes a beast to know a beast."

"Ow! Charlene, not *now*." Harry waved the blonde away. "Charlie? Stand up."

"Nope. You just want to hit me again."

"You're damn straight I want to hit you again."

Charlie began to struggle to his feet. "Then I'm gonna knock your block off," he offered. "I'm gonna shove your nose right down around your socks. I'm gonna—"

"Yeah? Well I'm going to sue the hell out of you and that sorry excuse for a fried-food franchise. I'm going to—"

"That's enough," Quill said. "Please, gentlemen."

"You better hope that Charlie doesn't sue *you*, Harry." The gray-haired woman sat on the farthest edge of the cream leather couch, one slim leg crossed over the other. Her voice was clear and crisp. "You threw the first punch. That's the correct expression, isn't it, Miss Quilliam? I want both of you to make your apologies to Miss Quilliam and go to your rooms and clean up. Charlie, I will want to eat dinner in an hour."

To Quill's astonishment, both men proceeded up the stairs.

Charlene took a half step toward Harry, then said loudly, "Where's the bar in this goddam place?!"

"Um. Kathleen?" Quill said.

Her head waitress nodded, and drew Charlene down the corridor that led to the Tavern Bar. Mrs. Kluckenpacker (Quill couldn't imagine that it was anyone else) surveyed the foyer, now crowded with waiters, waitresses, and everyone possible from the kitchen, including Bjarne. "Perhaps it would be better if we had a little more air, ladies and gentlemen. You will excuse us, please." The authority in her voice was so clear that everyone except Meg and Banion O'Haggerty melted away from the dining room archway, but not, Quill guessed, any farther than the maitre d' stand where they could still hear what was going on.

Quill turned to the gray-haired woman and said, "I'm impressed. Thank you very much."

"I'm Judith Kluckenpacker. It's Miss Quilliam, isn't it? Please call me Judith." She extended her hand to Quill. Mrs. Kluckenpacker was gloved; proper white kid gloves, the kind that had gone out with Mamie Eisenhower. Quill shook her hand. "Well, Judith. I'm sorry your welcome was so—um—frantic. This is my sister, Margaret Quilliam."

"Oh, yes. Maitre Quilliam. And Chef O'Haggerty, too, I see." Her tone was dry.

Meg, suppressing a grin, came forward and shook Mrs. Kluckenpacker's hand, too.

"I must apologize on behalf of my husband." Mrs. Kluckenpacker rose to her feet. She was wearing a neat double-knit suit in apple green. St. John, Quill thought, those double rows of brass buttons on the jacket a dead giveaway. Judith's double strand of pearls was heavy, expensive, and discreet. A handsome woman, with a strong nose and square chin, she was unabashedly in her mid-sixties. Quill would have bet a dozen of her best paintbrushes that Mrs. Kluckenpacker had never come near a jar of anti-wrinkle cream, much less visited a plastic surgeon.

She was impressed. She was also some years older than Charlie. Quill was impressed with that, too.

"Well," Quill said. "I seem to have—"

"Lost your aplomb?" Mrs. Kluckenpacker smiled. "It's no wonder. They don't mean anything by it, you know. Happens all the time whenever they run into each other. It's unfortunate that we all arrived at the same time. And what the devil is that noise?"

"The Hemlock Falls Volunteer Ambulance," Dina said. "I mean, you *told* me to call them, Quill."

"Oh, my," Quill said. "We'll just have to tell them to go away again. Remind me to send them a check for their trouble, Dina. Oh, *damn!*" She stared at Banion O'Haggerty in consternation. He stood close to Meg, one hand on her arm. Meg seemed not to notice.

"What?" Meg said. "What's the matter now?"

"Is Dr. Bishop with them, too, Dina?" Quill said, too loudly. "Meg, Andy came back rather unexpectedly—"

The front door opened with a bang. It was made of hundred-year-old oak, three inches thick and it made quite an impressive noise. And Andy was the first one through.

CHAPTER 4

"There must be a lot of self-defense courses around," Quill said to Myles McHale. "Are there special courses in subduing people?"

"Of course."

Myles, bless him, didn't laugh. But the wrinkles at the corners of his gray eyes deepened. "You're past the recruitment age, but I could probably get you into basic training at the Police Academy in Ithaca. But any commercial self-defense course would give you enough expertise to break up a fight. If that's what you're after."

Quill handed Myles his Scotch and sat down beside him with her own glass of wine. Max lay on the floor next to the couch, his muzzle across Myles's feet.

"I certainly didn't care for the way O'Haggerty broke up the one in the foyer," Quill said. "He kicked both of them, Myles. There's something really revolting about kicking a man when he's down. There's something revolting about *kicking*."

"That's true," Myles said. "I'm not sure why."

"They don't teach you that stuff at the police academy, do they? Kicking?"

"We try to avoid it."

Quill wasn't sure if this was an answer. She was sure that she didn't want to know.

Myles sipped his Scotch. "The reality's always tougher than the training, Quill. I'm sorry you had to deal with it.

But I can teach you some tactics, if you like."

Quill shuddered. "It wasn't the fight, so much, although that was unsettling enough. Mrs. Holcomb said they do it all the time. It was what happened afterward. When Andy came in."

It was late, well after midnight, and Myles had come to her rooms at the Inn to save her the drive out to his house. Quill was glad he was here. In the past, she'd been confused about her feelings over his presence in her private space. One of the benefits of her visits to Dr. Benziger was that she wasn't confused anymore.

Both she and Meg had three-room suites at the Inn; Meg's was cluttered with pots of herbs, bright posters, and cookbooks. She didn't spend much time in hers; she spent most of her nights with Andy.

Quill's rooms were uncluttered and serene. The carpeting and furniture were neutral shades of ecru and beige; black and white photographs of mountain and desert scenes were mounted on the cream-painted walls; off-white drapes framed the French doors that led to her balcony. She'd liked it this way for years. It was a home where everything was in its proper place, a place where there was no color or vibrant design to distract her. A place where she could shut everything out. Her easel was here. Her books were here. It was, to paraphrase Virginia Woolf, a room of her own.

In the past months, more and more of Myles's things had found their way in: a stack of current science magazines; his winter parka; a Mason jar of pennies and nickels on the birch bookcase; coffee cups with the logo of the investigative firm he worked for; a bottle of Grey Goose vodka and a bottle of Johnny Walker Black; a battery pack for his cell phone; a spare laptop computer. And of course, his shirts and socks and handkerchiefs took up space in her bedroom dresser.

Quill propped her feet on the pine chest she used as a coffee table and ran a mental list of the things she kept at his house: an extra sketchbook, charcoal pencils, shampoo, and a few items of clothing. Not as much. Not nearly as much as he kept here.

Myles drew the palm of his hand down her cheek. "Quill? I can stick around here tomorrow morning if you're worried about another brawl."

Quill looked at him and smiled. He slouched easily next to her, a tall, sun-weathered man in his early fifties with gray eyes and hair that became more salt than pepper every year. He'd spent twenty years with the NYPD, retiring as a senior homicide detective at forty-two. He'd lived hard, this man she'd come to love so much. She took his hand in her own and cradled it in her lap. The thumb was flattened and the middle finger scarred from a knife fight somewhere in his past. And there was a puckered scar on his chest, the relic of a gunshot wound. Like almost all the men she'd been attracted to in her life, he had a hard, muscled chest, strong arms, and a lithe, graceful walk.

"You don't have to go into the sheriff's office?"

He made a grunt of annoyance. He had agreed, with his usual imperturbability, to resume his duties as Tompkins County sheriff, part-time. The Town Council had approached him after the full-time sheriff Davey Kiddermeister had asked for his help. So he'd cut back on the number of assignments from Global Investigations and spent a day or two a week in his old office at the Tompkins County Courthouse, tactfully stepping in when Davey got in over his head.

"I could send a patrolman to stand in the dining room, but the uniform would be a little obvious."

"Oh. Sorry, Myles. No, I don't need any help, thanks. I wasn't thinking about that."

He waited.

"I was thinking that you have more of your stuff here than I have at your place."

He blinked. He raised one eyebrow. "Did you talk to Dr. Benziger about this? Is it significant?" He kissed her ear. "Should I be concerned?"

"Oh, no. Of course not." She leaned into him and kissed him warmly.

Myles had greeted her decision to go to a therapist with an abrupt, "Good." Followed by, "Tell him I want to marry you. And that I want you to make up your mind." Quill had, in fact, told Dr. Benziger just that. And he'd said, "What do *you* think?" which hadn't helped at all.

"Do you think it's helping?"

"What, seeing Dr. Benziger?"

Quill looked at him anxiously. If Myles said "I-don't-know, what-do-you-think," she would scream. "About some things, sure. About others? I'm not so sure. It's so spongy. And all he wants to talk about is how I feel. There's so much more to life than how I feel, Myles. And since half the time I don't know what I feel anyway . . ." She flung her hands up.

"Therapy's a pretty routine practice in police work, Quill. Every time there's a violent incident involving the force, the cops involved have to pay at least one visit to the department psychiatrist."

"You've been in therapy, then?"

"I've had a couple of sessions, yeah," he said warily. "You sound surprised."

"I don't know why I should be," she admitted. "You always seem so focused, Myles. Nothing ever intimidates you, or flaps you. You always seem to do the right thing at the right time. It's very . . ."

"Nice?" he said hopefully. "Attractive? You love me for it?"

"Frustrating."

"Ah."

"Don't do that. That's one of those 'I understand' sort of ah's. It's condescending."

"Hm."

"The 'hm' is a lot better."

"You know, Quill, a large part of life is knowing when to do nothing at all."

"It is, huh."

"Absolutely. Do you want to talk about . . ." he hooded his eyes slightly, which meant, Quill knew, that he was feeling self-conscious, "ah, about us? Or about what happened tonight?"

"About what happened tonight. I think I should go to Meg."

"And I think she's better left alone. Tell me again what happened after Andy came in the door."

Quill gave a short, involuntary sigh. "Oh, dear. Well. I started to babble, you know, the way I do when I'm a little anxious, and I think I said, 'Oh, Andy, so good of you to come, and you too, Denny.' Did I tell you Denny was there? The ambulance driver? I did. Anyhow, then I said, 'Oh Meg, look Andy's back from the conference. Andy, have you met Banion O'Haggerty?' And then . . ." Quill took a deep sip of her wine. "Then that *jerk* O'Haggerty ran his hand up and down Meg's arm in this . . . this . . . disgustingly obvious, intimate way and said, 'Catch you later, Meg.'" Quill set the wine glass down on the coffee table with a thump. Red wine splashed onto the cream Berber carpeting and she glared at the stain.

"Then what happened? Just the facts, Quill. Don't editorialize."

"Andy came in with a big smile for Meg. He saw O'Haggerty. He stopped smiling. Meg looked at Andy, and I'm *not* editorializing Myles, and there was guilt all over her face. It could have been written in foot-high letters: I Have Slept With This Man. Andy spun around on one heel and walked out the door. Meg ran after him. Banion slouched down to the Tavern Lounge where I bet you fifty cents he's smooching up to that blonde bimbo who showed up with Harry Holcomb." She looked at her watch. "Except not now. The bar's closed. Anyway, Denny hung around for half an hour and when neither Meg nor Andy came back he took off down the driveway *with*, I might add, the stupid siren on. Why does Denny run that damn siren every time he gets in the ambulance, Myles?"

"He likes it," Myles said. "It's why he volunteered."

"So Bjarne handled the kitchen tonight and I helped. I didn't know where Meg was until about eleven-thirty or so, when I came up here. I heard Meg in the hall. She walked to her room about twenty minutes before you got here. I heard her."

"Heard her or saw her?"

"Heard her."

"Hm."

"It's the wrong time to say 'hm.' I know my own sister's footsteps, Myles."

Myles didn't say anything. Quill was so anxious she bit her thumbnail. "Meg in her room is not a good sign. She's *always* at Andy's, Myles. Always. And," Quill concluded, "there's forty pounds of shrimp in the Zero King getting wonkier and wonkier because Meg was supposed to be trying out new shrimp recipes today and poor John's budget is going to be blown for the third time running."

Myles shook his head ruefully.

"So what do you think I should do?"

"Stay out of it."

Quill closed her eyes in complete exasperation. "That is so *gender specific!*"

"So what?"

The look on his face would have been funny if she weren't so irritated. "I don't want to fall into cliché here, Myles. But that's a very guy thing to say."

"Oh."

"When women are upset, they want support. Reassurance. Kindness."

"They don't want to be left alone? My guess is that if Meg is alone in her room, Andy's just as alone somewhere else. And he'll want to keep it that way. I mean, I'm just trying to understand the differences in handling the—ah—genders, here."

"So you are. I appreciate it. Let's try this. What if what happened tonight had happened to me? What would you have done?"

He looked at her warily. "Is this a test? Of course it's a test. I should have punched O'Haggerty out?"

"No! That would have been the worst thing you could do."

"Well, I couldn't have punched you out, Quill. That's the other total male response."

"You're not taking this seriously."

Myles rubbed his chin. "Okay. Maybe I'm not. Sorry. But either this will all blow over, Quill, or it won't. I don't see what talking to Meg is going to do to solve the problem. It's between Meg and Bishop. Leave it alone."

"Wrong answer!" Quill said. "I am going to my sister. She needs me to hug her. To tell her she's wonderful. To let her know that men are jerks."

Myles threw his hands up. "Okay."

"I can't solve it. But I can soothe it. Got that?"

"Got it." He grinned. "If I'm awake when you get back, I've got some soothing of my own to suggest."

Quill paused on her way out the door, Max at her heels. "I'll be as quick as I can."

Meg didn't respond to her knock. When Quill opened the door and looked in, it was clear her sister had been there. Her sweatshirt lay on the floor. The sweatpants and socks were nowhere in sight. A bottle of aspirin stood open on the kitchen sink. Quill called, "Meg?"

No response. Max went "whuff" and turned back to the hallway.

"I don't believe you for a minute, Max," Quill said. "I asked you to find her twice before today and you booted it each time. And the park doesn't count because I saw her first."

Nevertheless, she followed Max down the hall and down the two flights of stairs to the foyer. As usual, John Raintree had left the lamp on behind the reception desk when he locked up for the night. The yellow light only served to make the rest of the Inn more deeply dark.

Max trotted purposefully through the dining room and toward the kitchen. Quill walked behind. He nosed the swinging doors open, and fluorescent light washed out. Quill heard the rhythmic "snick-thump" of a knife hitting the wooden chopping board.

"Hey," she said as she came into the kitchen.

"Hey." Meg was chopping shrimp. She'd changed into the T-shirt she wore to sleep in: a cranky little duckling was on the front with the legend "I'm Bad!" printed beneath it. Quill looked at her feet. Barefoot. No socks at all.

Quill drew a stool up to the prep table and sat down. "You look exhausted."

"I'm fine." Meg swept the chopped shrimp aside.

Quill inhaled. "Meg! Are you drunk?"

"Somewhat." She started to grate ginger root. The pungent scent was pleasant.

"I like shrimp and ginger together."

"It's banal. Or can be. I'm going to try some edible flowers with it. And a tomato mayonnaise."

"A tomato mayonnaise? With edible flowers? We can call it May Time Mayonnaise."

Meg made a face.

"Okay. I'll leave the menu description to you; how's about if I try sympathetic sister, instead."

Meg looked up at her. Quill bit her lip. She blinked back sympathetic tears. "That bad, huh?"

Meg held up her left hand. Her ring finger was bare.

"Oh, Meg." Quill was afraid to get up and hug her. Her sister might break. "Listen. He'll get over it. My gosh, it isn't as if you were married, Meg. Jealousy is a terrible force. But it spends itself."

"Spare me the bromides, okay?"

"Okay," Quill said meekly.

Meg whacked away at the shrimp. "He wasn't jealous," she said after a while.

"He wasn't?"

"No. It wasn't my fault, he said."

"He did?"

"I'd been seduced, he said."

"Seduced?"

"Women like me just kind of . . . what was it?" Meg paused, considering. "Oh, yes. Lose what little control we have sometimes."

"Andy said that!?"

"So, under the circumstances—"

"The circumstances being that you are a weak, mindless woman who lost all control when confronted be a powerful male force—"

"Precisely. Under those circumstances, Andy forgave me."

"I sincerely hope," Quill said passionately, "that you shoved that engagement ring right up his nose."

"Actually, I threw it in the parking lot next to the Croh Bar."

"Marge will find it," Quill said in a practical way. "That was a lovely ring. I mean, of course you have to give it back to him. But to do that, you have to have it. If you see what I mean. Oh, Meg. Don't cry. Please don't cry."

Meg put her shrimp-covered hands up to her face. Quill came around the end of the prep table, then took her sister to the rocking chair by the fireplace. She took a hand towel from the stack by the vegetable sink, wiped Meg's hands and face, and searched in the pockets of her skirt for tissue.

"I'll make some tea."

Meg scrubbed at her face. "I'm thirty-two," she said in a quavering way. "I thought it was time to get married."

"The biological clock," Quill offered.

"That and, I don't know. I love to cook, Quill. But it's a life that eats you up, you know? No pun intended."

"I know."

"Professional chefs . . ." Meg shuddered. "Ugh! The competition's awful. The spite and malice are not to be

believed. And it's a popularity contest, Quill. I mean, let's
face it. There's only so much you can do to food before
you start getting just plain stupid about it! Black bean ice
cream? Crushed bean sprouts and meringue? Raw tuna in
pastry? You know, Marge has a point about gourmet food.
As far as the state it's in these days."

"You're right," Quill said.

"And the demands for presentation are ridiculous! Do
you know I've been seriously thinking of asking you to
design the pattern for the dessert plate presentations?! I actually *contemplated* being able to tell the editor of
L'Aperitif that the food art was by Quilliam?"

"I wouldn't have minded," Quill said. Although she
would have. A lot.

"The competition for recipes is not only insane, half the
time the results taste terrible. *Terrible! No human can eat
them!* And to keep up I have to do TV and interviews and
all the time, Quill, all the time, *I just want to cook good
food!*"

Quill decided to get straight to the point. "Do you love
Andy?"

Meg jumped up from the rocker, grabbed the eight-inch
sauté pan and threw it against the wall. *"Yes!"* Then she
sat down again. "So," she said, calmly. "Half the time I'm
thinking this way. I marry Andy. I retire from the really
fierce competition, you know? I mean, I'd have a baby, too.
Have Bjarne handle the day-to-day stuff in the kitchen.
Concentrate on growing some really great vegetables and
herbs."

"Sounds like a great plan to me."

"Well, it *was* a great plan." Meg began to rock, furiously.
Max, who'd been sitting at attention once the shouting
started, sniffed the floor for any stray bits of food, then
curled into a ball near Quill's feet and heaved a deep sigh.

Meg contemplated the dog with an expression of gloom.
"That's right, Max. Just give it up. Don't you want a treat,
Max? A treat?"

Max jumped to his feet.

"I'll get it," Quill said. "What do you want to give him?" She knew better than to rummage in Meg's refrigerator without asking first.

"Some fool in the dining room sent back Bjarne's Beef Wellington," Meg said. "I told him to back off the mustard, but no. Would he listen to me? Stubborn Finn. Anyway, whack off a piece of that. Don't use the boning knife, Quill. Use the butcher knife."

Quill opened the knife drawer. "It's not here."

"Of course it is. It's always there."

"It isn't here, Meg."

Meg jumped up and shoved Quill aside. "The butcher knife isn't here."

"I just told you that."

"Use the boning knife then. I'll resharpen it tomorrow." She sank back into the rocker, folded her arms across her stomach, and started to cry again. Quill fed Max, took the now-boiling kettle off the hob, and prepared some chamomile tea.

"Andy and I never argue. This was our first argument."

"All couples argue, Meg."

"But who knew he'd be such a *pig!*"

Quill handed her the tea and crouched by the rocker. "You know what?"

"What!"

"Is this the first time Andy's ever pulled this weak little woman stuff on you?"

"Yes. But since I never want to see his stupid face again, who cares? Why even discuss it?!"

"I was just thinking about the times you guys go camping."

"So?"

"Does Andy insist on carrying all the heavy stuff?"

"No."

"And you taught him to shoot skeet."

"Yeah. I did. So what?"

"He told me you were a superb shot. He thought you could make a national competition if you ever wanted to."

"So what, Quill?"

"And you beat him all the time at tennis."

"Regularly."

"But he's always ready to go back and get trounced again."

"So what? Who cares? I made more money than he did last year, too . . ." Meg stopped in midsentence. "Oh. I'm beginning to see where you're headed."

"Good. Andy likes strong, independent women. Or at least, his behavior seems to point that way. This was an argument, Meg. A quarrel. People say things in a quarrel that they don't mean. What's more, they say the most hurtful things they can think of."

"Even Andy?"

"Even Andy."

Quill rinsed the kettle out, wiped down the prep table, and threw the shrimp in the garbage. The wall clock said one-forty-five. She'd make Max go out for his final walk and get Meg to bed.

Meg said dismally, "He'll never speak to me again after tonight."

"I don't know what you said to each other, but I'd be amazed if he wasn't feeling as awful as you are."

Two sharp knocks sounded at the back door. Max flattened his ears and wagged his tail. Quill looked at Meg. "It's somebody we know," she said cheerfully. "Look at Max."

"Who'd be up this late?"

"We won't know until we open the door, will we? You go, Meg."

Quill was so certain that it was a contrite and repentant internist that she was halfway out the swinging doors when Meg called her. She went back to the kitchen. Davey Kiddermeister stood there, John Raintree beside him.

Davey was in uniform. "Myles here?" he asked abruptly.

Quill smiled at John, who said, "I saw the lights. Knew you were up. Davey wanted to call but I thought it'd be better if we came over."

"You know that TV chef?" Davey said.

"Banion O'Haggerty?" Quill said. "He's asleep upstairs. I think. Shall I wake him up? I wouldn't mind doing it with a frying pan, either. I hope he's done something awful. I hope you're here to take him to jail."

"He's not going anywhere but the Tompkins County Morgue," Davey said. "Betty Hall found him back of the dumpsite at the Croh Bar. He's dead."

CHAPTER 5

Myles sent Meg to bed. He told Quill that she'd just be in the way at the crime scene. And all she could get out of Davey Kiddermeister was that it was a crime scene.

Quill went up to Meg's room and knocked on the door.

Meg refused to talk to her. She wouldn't let her in.

She'd been out, that's where.

Quill thought she'd murdered Banion O'Haggerty, didn't she? Her own sister was a jerk and a creep. Fine. Just fine. Just leave her alone.

Quill left her and prowled restlessly around the Inn. Visions of Banion O'Haggerty's corpse lurked in every shadowed corner. Had he been shot? Strangled? Quill stood in the darkened dining room and her heart went cold. The knife. Meg's butcher knife. She remembered how O'Haggerty had refused to let his own case of knives out of his hands. All chefs were like that about their knives. Nobody used a chef's personal knife. Meg's fingerprints were all over it.

She was scared to death that her sister had cut Banion O'Haggerty's throat. She ran to the kitchen and began a frantic search. She went through all the drawers, the shelves, the pantry. She checked the dishwashing machines, in the hope that one of the staff might have had temporary loss of all common sense and put the knife in one.

Nothing.

Quill sat at the prep table and buried her face in her

hands, trying fiercely to concentrate. She'd been standing here when Banion himself had waltzed into the kitchen.

And he'd brought his own knife case with him.

Quill raced as noiselessly as she could back through the dining room and to the reception desk. They kept a set of master keys locked in the top drawer. She spent agonized minutes searching for the drawer key and finally found it in the cloisonné bowl she kept on the desk in her office.

What room had they given him? 212? 214? 212. She was certain it was 212.

She went up one floor and slipped the key into the lock. The door swung open and she peered around the edge. The light from the hall was dim, but she could see that the bed was still made. Banion's Vuitton luggage sat unopened at the luggage rack.

She stepped into the room, closed the door softly behind her and flipped on the light.

The knife case was under the bed. She popped it open. And there it was, tucked into the top of the velvet-lined case.

She held it under the light, searching for remnants of blood. The metal edge was honed to a lethal whisper of steel. But it looked clean. She took the knife into the bathroom and scrubbed it under the tap until she was sure it could have been used in surgery. She let it air dry, then used a hand towel and grasped the blade gingerly.

She went down to the kitchen and replaced the knife in the drawer. Then she threw the towel down the laundry chute and went to bed.

Quill woke at nine o'clock, feeling ill prepared and unready for the day, as if she were about to start a marathon with bare feet. A cup of strong coffee helped a little; a hot shower helped a lot. Wrapped in her bathrobe, a second cup of coffee in her hand, she opened the French doors to her balcony and stepped outside. The day was overcast and cool. And Myles was outside the back door to the kitchen.

He was in the same black pullover and sports coat he'd

pulled on the night before, although Quill noticed he'd had time to shave. She leaned over the railing, pulling her robe tightly against her.

"Myles?"

He looked up and smiled briefly. "You're beautiful against the light. You ought to wear your hair down more often."

Quill felt so guilty she wanted to jump off the balcony. Instead, she said as lightly as possible, "Is that your way of telling me to butt out? What happened? Do you have anyone in custody? Are there any witnesses? Did you find the knife?"

He frowned. "What knife?"

"His throat was cut, wasn't it?"

"He was strangled," Myles said briefly. "By someone who knew how." He shaded his eyes against the glare of the morning sun. "Why did you think his throat was cut?"

Quill bit her lip.

"Quill?"

"Nothing." She smiled down at him. The morning suddenly seemed much brighter. "Why are you coming in the back way?"

"You know I have to take Meg's statement, Quill."

"Not without me, you're not!" He disappeared into the kitchen. Quill raced into jeans, a pullover, and a pair of Docksiders and ran downstairs. Dina wasn't at the reception desk. John was. Quill stopped at the foot of the stairs and took a deep breath. "Well?"

He shook his head. "I don't know much." His thick black hair was, as usual, neatly combed, his shirt crisply pressed, and the dark gray blazer he always wore hung elegantly on his wiry frame. "The body's been taken to the morgue in Ithaca."

"I should have gone with you guys."

John pressed his lips together. "Not a pretty sight," he said. "You were better off here."

Quill crossed the foyer and glanced into the dining room. It was full. "Any reporters yet?"

"Not yet. Stoke turned up, of course, so there'll be a story in the *Gazette*. But I don't think the guests know anything yet. Can't say the same about the village. I stopped by Marge's diner for breakfast with Myles and Davey. The town's full of the news, of course."

Quill rubbed her forehead. "I've got to get back to the kitchen. Myles just came in. To talk to Meg. Has he talked to . . . I mean. What about Andy? He's the coroner. I assume he was there last night. With you guys, I mean. As part of the investigation. Myles said Banion was strangled. By someone who knew how."

John didn't say anything for a moment. Then, "Myles called the Tompkins County coroner in, Quill. He thought it best. Under the circumstances."

Quill swore. Then she said, "What are we going to do?" Then she swore again.

"Wait," John said. "There isn't anything *to* do at the moment. We have to let the sheriff's office handle it."

"Men!" Quill exploded. "We have to do something, John. We can't just let Andy . . ." she trailed off. If she said it aloud, it would make it more real.

"Do you really think either Meg or Andy murdered Banion O'Haggerty?" John asked.

"Of course not! But John, it looks like—"

"I know what it looks like. But Davey isn't in charge of the investigation, Myles is."

"That's true, Myles is."

"We'll get through it, Quill. We always have before. Go on. See to Meg."

"What about the guests," Quill said distractedly. "And this *bloody* cooking contest. And there's a Chamber meeting this afternoon, too, Oh, ugh!"

"There's always the patented Sarah Quilliam Last Resort." John smiled.

"You mean gain twenty pounds, dye my hair blonde, and move to Detroit? That one?"

"You could always run away and marry me."

"Tricia would have something to say about that."

John's smile widened to a grin. "She probably would, at that. Go on, Quill, go. Everything's under control here."

The shortest route to the kitchen was through the dining room and the tables filled with guests. Nosy, inquiring guests. Nosy, inquiring *paying* guests, Quill reminded herself. She briefly considered going through the front door and walking all the way around to the kitchen that way, then rejected it. "Ma Quilliam didn't raise no cowards," she muttered, and with a wave to John, she plunged into the dining room.

The Holcombs and the Kluckenpackers were seated at opposite ends of the room. The Holcombs had table seven by the windows that overlooked the waterfall; the Kluckenpackers were against the wall that held the wine. Quill could get to the kitchen without passing either of them. That was good.

Mayor Henry and Marge Schmidt occupied table twenty by the swinging doors. That was bad.

Quill forced herself to a leisurely, Competent Innkeeper stroll. She paused at a few tables to inquire after the patrons' well being, raised a friendly hand to Judith Kluckenpacker, and managed to appear as if nothing whatsoever was wrong.

"Hold it," Marge said as she reached the doors to the kitchen.

"In a minute, Marge," Quill said, and made her escape. Meg wasn't there.

"Where's Meg?" she demanded. "And where's Myles?"

Bjarne, fully occupied with the hollandaise for Eggs a la Quilliam, jerked his chin at the back door.

"The sheriff took her," Elizabeth Chu said. "I mean, not in handcuffs or anything. He just said it'd be quieter if they talked somewhere else. Quill! Can you believe it? Do you think that Andy . . ." She faltered under Quill's fierce gaze. "Um. Never mind."

"Everybody in this kitchen listen to me *right now!*" Quill said. "There has been an unfortunate incident. We will conduct business as usual. And my sister didn't do it. Andy didn't do it. And there will be no gossip about this. You guys hear me? No speculation, no rumormongering. Our collective lips are sealed."

"There's lots of other suspects other than Andy and Meg," Elizabeth said stoutly. "If anyone was asking to be murdered, it was Banion O'Haggerty. Did you hear what happened in the Tavern Lounge last night?"

"No. What?" Quill demanded. "The last I saw O'Haggerty, he was headed there with Charlene. And you know where I was last night, I was here in the kitchen with you guys."

"Charlene?" Bjarne asked.

"The blonde babe with Wholesome Harry," somebody said.

"What?" Quill said. "What happened?"

"I didn't see it," Elizabeth said with a scrupulous air, "but Kathleen Kiddermeister did. I guess Banion was all over Charlene. And I mean all over, Quill. You know that skimpy little halter-top she was wearing when they checked in?" Elizabeth rolled her eyes. "Do you know what he was doing with his hands?"

"Oh, dear," Quill said. "I suppose Harry came looking for his wife."

Elizabeth nodded vigorously.

"And then what?"

"Pow!" Elizabeth smacked her right fist into the air. "Banion ducked, of course, and then he socked Harry."

"Wow," Quill said. "Not in the nose, I hope. Charlie Kluckenpacker already socked him in the nose."

"In the nose," Elizabeth said with satisfaction. "Nate broke it up."

"How?" Quill asked. Maybe she could get a few pointers from Nate. "Tactfully, I hope."

"Grabbed Harry by the back of the neck, pulled him out of the way, and shoved Banion onto a bar stool. Then he gave Banion a whiskey, and the blonde—Charlene you said her name was?—he gave Charlene a bar towel to stop Harry's nosebleed and sent her and Harry on their way."

"Did they go back upstairs?" Quill asked.

"I don't know."

"How long did Banion stay in the bar?"

Elizabeth shrugged.

"How much did Banion have to drink after that whiskey? And where did Charlene go? Did anyone see her actually go into her room?"

Elizabeth's eyes lit up. "Are you going to investigate this case, Quill? 'Cause if you are, I could like, give you a hand."

"Meg is the other detective," Bjarne said. "You, Elizabeth, are a cook. Somebody give me those poached eggs."

"But Meg's a suspect. She can't . . ." Elizabeth clamped her mouth shut. "Forget I said that, Quill."

"I certainly will," Quill said coolly. "I'm going out for a while, Bjarne."

"If it is to the sheriff's office, Sheriff McHale says please not."

"What?"

"Sheriff McHale said it would be better if he talked to Meg alone. Otherwise there might be an appearance of improperness."

"Impropriety," Elizabeth said helpfully. "He said you would understand that frequently it's better to do nothing."

"I can't just stand here," Quill said furiously, "while my sister's being interrogated by the police."

"You could shave prosciutto," Bjarne suggested.

Quill banged out of the kitchen and into the dining room before she remembered that Marge and the mayor were lying in wait.

"Quill!" Marge said. "Sit! Now!"

Quill sat.

"This is a fine kettle of fish." Marge was stolid as a Buddha, but her eyes glittered. "Elmer, will you *stop* that fidgeting. Nothing's going to happen to your precious contest. We'll just get Meg to judge it."

"That letter of agreement have anything to say if the fella who signed it's dead?" The mayor wiped his face with his napkin. "He signed it, didn't he? Do I have to pay the estate?"

"Will ya stop fussin' for cripe's sake? I drafted the letter myself," Marge said. "You're off the hook, Elmer." She laughed heartily. "Unless *you* killed him to save yourself the twenty-five thousand bucks."

Quill's eyes widened. She knew that people had killed for much less.

"I'm not fussin'," he complained. "And I'm not worryin' about the contest. And I know Meg wouldn't kill Andy and that she'll be a trouper and judge this-here thing for us. Unless Andy killed O'Haggerty. She might not be in the mood, then. But nah, she didn't kill him."

"Thank you, Mayor," Quill said. "I hope you tell everyone in town the same thing."

"Don't thank me. She and Howie Murchison were singing the roof off at the Croh Bar last night. Only time Meg shut up, beg your pardon, Quill, was when Miriam Doncaster walked her to the ladies room. She didn't have time to do it."

Quill closed her eyes for a minute. Marge gave her hand a friendly squeeze. "You know she couldn'ta done it."

"I know. But under the circumstances . . ."

"Yeah. Elmer, sit *still*!"

The mayor had been moving restlessly back and forth in his chair. He stopped. "But I'm distracted, naturally, what with this murder and all."

"Hush," Marge ordered. She swept her gaze around the dining room. The room was filled with the happy chattering hum of satisfied diners. "Far as I can tell, the news hasn't reached 'em yet."

"It will," Quill said gloomily. The wait staff was far too well trained to drop gossip while food was being served, but she knew she was right. A family of four was leaving their table now, and they'd stroll down to the village to admire the quaint cobblestone buildings. Inevitably, they'd all end up at Adela's gift shop or Marge's diner for coffee. Some of them would pick up the *Hemlock Falls Gazette*, too. Quill was certain Stoke would publish a special edition. He always did. "It doesn't matter when they find out, anyway. They will. Sooner better than later, I suppose."

"That's just it." Elmer leaned toward her earnestly. "Marge and I were hoping we could keep the lid on it for a while. Especially concerning our friend, there."

"What friend?" Quill asked.

"He means Harry Holcomb." Marge took a large slurp of coffee and an even larger bite of a chocolate-filled croissant. "The mayor here's afraid he's gonna back out."

"Of the deep-fat frying contest?" Quill said hopefully. "I think that's a very good idea, Elmer. Meg, I mean none of us is going to be in much of a mood for a festival."

"Not the contest," Marge said flatly. "The contracts are signed and the tents go up as soon as the Zoning Commission approves it and Holcomb's ad campaign is all set to go. Nah. It'd cost him too much to back out now."

"It won't cost him a dime to back out of the chicken business," the mayor said. "And I know for a fact the folks over in Trumansburg would be as happy as spit to get him to move it over there."

Quill looked at him curiously. "You don't sound too upset about it."

"I'm a businessman," he said loftily. "I got a head on my shoulders." He scowled. "This whole thing requires a lot of delicate negotiation, is all! And I'm in charge."

"This whole thing? What whole thing?"

"It's just a deal, Elmer," Marge said.

"I don't do that many of 'em."

"Are you talking about the contest or the chicken franchise?" Quill asked. "I thought you wanted the Holcomb's Wholesome here." She was still trying to catch up on the conversation. "And you said there's a zoning meeting this afternoon? I thought there was a Chamber meeting this afternoon. Do I have to be at both of them?"

"Chamber's at four. Hearing's at two. Just a formality, to approve the license for the tents. Elmer ain't even goin' to be there. They can vote with just the two members, and nobody's gonna object to the tent license." Marge set her coffee cup on the table with a thump. "So. Elmer here was thinking you could take Harry and what's her name, Charlene, on a wine tour this morning. Maybe show him how the resort construction's going down at the bottom of the river. It's not a bad idea. I'd do it myself but I got the diner to tend to at noon."

"You know, schmooze him a little," Elmer added. "He loved that slide show about Hemlock Falls that Harvey put together, but it's not a patch on the real thing. I mean to say, Hemlock Falls sells itself."

"Then you don't need me," Quill said. "You'd be a perfect tour guide."

"I'm not a famous artist who looks like Katharine Hepburn," the mayor said. "And Marge ain't, either."

"I'm sorry, guys, but I just can't. Not today."

"Meg'll be fine," Marge said, with unexpected sensitivity. "The sheriff'll take care of it."

Quill looked at her gratefully. "But you do understand, Marge, I can't just waltz off and leave her."

"Why not? She was in my bar all night. She sings like a Buick with a bad muffler."

Well, that was the familiar Marge. Quill bit her lip. "I just can't."

"And what are you gonna do? Hold her hand all day?" Marge slapped her heartily on the back. "Let her get back to work. That bozo from the magazine's coming in day after tomorrow, isn't she? Meg's got a long way to go with that shrimp if what I tasted yesterday is any sample. And it's a darn good thing. Keep her mind off it."

"Please, Quill." The mayor showed all his teeth in a hope-filled grin.

"I really doubt that a tour of Hemlock Falls is going to make one bit of difference to Harry Holcomb's plans, guys." She glanced over to his table. He was on his cell phone. His nose looked awful. Charlene stared out of the window, bored and occasionally sneezing. The table was littered with damp Kleenex. Ugh. "I'll bet he already knows about the murder anyway."

"So, you can schmooze him out of bein' upset by it," Elmer said ingenuously. "Please, Quill. For the town."

Quill clutched her forehead. "Okay. Look, I'll go over and ask them if they'd like a tour. Okay? But I'm not leaving here until Meg gets back."

"Back from where?" Elmer said. His eyes widened. "What I heard down to Marge's this morning true? She did it after all? Has Meg been arrested?"

"No, she has not been arrested," Quill said heatedly. "She has an alibi."

"Alibis can be broken," Elmer said wisely. "I mean to say, she coulda snuck out of that singing, maybe."

"And if you're going to spread stories like that, Mayor, if you're even going to listen to stories like that, you can take your stupid wine tour and—"

"Hold it," Marge said. "Don't be a damn fool today, Elmer, okay? Just once, try for twenty-four hours without puttin' your size eleven's between your teeth." She sat back with a sigh, "Meg didn't kill anybody. Now, Doc Bishop . . ." She shook her head. "Never can tell what a jealous man might do."

"The gossip mill *has* been busy," Quill said sweetly. She twisted her napkin hard, to keep from losing her temper. "Look here, you two—"

"Miss Quilliam?"

Quill knew that crisp, clear voice. She turned and rose from her chair. "Mrs. Kluckenpacker, I mean Judith. And Mr. Kluckenpacker."

"Call me Cap," Charlie Kluckenpacker said. "Everyone does."

"Everyone calls you Charlie," Judith said. "Nobody calls you Cap." She nodded graciously at Quill. "We have a favor to ask."

"Certainly." Quill was very glad to be back on familiar innkeeper's ground.

"Jude and I were thinking maybe we could join you and Hotshot Harry for that tour this morning."

"Charles overhead the mayor's invitation to the Holcombs this morning," Judith said. "And as is usual with Charles, impulse wins out over manners. But I, too, would like to see more of Hemlock Falls."

Quill stared stonily at Marge (who winked) and then at the mayor, who started shifting back and forth in his chair again.

"About eleven o'clock, then?" Judith said. "Is that correct, Mayor Henry?"

Quill, exasperated, wondered why the heck the mayor hadn't panicked over the prospect of the rival chicken entrepreneurs spending time in the same van together. Then she thought about it. It was typical of Elmer's scatterbrained approach to his deals. "You realize that Mr. And Mrs. Holcomb will be with us," she said. "In view of yesterday's—um—incident, you might want to arrange to go another time."

"There will be no further incidents," Judith said with the authority of MacArthur promising to return.

"That's all set, then," Elmer said breezily, "Eleven. That's what I told the Holcombs. They're gonna be at the reception desk." He avoided Quill's furious eyes and bounced to his feet. "You're going to have a great time in Hemlock Falls, Judy."

"Mrs. Kluckenpacker," she returned icily. Her gaze

swept over Quill's jeans and pullover. "Will we be—er—climbing around outside? If so, I shall change." She was dressed in a periwinkle blue St. John's double-knit this morning. And the double strand of pearls around her neck was at least eight millimeters. Her husband, on the other hand, was the kind of man who always looked as if he'd slept in his clothes. His striped shirt had obviously started out the morning fresh from the dry cleaners, but there were specks of egg on his starched shirtfront, and the shirt buttons gaped over his belly. The remnants of last night's scuffle were evident in a large bruise over one watery eye and the inflamed scratch on his cheek.

"No, we won't be hiking anywhere. I was in a hurry to get downstairs this morning," Quill said, "I'll just go back upstairs to change. I'll see you both about eleven in the foyer, then."

"That will be fine." Judith nodded pleasantly to them. "Come, Charles."

"It's wonderful, ain't it?" Elmer breathed. "That lady has class."

"That lady's a natural general," Quill said wryly. "Elmer, next time you have an impulse to arrange my morning for me, please don't, okay?"

"The town'll be eternally grateful to you, Quill."

"It'll do you good to get out, too, Quill." Marge's naturally belligerent expression softened. "It's gonna be okay. You'll see. Meg's gonna come out of this just fine. Andy? I ain't so sure about Andy."

Quill went back to her room and called Meg.

"I'm just fine." Meg's voice was a bit distorted by the cell phone line, but Quill couldn't detect anything but fatigue in her voice. "I'm leaving the sheriff's office now."

"Do you want me to come and pick you up?"

"No. I've got my car. I followed Myles here. I want a little time by myself, Quill, okay?"

"Are you sure? I can cancel this stupid tour in two seconds flat."

"I'm positive."

"Have you seen . . . I mean did you talk—"

"To Andy." The pause was so long, Quill thought they'd been disconnected. "Not yet. I want to think about it."

"Listen, you need me you call me. Right?"

"Right."

"Are you coming back here?"

"In a while. You'll tell them in the kitchen."

"Sure. Meg . . ."

But her sister had clicked off.

Quill tossed the cell phone in her purse and closed her eyes for a long moment. She was going to bug out of therapy. Instead, she was going to find a Zen center somewhere, and learn to float with the cosmic tide. She counted backwards from one hundred, got bored by the time she reached fifty-three, looked at her watch, and said, "Darn!" Judith Kluckenpacker didn't strike her as the tolerant type. She was already late.

She jumped in the shower and put on a skirt and light sweater.

She was downstairs with her hand outstretched in greeting when she remembered that MacArthur never had gotten back to the Philippines. But both Judith and Charlie were there, and so was Harry Holcomb. Dina was behind the reception desk, and her cheerful nonchalance seemed to be keeping both Charlie and Harry from each other's throats. Judith sat coolly remote on the couch. Charlene wasn't in sight.

"Freshwater pond ecology," Dina concluded as Quill came toward them. "Hi, Quill! I was just telling Mr. Holcomb about my dissertation."

One of them, Quill thought, is going to say "What's a cute little lady like you studying all those muddy ponds, for?"

"A cute little lady like you," Charlie said, "ought to think about a career in fried chicken."

Dina wrinkled her nose. "Ugh. All that hydrogenated fat."

"As far as the bottom feeders in our business are concerned, you're right," Harry said with a vicious look at Charlie. "But Holcomb's Wholesome uses canola oil—"

"Which is why your chicken is soggy, pal," Charlie said. "Thing is, Dina, you can't get canola hot enough to get the chicken fried crisp, the way folks like it."

"Motor oil," Harry said, "has a higher boiling point than canola, too. And you might just as well soak chicken in that as in that crap vegetable oil you get."

"Dina!" Quill interrupted a little desperately. "I forgot to ask Mike to bring the van around."

"I didn't," she said. "Mike's got it right outside." She looked at Quill over her big round glasses and said in a meaningful way, "You're touring Hemlock Falls with all of them? Together?"

"Yes," Quill said firmly. "And we're going to have a wonderful time. Except, oh, darn it, Dina, I forgot to ask the kitchen for a hamper."

"Taken care of," Dina said. Quill was pleased. Really, when she wasn't distracted by cocephods or Davey Kiddermeister, Dina was a terrific employee.

Quill made shooing motions to get the two men out the door. Mike had parked the van conveniently near the entrance. "Judith?" she called. "We're ready." She slid open the side door. "It seats eight very comfortably. Perhaps you,—um—Captain—might want to sit way in the back and you, Mr. Holcomb, can sit up with me. And Judith and Charlene . . ." She looked around. "Where's Charlene?"

"Sleeping in," Harry said flatly. He held the front door open for Quill and Judith, but let go as Charlie came through.

"Don't think so, pally," Charlie said, shoving Harry slightly aside. "Saw you two at breakfast, didn't we, Judith? If she don't want to breathe the same air as me, I got no problem with that. 'Sides. I tell you where I think she is. She was chatting up that good-looking Indian you got as business manager, Quill."

Quill bristled, but kept silent. John was an American Indian, and proud of it, too. But wasn't there the slightest hint of contempt in Charlie's voice? Attitudes like good old Charlie's were the toughest to battle.

The four of them reached the van together. Quill wasn't sure how much she liked the van. The Inn at Hemlock Falls was discreetly lettered in a small bronze logo on the passenger door. It was very useful if Mike had to pick up guests at the train station or the airport in Ithaca. It was new, a testament to their recent (and welcome) prosperity, but it was big and she tended to forget how long it was, especially when she was backing up. And even though it was a Honda, it seemed to guzzle gas, which always made Quill feel guilty.

"I'll get in the front," Charlie said.

"I'll get in the front," Judith said. "Charles. Sit in the back. Miss Quilliam has a hamper there. Harry? I don't care where you sit, as long as it isn't within striking distance."

Firmness and clarity were all, Quill decided. She should call up the Cornell School for Hotel Management to recruit Judith to give a course. It could be titled "Battlefield Rules! Managing the Unmanageable Guest," or something. She buckled her seat belt, turned the ignition, and pulled down the driveway. She said, "We'll drive through the village first, on our way to Route 15."

"You don't mind if we have a few unscheduled stops," Judith declared.

"Not at all. This is one of the most beautiful spots in upstate New—"

"Stop right here. Please."

"But we haven't gotten out of the driveway yet."

"And I haven't truly appreciated your inn yet."

Quill turned off the ignition.

"Everybody out," Judith said.

Everybody piled out. Quill had gotten far enough down the drive so that they had a full view of her inn. The weather had cleared, and the sun was out. The building sprawled across the thick green lawns under the spring sun. The copper roof had a perfect patina. The old stone walls were a soft and mellow ochre. Mike's first spring job was to clean up the winter debris from the flagstone gardens, so the first new leaves on the rose bushes stood free. The fountain in the fishpond sent sparkling sprays of water into the scented air. The waterfall was behind them, the gentle rush of the waters a perfect aural complement to the whole view.

"Is this land all yours?" Judith asked.

"We have seven acres. There's a large herb and vegetable garden in back. My sister . . ." Quill flashed on a memory of Meg in the kitchen the night before. Poor Meg. All her sister wanted was to cook and garden and marry Andy. "My sister likes to garden, but she doesn't have a lot time, as you can imagine. But we grow a lot of our own produce— most of the lettuces, peas, beans, and all of the herbs that can handle this climate. We've thought about adding a greenhouse to the maintenance sheds out back."

"You seem to occupy a great deal more than seven acres." Judith shifted the Prada bag she was carrying from her left arm to her right.

"The whole effect is much larger than that," Quill admitted. "Our property abuts Peterson Park on the south, and the Gorge on the east, of course. But the property out back and the woods to the side belong to somebody else. A Peterson, I think. I'm not sure. But we're lucky. No one's built on it, yet."

"Very beautiful," Judith said. "And the Inn has been here how long?"

Quill had this particular speech ready to roll. In the dark, debt-ridden days of the past, she'd tried running paid tours of the Inn (which did have an interesting history). So she talked about the Civil War general C. C. Hemlock who built the Inn to its present size, and Turkey Lil, the half-

Onondaga entrepreneur who'd run a trading post for trappers in the late seventeenth century, until Charlie disappeared into the back seat with a comment about the hamper and Harry Holcomb began kicking the Honda's tires one by one.

"This is extremely interesting," Judith said with a surprising degree of warmth. "But yes, we are losing the gentlemen. Perhaps you can give me a private tour, later. Your receptionist said the upstairs rooms are beautiful."

"She did?" Quill said, pleased. She chatted easily about the Provencal suite, and how the Federal suite, while in period, was not one of her favorites as they all piled up in the van.

"Now," Quill resumed, as she buckled her seat belt. "We'll start by going through the village on our way to—"

"96," Harry said abruptly.

"Excuse me?"

"There's a grower on Route 96. I'd like to go there, next."

"A grow . . . oh! You mean a chicken farmer." She thought a minute. Heavenly Hoggs Pig Farm was on 96. And there were half a dozen dairy operations within several miles of one another. But she didn't recall any chicken farmers. Meg would know, but Meg wanted to be alone for a while. "*Do* you know where on 96?"

Harry waved his hand dismissively. "On the edge of town."

"96 goes east all the way to Rochester and west all the way to Covert," Quill said dryly. "And I have a meeting back here at four."

"Ask somebody," Judith said.

Quill took a moment to mentally run through the laws of innkeeping she'd recited to Dr. Benziger the day before. She'd forgotten rule four: You Must Tolerate Ordinary Rudeness. She and Meg had gotten into a major squabble over what ordinary rudeness was.

"Quill?" Judith said. "Are you with us?"

"Oh. Yes. Sorry. If anyone would know where the chicken grower is, it'd be Harland Peterson."

"Who he?" asked Charlie, who'd decided to be cute. "Harland? What kind of name is Harland?"

"A distinguished farming name around here, I'm sure," Judith said in her measured way. "And where would this Harland be?"

Quill looked at the clock on the dashboard. "Good grief! It's noon already! Well, he'll be at Marge's diner for dinner."

"Dinner. Dinner's at eight," Charlie said. "Har-har."

"Another farming tradition, I believe," Judith said. "To refer to luncheon as dinner."

"Yes," Quill said.

"And what we know as dinner, Charlie, is referred to as supper."

Quill gritted her teeth. Everybody in town went to Marge's at lunchtime. It was where all the gossip was exchanged. If the mayor was worried about Harry's reaction to the murder, it was the last place she should take them.

"Quill?" Judith said. The warmth in her voice was noticeably cooler.

"Sure. Yes." Quill put the van into drive. They were at the curb by Marge's diner, A Fork in the Road, in less than three minutes.

There was a large parking spot available between two pickup trucks. Quill regarded it dubiously. She avoided parallel parking whenever possible. If she double-parked, ran in, got directions from Harland, and ran out again, there wouldn't be time for one of Myles's deputies to drive by and give her a ticket.

"This looks like my kind of place," Charlie said. "And I could use a decent egg salad sand-widge. Pull in, why don-cha."

"There's quite a bit of food in the hamper," Quill said, although she hadn't checked. "And there are a number of terrific picnic spots by the Hemlock River—"

"Not as much stuff as you thought," Charlie said from the backseat. Quill heard rummaging sounds. "A little beef, but I took care of that. A little mousse. I took care of that, too. There's a bit of bread left, maybe. And you only gave us one bottle of wine."

Quill said, "Fine." She was so annoyed she parallel parked without any trouble at all.

One of the mysteries about Marge's diners—and Quill had eaten in at least three of the places Marge and Betty Hall had owned over the years—was that no matter how crowded it was, a table always turned up. The last hope Quill had that the topic of the murder could be avoided evaporated.

Marge herself greeted them at the door. "Come to eat? Good. That's more like it," she said in satisfaction. "Got tired of that goure-may food up to the Inn, did they?"

Marge always drawled the word "gourmet" out, an insult. She'd done it as long as Quill had known her. "That's why we're here."

"Ready for some good down-home cooking, Holcomb? Oh. It's you, Kluckenpacker. You've come for lunch, too. Good. Maybe you can learn something about frying chicken here."

And just when you wanted to belt Marge for her truculence, she'd do something stand-up and heroic, like insult the wealthiest fried food chicken king in America because of the weasely way he ran his business.

Marge bullied a few straggling customers from a table, cleared it with alarming efficiency, and motioned them all to sit down. "You want menus or the special?"

"The special," Quill said. Marge and Betty were both outstanding cooks.

"What is the special?" Harry asked suspiciously.

"Fried chicken," Marge said.

"Huh!" Charlie said.

"Betty!" Marge bawled. "Four specials." She narrowed her eyes at Charlie, "Now *you* are going to learn something about chicken." She swung her gimlet gaze to Quill. "I thought you were taking these guys on a tour of the countryside."

"I was," Quill said. "We've been sidetracked. Actually, we came in to see if Harland's here."

"Nope." Marge smoothed her gingery hair. "Not yet, anyways. He must be a little late today. What you want from him?"

Harland Peterson, president of the local Agway, and a widowed dairy farmer of considerable substance, was high on Marge's list of potential husbands.

"There's a chicken grower out on Route 96, if my information is correct," Harry Holcomb said. "I'd like to drop by."

"We thought Harland might know who and where," Quill added.

"Both of you?" Marge said, ignoring Quill. "You *and* Charlie here goin' to talk to the same supplier?"

"Just along for the ride," Charlie said, showing yellowed teeth in a wide smile.

Marge stopped snapping her gum. Her face went blank. Quill had seen her do this before, when Marge calculated just how much to offer for the Inn at Hemlock Falls. And when she offered to buy out Mr. Kurosawa's golf course. Quill had always wished the business part of Marge's brain could be marketed as software and that she could buy it.

"Hel-lo, there." Charlie waved both hands in front of Marge's face. "You switch off, or what? You know where this place is or not?"

"You'd be thinking of Derek Maloney's place," Marge said after a long moment. "It's just past that Amish harness shop, Quill. Take a left on the towline road and go down about three miles." A bell shrilled. "Your order's up." She whirled and stumped off to the pass-through window at the back.

"Local yokels," Charlie said. "Honest to God, Jude. I

thought Appalachia was bad. The woman's dumber than mud."

Judith shot a quick look at Quill. "That's enough, Charlie."

Quill had never stopped being astonished at the insolence of the Inn's guests. It was the casualness that bothered her most. And if there was an effective way to fight it directly, she hadn't found it yet. "You're very wrong about that," she said aloud. "And Marge is a friend of mine."

"No offense meant," Charlie said hastily.

"Quite a lot taken." Quill switched smoothly to Sociable Innkeeper mode. "I think you'll enjoy Marge's fried chicken, Judith. You, too, Harry."

"We are always interested in the competition," Judith said.

Harry shot her a nasty look.

"Thing is, there's a lot goes on in these small towns that you wouldn't expect." Charlie apparently felt the need to explain himself. "Norman Rockwell they ain't, if you get my drift. You get your morons, your drug dealers, your murderers, even more than you do in the big city. Inbreeding, see."

"Shut up, Charlie." Harry Holcomb jabbed him in the arm. "Just keep your opinions to yourself."

"He's hungry," Judith said dispassionately. "Low glucose always makes him this way."

Quill turned to see if she could reasonably get away from this idiotic conversation. The customers seemed to be minding their own business. Marge was deep in conversation with Esther West, who was sitting at the counter. But Betty Hall was at the pass-through window with four plates of fried chicken in front of her. Quill waved at her, and called, "I'll come and pick those up!" Betty, who was getting a little deaf, waved back and shouted, "I'm fine thanks! How's Meg doing? Heard Myles had her down to the station this morning about the murder! Heard she was arrested!"

"Murder?" Judith turned a sharp gaze on Quill. "What murder? What's she talking about?"

"Told you," Charlie said in satisfaction. "Small towns."

"Who's dead?" Harry Holcomb asked.

"You just sit right there!" Betty expertly stacked all four platters—two on each arm—and backed through the swinging gate that separated the kitchen from the diner proper. She bustled up and set the plates down. "Here you are folks. Enjoy. So, Quill. What about Meg?"

"Your sister kill somebody?" Charlie stuffed his mouth with chicken. "That's a good one on you, Holcomb. Heard that pinhead mayor asked her to judge instead of O'Haggerty. Big mistake." He stopped and concentrated on chewing. "Oh, shit," he said. "Damn it all. This is good."

"Best in upstate New York," Betty said matter-of-factly. "Who are you folks?"

"Who's dead!?" Harry demanded loudly.

"You haven't heard?" Betty took a deep, satisfied breath. Quill loved Hemlock Falls and almost all the people in it, but she had to admit that everyone in the village lived to gossip. And there was nothing better than to be first with the gossip. "Why, that good-looking guy from TV, that's who. Banion O'Haggerty." Betty adjusted her rhinestone glasses, put her hands on her skinny hips, and began dramatically, "It was Quill's dog that found him first, I got to say that right up front. But then I was the first human to find him."

"Max?" Quill said, dismayed. "I didn't know that."

"On account of he's always at the dumpsters," Betty said. "And that's where it was, the body. Right by the dumpster in the back of our bar. Well, Max set up a-barking and a-barking. So I come out to chase . . . ," she shot a quick, guilty look at Quill, "to give him a bone from the kitchen and *there he was!* Dead as a doornail!"

Quill had always wondered what that expression meant. She'd never encountered a sentient doornail.

"And that young Davey Kiddermeister was driving

around in his patrol car on account of the kid that should have been on the late shift didn't show up. So I flagged him down. Banion O'Haggerty. Dead," she repeated, "as a doornail."

Judith shoved her plate to one side. She'd eaten nothing on it. "May I have some coffee, please?"

"Thing is," Betty sailed on, "it seems that *Banion* and Meg had—"

"Betty," Quill said desperately, "I'd like some coffee too."

"I . . . sure, Quill. Justa hang on a bit."

"I'll be right back." Quill got up. She grabbed Betty's arm and steered her back to the kitchen. "If you set up the coffee, I'll take it back," Quill said. "And Betty, Meg had nothing to do with this murder."

"Well, I don't know, Quill. What I heard was—"

Quill shook her head. "You know what kind of talk goes around."

"Sure."

"And half if it's wrong."

"True," Betty said. "To tell you the truth, Quill, I don't see how Meg could have done it anyways. She was doin' some mighty painful singin' in the bar all night long. You know who it must have been? It must have been Andy."

"You know Dr. Bishop," Quill said. "Do you really think he could have killed a man in cold blood?"

"Sure," Betty said.

"It's absurd," Quill said shortly. "Think about this. Banion O'Haggerty is, was rather, six feet, two inches tall and built like Sylvester Stallone."

"Sylvester Stallone's five-six," Betty said. "I read that in *People*."

"Andy," Quill persisted, "is five-nine. And he's slender."

"He's a doctor," Betty said, with superb illogic. "So he could have anyways. But I see what you mean."

"So you know it's not Andy. And it certainly isn't Meg."

"I'll allow that it isn't Meg," Betty conceded. "Besides,

you two usually solve crimes, you don't commit 'em. You two gonna solve this one?"

Quill sighed. She hadn't gotten enough sleep last night. She absolutely understood why Harry Holcomb kept trying to punch Charlie Kluckenpacker out—he was the most hateful guest they had at the Inn and Quill wanted to punch him out, too. She was tired, irritated, and worried about her sister, who was not engaged anymore to someone who might be a murderer. She didn't have time to investigate this murder.

"Yes," Quill said. "Meg and I are going to solve this one."

CHAPTER 6

"So are we going to solve this one?" Quill sat behind the desk in her office. Meg was curled up on the couch facing her.

"Everybody thinks Andy did it? You said you went down to A Fork in the Road and everyone thinks Andy did it?"

"Betty's a pretty good barometer. Now here's what I think we should do . . ."

Meg sucked her cheeks in, then blew out sharply. "Something happens to you when you get behind that desk."

"What do you mean something happens to me when I get behind this desk?!"

"You become Competent. Did you hear the capital?"

"I heard."

"It's very annoying. Because you aren't any more Competent than you are when you're not sitting at the desk. You just act like it."

Quill rubbed her face with both hands. "I have to go to the Chamber meeting in about twenty minutes. If you aren't going to investigate this case, go away."

"That's a fine way to talk to someone who's been interrogated by the police. Not to mention someone whose life has been wrecked by a trashed engagement."

"You said Myles was kind, sympathetic, and firm. And he said you weren't a suspect."

"I had an alibi."

"Sitting at the Croh Bar drinking six wine spritzers in a

row in full view of half of Hemlock Falls is quite an alibi. So is the fact that you and Howie Murchison started singing show tunes. And that Miriam Doncaster had to help you to the ladies room. Twice. Not to mention the fact that Davey Kiddermeister drove you home. Why," Quill said crankily, "you didn't tell *me* what your alibi was I'll never know."

"Why should I tell you my alibi? You knew I would never kill anybody."

Quill decided she would never tell Meg about the frantic search for the butcher knife. "And as for the trashed engagement? 'Is that a dagger I see before me?' or a ring?"

Meg held her left hand up and admired the ring. "It's kind of creepy. The way I got it back, I mean, not the fact that Andy and I made up. Davey found it while they were searching the dumpster area for clues. I mean, Andy and I had our argument in the very spot where poor Banion bought the farm."

"And what's Andy's alibi?"

Meg became very still.

"He has one, hasn't he?"

"He has the truth," Meg said stiffly. "He went back to the medical center and caught up on some patient charts."

"Did anybody see him?"

"For heaven's sake, Quill! He's not on the witness stand and I'm not either!"

"So no one saw him."

"Nope." Meg ran her hands through her hair, which made it stand up in little spikes. Her eyes were gray and her complexion fair. She looked like a lemur caught in a searchlight. "And Myles doesn't like it at all."

"Did he say so? It wouldn't be like Myles to say that."

"He didn't say a word about it to me. But he talked to Andy right after I saw him. Andy said Myles suggested he get a lawyer, a good one. And Myles said he couldn't go to Chicago next weekend for that cardiologist's convention."

"Wow," Quill said soberly.

Meg jumped off the couch and made two rapid circuits around the room. "You have to talk to him, Quill."

"Myles, you mean?"

"Yes. You have to tell him to back off. Anybody could have killed Banion. He was a class A, number one womanizer. And he was arrogant. Half the chefs in the business wanted to kill him. For all I know each one of his ex-wives wanted to kill him. Anybody," Meg's voice rose to a shriek, "that ever *met* the son of a—"

"Meg." Quill didn't use this particular tone of voice often, but it worked. Meg sank back onto the couch. "You know I can't talk Myles out of anything to do with this case."

"If you could, would you?"

This was a sister-loyalty test. Quill bit her lip. "No, I wouldn't."

"You wouldn't save Andy?! What kind of a sister are you?"

"If Andy had killed someone, which I know he didn't, why would I want my sister to be with a killer? And Myles is not the kind of man to accuse an innocent person."

Meg stared at her crossly. "At least you're not lying to me anymore."

"Never again," Quill promised. "But I do think Myles could solve this a lot faster if we helped him."

Meg grinned a little. "He hates it when you help him."

"We won't mention it until we uncover some relevant information. Now. Did they find the murder weapon?"

"Yes. He was strangled. With a piece of wire with handles on it. Like a little teeny jump rope."

"Right by the body?"

"Embedded in the neck."

Quill shuddered.

"No prints on it. At least, that's what Davey told Kathleen."

Quill pulled a notebook out of her desk drawer and wrote "MEANS/ MOTIVE/ OPPORTUNITY." Then she drew a line under all three and wrote "Action Items 1. Chat up Kathleen."

Kathleen was their head waitress. She was also Davey's older sister. She could make Davey tell her anything. And if he didn't tell Kath, he would probably tell Dina. Quill regarded the beginnings of her chart with pride. "Okay. Now, who had access to the . . . thing that strangled Banion."

"Anybody in Hemlock Falls could have made one," Meg said promptly. "And it's called a garrote."

"I knew that," Quill said, who suddenly remembered that she did.

"The weapon isn't going to tell us a thing, Quill. We have to look at motive."

"The law ignores motive. Forensics makes the case."

"Then we can quit being detectives right now. We don't know a hoot about forensics. Myles and the Tompkins County Sheriff's Department will know all there is to know about forensics. If this case can be solved by forensics, than we can just forget it."

"You're probably right," Quill said. "Let's look at motive."

"That's what I just said," Meg said. "Honestly, Quill. If you're going to be bossy and Competent all at once, I'm going back to the kitchen. I can't stand it. And forget looking at motive. The only people with motives here in Hemlock Falls are Andy and me."

"It's Andy and I, isn't it?" Quill said.

"*You* had a motive? Oh, you're talking about my grammar. It's Andy and me."

Quill looked doubtfully at her notebook. "That leaves opportunity."

"Good one. We can start there. We already know a few things about the evening in question."

"I don't."

"Well, I do. I really pumped Kathleen. First, Myles has

narrowed the time of death to between nine and ten o'clock."

"He has?" Quill was impressed. "I didn't think it was possible to be that precise."

"The coroner couldn't do it, that's for certain. Although they're getting more precise as technology advances. Anyhow, the dumpster guy was late with the pickup. He emptied the dumpster around nine. He has a computer thingie he punches so that his bosses know that he's actually picking up garbage. Esther West confirmed that because she was out walking that little poodle Max chases and she got cross because of the noise. So that's about as credible as you can get. And Marge yelled at the short-order cook because the garbage cans in the kitchens were full, and she stomped out of the back about nine with a pile of garbage which—"

"Ended up on top of the body."

"Right. And both Marge and the cook confirmed the time. Or rather Marge did, the cook quit and Myles hasn't—"

"The cook!" Quill said eagerly.

"Nope. It's Clara-Alice Peterson."

"Oh." Clara-Alice Peterson was sixty-two years old and arthritic. "Why did she quit? Maybe she knows who did it!"

"Maybe. But she said she wasn't about to work in a place where they threw dead bodies into the dumpster like so much trash."

"Would she work at a place where dead bodies landed up somewhere else?"

Meg ignored this and steepled her fingers under her chin. "Now. Make a list of who knew Banion personally. I take it we aren't looking at the wandering tramp solution here."

"Not until we get stuck." Quill flipped to a fresh page in her notebook. She wrote one name.

"It's more than just me," Meg said.

"It's not you. It's Charlene Holcomb."

"Char . . . ?" Meg's brow cleared. "You mean the blonde?!"

"Better than the butler," Quill said obscurely. "Yes, the blonde. Banion followed her into the Tavern Bar. And look." She wrote Harry Holcomb's name under Charlene's. "Nate broke up a fight between Banion and Harry about seven-thirty. The fight was over Charlene."

"Fabulous!" Meg said.

Quill glanced at the clock on her desk. "I've got to get to the Chamber meeting. Harry's going to be there to talk about the Fry Away Home contest. I'll corner him and charm him into talking about where he was last night."

"Sounds like a plan. I can find Charlene and engage her in seemingly idle conversation. Then we can match the stories up. If there's a discrepancy, we're in like Flynn."

"John would be better at getting information out of Charlene than you would," Quill said. "Let's ask him."

Meg grimaced. "Oh, ugh. Poor John."

"Poor John? He's helped us before."

"I know. But every single female guest under fifty-five falls all over John. Quill, don't you think if we ask him to do this, we're treating him as a mere sex object?"

"There is a fundamental difference between men and women, Meg."

"No kidding."

"Men are quite used to being treated as masters of the universe. It is a far different thing to ask a master of the universe to wield the power of sex than to cajole an oppressed victim of sexual injustice to do so."

Meg rolled her eyes and shook her head.

"I think John will be flattered."

"Maybe. I think he'll be insulted."

"He might." Quill shoved her detecting notebook into her purse. "Okay. Let's leave John out of this. But let me talk to Charlene, okay?"

"I can do it," Meg said.

"Oh? Try it."

"Huh?"

"Go on. Pretend I'm Charlene and you want me to tell you where I was last night. And with whom."

Meg scowled, but said, "Hi, Charlene."

Quill pitched her voice lower, in a Charlene imitation. "Hi. It's, like, Meg, isn't it?"

"I'm the chef, yes. So. How'd it go with Banion last night?"

"None of your business." Quill raised her eyebrows and dropped into her normal tones. "See? You have no tact, Meg. Tact and intuition, that's the ticket."

"I suppose you think you're better at it."

"I'm brilliant at it. Never once, in all my years as manager of the inn, have I belted a guest. True?"

"Oh, all right," Meg grumbled. "So you're more tactful with people than I am. But not by much."

"You're better with food than I am. By quite a lot."

Meg looked at her watch. "And you're past due to go bat your eyelashes at Harry Holcomb." She sighed. "Good luck."

Quill was halfway out the door before she remembered to ask Meg if she was going to judge the contest.

"No way. No how."

"Meg. It's twenty-five—"

"I don't care."

"We're in a bind."

"*I'm* not in a bind."

"What if we get Betty Hall to be one of the contestants?"

"Betty Hall makes the best fried chicken in New York State." Meg glowered. "Okay. I'll do it. But I'll tell you right now, the fix is in."

Chamber of Commerce meetings were almost always held in the Inn's conference rooms. The Conference Center was the only public place in Hemlock Falls large enough to hold twenty-six people and didn't have linoleum floors. Adela Henry, the mayor's formidable wife, had strong objections to linoleum, on the grounds of good taste. (Freddie Bellini's Funeral Home was carpeted, but Adela couldn't count on the visitation parlor being free of coffins at the appropriate times. So she nixed that.)

Quill came in a little late (as usual) and was relieved to see that neither the mayor nor Harry Holcomb had yet arrived. It was a good turnout: she waved at Harland Peterson, wiggled her eyebrows at Harvey Bozzel (Hemlock Falls's best, and only, advertising executive), and took a vacant chair next to Howie Murchison, the town attorney.

Howie was a comfortably rumpled man in his late fifties, long-divorced. He served as town justice off and on. This year was one of the on times, for which Quill was thankful. He was a large part of Meg's alibi, and in a town like Hemlock Falls, position counted a lot, as much as she hated to admit it.

Howie peered at her over his half-glasses. "And how are you this afternoon? Business as usual? Dead bodies, as usual?"

"That's not funny, Howie," Quill said crossly.

Howie had a nice smile. "Sorry. You're right. I'm not really with it today."

"You were pretty with it last night, from what I hear."

"Now be nice to me, Quill. I'm Meg's chief bulwark against the majesty of the law."

Quill made herself relax. "I'm tired," she admitted. "And a little worried."

"You don't have to worry about Meg. When she wasn't with me she was in the ladies room with Miriam. We went through the entire Sondheim repertoire last night." He winced, either at the memory or from his hangover. "Quill, I love Meg. Everyone does. But why does she think she can sing?"

"She knows she can't sing. She just doesn't think anyone else can, either."

"God. Here's hizhonner. I hope this doesn't take too long. I need a nap."

Elmer bustled in, one hand draped familiarly over Harry Holcomb's shoulder. Charlene trailed along behind. Quill hadn't paid a lot of attention to her the night before, except to register the fact that she was lovely, slim, and twenty years younger than Harry. She wore tight white jeans and a tank top. When she settled next to Harry at the head of the long conference table, Howie smoothed his hair and sat up a little straighter.

Elmer whacked the official gavel against the mahogany table, to Esther West's inevitable distress. "Use the *rest*, Mayor!" she hissed. The Reverend Mr. Dookie Shuttleworth gave a short prayer. Harvey Bozzel fussed importantly with his portfolio. Miriam Doncaster batted her eyelashes at Howie. Marge sat like a stolid pillar, brooding. Freddie Bellini stared at nothing in particular. And of course, there was the horrible Carol Ann Spinoza, no longer tax assessor (Hooray!), but now a member of the Zoning Committee, which she'd insisted, based on no precedent at all, made her eligible for Chamber membership. She gave Quill a huge, white-toothed smile, which discomposed Quill so much she dropped her pencil.

It was business as usual.

Quill drew her Minutes notebook from her skirt pocket. She'd lettered the cover HEMLOCK FALLS CHAMBER OF COMMERCE *Official Minutes*, Sarah Quilliam, Secretary. She flipped to a clean page and made a quick sketch of Howie and Miriam at the Croh Bar, dressed as the Prince and the Maiden from *Into the Woods*. Then she drew Carol Ann's face on the body of a long ugly snake.

Howie nudged her in the ribs, and she glanced up.

"The minutes from the last meeting, Quill." The mayor sounded as if he'd been repeating himself for some time.

"Sorry, sorry. They're right here." Quill paged through the notebook and found her notes of last week's meeting: ASK M.Q!!!!! (Ban O'H?) 25 plus 5. LSC. TNT. "Um," she said.

"It's all right. Take your time," Elmer said genially.

Quill appreciated his tact, especially in front of Harry and his wife. Then Elmer said, in a loud aside, "Artists, y'know. M'wife will prob'ly take the job over next year."

This made Quill cross, so she faked it. "The Chamber moved as one to ask Margaret Quilliam to judge the Fry Away Home fried food cooking contest, sponsored by Holcomb's Wholesome Chicken."

"Huh," Elmer said.

She skipped over the reference to Banion O'Haggerty, which would have started a riot. The Chamber members had been furious over Elmer's faux pas. And they flatly refused to authorize more funds than Harry Holcomb was willing to pay. True. Banion was dead and the twenty-five thousand moot. But that wouldn't stop the members from a brouhaha. It never had before.

Quill equivocated. "We all know about the judging fee and having to come up with a little more if Meg declined, but she hasn't, she's accepted. So that's okay."

There was a hum around the table. Carol Ann's hand shot straight up into the air. "Your Honor. Your Honor!"

"Carol Ann, nobody interrupts the reading of the minutes," Miriam Doncaster said. "We have several copies of *Robert's Rules of Order* if you want to come by the library. I'll set one aside for you."

"But we don't want an accused murderess to judge this contest," Carol Ann said sweetly. "Do we? I mean, it makes absolutely no difference to *me*, personally. But as a loyal citizen of this town, and as an official member of the Zoning Commission . . ."

Howie muttered, "Jesus Christ!" He stood up. He had quite an impressive courtroom demeanor when necessary, and he used it now. "Anyone who implies that Margaret Quilliam is implicated in the death of Banion O'Haggerty is guilty of slander." His voice would have reached to the farthest corners of the County Court House. "And if it's written down, it's libel. She has an alibi. I don't want to hear another word about it."

"Does that mean we got to use her as a judge?" the mayor asked. "No offense, Quill, but Carol Ann and I got to thinking about it, and I don't know. I just don't know." He broke off and turned to Harry Holcomb. "It depends on you, Mr. Holcomb."

Holcomb, clearly bored, said, "Any publicity is good publicity. It's fine with me. And with my wife, of course," he said as an afterthought.

Charlene said, "Fine," and sneezed.

"As a matter of fact, we might be able to get better media coverage this year than we have before. Banion's death was news." Harry referred to O'Haggerty in a casual way. As if he had known him for years. As if he weren't dead. Quill paused to scribble a note to herself: DID HH KNOW BO'H BEFORE? Howie glanced over and raised one eyebrow. Then he mouthed, "Stay out of it."

"True about the media coverage," Harvey Bozzel agreed eagerly. "Very true, Mr. Holcomb. I can see the interview with Geraldo now. Just give me the word. I can access him in no time."

"Wait a minute," Quill said. "I don't think we want to capitalize on this. As a matter of fact, I won't have anything to do with the festival at all if we use the murder as a publicity gambit." She half-rose out of her chair. Howie pulled her back down.

"I'm town justice this year," Howie said. "And I'm ruling that no more is to be said about it." He winked at Quill.

Harland, Marge, and Harry Holcomb all chuckled. Everybody else looked properly repentant. Except for Carol Ann. "Well!" she snapped. "If you say so. But I really don't know. I really don't know. So what do I know?"

"Not much," somebody muttered.

Carol Ann gazed accusingly at Quill. "Right. Miss High and Mighty Meg's the judge. I'm not going to say one more word about it." Carol Ann pressed her lips tightly closed. But she didn't look as nasty as she should have. She hated being balked. She should have been furious. Quill observed her thoughtfully for a moment.

Elmer cleared his throat. " 'Kay, then. What's next on the minutes, Quill?"

Quill frowned at her notes. LISC TNT. Was someone supposed to apply for a license to blow something up? "Oh! Sure! The license for the tents. Elmer, I mean, Mayor, you said that you'd take care of it at the zoning meeting today."

"Yes, well. So I did. Had a good zoning meeting." He rubbed his hands together nervously. "Just two of the three members present, but it's all nice and legal. The Zoning Commission issued a permit today for the contest grounds. Only there were a lot of problems having it at the school."

"What kind of problems?" Harry Holcomb asked. "You didn't tell me this, Henry."

"Those hot fat fryers are too dangerous around kids," Esther West said. "I'm a member of the school board and we discussed it at our meeting last week. We really would prefer that you find another venue."

"I didn't agree to this," Harry Holcomb said with dangerous calm. For the first time, Quill could see how he'd climbed all the way to the top of the fried chicken business.

"Nossir. You didn't." The mayor was sweating profusely now. "Way your contract reads, and I checked it and rechecked it, you have to oblige us as long as we provide a suitable venue for the contest." He took a deep breath. He shouted, "But we've found a much better place for the contest. Much prettier, with better parking, better view. Thing is, we got a buyer for that property right next to the Inn here."

Quill blinked.

Elmer let the rest of it out in a rush. "And that buyer's graciously agreed to let the Fry Away Home cooking contest be set up right next to one of the most beautiful places in this town."

"The Inn?" Quill said.

"Now, Quill, it's gonna mean a lot more trade for you."

"Somebody bought the property next to my inn?"

"Yes'm, they did."

The sweat was pouring off the mayor. Quill, puzzled, said, "Oh."

It was Marge who asked the next two questions. "Who bought it, Elmer? And what did you guys zone it for?"

"That'll be disclosed in due time," the mayor said. "Right now, I think we should move on to new business."

"It'll be disclosed right now," Howie said. "What the hell's going on, Elmer?"

"I don't mind if the contest tents are set up next to the Inn," Quill said.

"*Elmer!*" Marge roared. "Goddammit!"

"All right, all right. Charlie Kluckenpacker bought it. And it's zoned commercial. Restaurant commercial. The contracts are all signed. It's done." Elmer whacked the gavel on the table. "Next order of business!"

CHAPTER 7

"A Captain Cluck fried chicken shack?" Meg said. "In the hemlock grove?" She hadn't quite taken it in. They stood outside in the deepening twilight, staring at the woods.

"You should have seen the way the Chamber meeting broke up." Quill was still bemused, herself. "Elmer tried to run out the door. Marge grabbed him and shook him by the back of the neck. Harry Holcomb yelled into his cell phone. Then he yelled at Elmer. Miriam Doncaster jumped on top of the conference table and tried to start a petition. Howie backed Freddie Bellini into a corner and shook his finger in his face. And Carol Ann just sat there." Quill kicked at a clump of grass. "Snakes are lipless. I didn't think they could grin. But that's what she looked like, a grinning snake."

"The Captain Cluck chicken shacks are topped with a big huge chicken head," Meg said. "The beaks are *neon*!"

Quill kicked at another clump of grass. "Yes they ... ow!"

"What?" Meg asked testily. "This can't be happening, Quill. Why don't we own this parcel? We maintain it! Mike keeps the path through the grove raked and weeded. The guests use it all the time. We put it in our brochures. We have *al fresco* parties out here! And now it's going to be a parking lot with a big fat chicken head in the middle of it! *I'll see the beak from my kitchen!* This can't be happening!"

"Well it is." Quill knelt and pushed through the grass. "Look at this."

"What?!"

"It's a surveyor's flag. See?"

Meg crouched and squinted at it. A short stake had been pounded into the ground. An orange red plastic flag was stapled to it.

"So?"

"Before anyone buys a piece of property you have to have it surveyed. If we walk around the hemlock grove we'll probably find more of them." Quill stood up and helped Meg to her feet. "I wonder when they did that? And who did it?" She frowned. The plastic flag was clean. The stake looked newly planted. Yesterday had been the first sunny day for a week. Mike had mowed in the afternoon. There were no grass clippings on the flag. And the mower would have run right over the flag. Even if Mike hadn't noticed, which he surely would have, the stake would have been broken off.

"We'll sue him," Meg said firmly. "We'll sue everybody."

"Yuck," Quill said absently. "That's way too tacky. We'll just have to figure this out. We can put up a big huge fence if we have to. Listen, Meg, this whole plot was surveyed last night."

"So? Elmer got some creep to crawl in and survey it behind out backs. It figures!"

"I wonder if he used that engineering firm from Ithaca. Roebuck & White. Not that it matters. But they might have seen something last night. Meg! You were at the Croh Bar getting blotto last night."

"I was *not* blotto." Meg cocked her head in a considering way. "Slightly fizzy, maybe. I was drinking wine spritzers, Quill, not the hard stuff."

"And Davey brought you home. About eleven-thirty, right? You two would have noticed a surveying crew over here."

"Would we? We didn't."

"They use infrared lasers to do the measurements. I know that. And there was a full moon last night. But there had to have been some light over here, some movement, even if the surveying crew was trying to avoid discovery. Which they most certainly were. If you didn't see them at eleven-thirty, it must have been done before that."

"Or after," Meg pointed out.

"Maybe not. Meg! Look at this!"

She shoved at a ball of damp tissue with her toe.

"You're more interested in used Kleenex than a flipping chicken hut?! You're not outraged by all of this? Earth to Quill! We've got a huge ugly problem here!"

Quill took Meg's arm. "Let's go back inside. I want to make some phone calls to see if I can find the surveyors that did this."

"I'm not setting foot in that kitchen again! I refuse! I quit! I'm not going to work next door to a chicken hut."

"We'll put up a hedge," Quill said.

Meg jerked her arm away and stamped off toward the Inn. Her back was rigid with anger. Quill trotted to keep up. Meg increased her pace. By the time they reached the backdoor, they were both running. Meg burst into the kitchen first,

"What?! What?!" Bjarne shouted. "Have they started? Are the chicken people here?!" He waved a pot lid in a threatening way. "Come! All come with me!"

"We've figured it out," Elizabeth Chu said breathlessly as she untied her apron. "We're going to sit in."

"Sit in?" Quill shook her head to clear it. "Sit in what?"

"My mom talks about it all the time," Elizabeth said. Her eyes gleamed excitedly. "She was at Berkeley in the sixties, you know? Bjarne figured it all out. When the excavator guys show up, we're all going to sit right down in front of them."

"Yeah!" said one of the dishwashers. "It'll be cool."

"It'll be dangerous," Quill said. "What if they squash you

flat? Bjarne! Put down the pot lid. Everyone settle down and listen to me."

"You know the Captain Clucks have like, a neon chicken head on them?" Elizabeth said.

"I know that."

"That is so gross."

"All right!" Quill called out. "Staff meeting. Everybody stop. Everybody sit down. If you can't find a place to sit down, just stand still."

After a series of thumps, clatters, and mutters, everybody in the kitchen settled into relative quiet. Meg sat at the prep table, arms folded.

"We will sue them," Bjarne said confidently. "This is the American way."

"We are not going to sue them," Quill said quietly. "We are not going to sit in. We are not going to harass them. We are going to accept this."

"Never!" Bjarne shouted. "Finland Forever!"

"Stop," Quill ordered. "I mean it."

This silence was absolute, except for the ticking of the kitchen clock.

"As far as I know," Quill said carefully, "Charlie Kluckenpacker bought this land legitimately. As far as I know, the Zoning Committee acted properly in allowing a commercial building to go up there. We're zoned commercial, aren't we? We're a restaurant too, aren't we?"

"We don't try and pass rat meat off as chicken parts!" the dishwasher shouted.

Quill narrowed her eyes at him. Richie Peterson, that was his name. Eighteen, pimply, with a stud in his nose. A nice kid. Quill struggled a second with his relationship to Harland and gave up. Even the Petersons couldn't keep track of the Petersons. "You don't believe all that stuff, Richie. None of us do."

"So we don't do anything?" Elizabeth said, her black eyes wide with dismay. "What about legitimate protest? What about our rights!"

There was a chorus of "yeahs!" and, of course, a lone "Finland Forever!"

"What rights?" Quill demanded. "We. Don't. Own. The. Property."

The silence this time was tentative. Quill relaxed slightly. She was getting through. Even Meg looked less angry.

"Let's *us* buy the property!" Richie said.

"That we can try." Quill rubbed her face. "That bothers me, I admit. That we didn't get a chance to bid on it."

Meg scowled. "Who owns it?"

Quill shook her head. "I don't know."

"Whoever it is, they'll never set foot in *this* Inn again!"

"Whoever said that, forget it." Quill looked at each of the staff in turn. "Let's get back to work, guys. It's going to be fine."

"It's not going to be fine," Bjarne muttered. "Things will never be the same again."

Quill walked through the dining room without greeting anyone. It was six o'clock, and the room was just starting to fill up, but she never felt less gracious in her life or less inclined to innkeeperly behavior. She forestalled Kathleen's anxious questions with a quiet, "Later, Kath, okay?" and went into her office. She sat down on the couch, grabbed a toss pillow embroidered "I'm Fine!" and screamed silently into it. Then she grabbed it by the corner and pounded the top of her desk, counting each whack.

"Fifty-two, fifty-three!"

"Does it help?" John closed the office door softly and quirked an eyebrow at her.

"Sure. Want to try it?" She threw the pillow at him. He caught it, placed it on the couch, and then settled behind her desk. He began sorting the mess Quill's fury had created, picking her enameled bowl off the floor, stacking the papers back into her in and out tray, replacing the receiver on the phone deck. "You've got a message."

Quill leaned over and punched the play button. Myles, telling her he was gone overnight to Syracuse.

The message clicked off. Quill, her rage spent (at least for the time being), sat cross-legged on the couch. "Who owns the hemlock grove, John? Someone from Hemlock Falls?"

"I checked our copy of the surveyor's map. It doesn't say. I'll go down to the town clerk's office in the morning and pull the tax rolls."

"I think I know already."

"Elmer."

"Elmer," Quill said. "His behavior's been truly peculiar ever since the whole Fry Away Home contest started. What I want to know is *why*!? Why couldn't he offer the land to us?! We're doing well, John. We could've afforded it, couldn't we?"

"We don't know that it's Elmer."

"I'll bet you five bucks it is."

"I won't take it. And could we have afforded it, Quill? I don't know. Probably not."

"But we're profitable! We've got money in the bank!"

"Hemlock Falls is growing. The new resort downriver will be open by the end of the year. Real estate values are going up. Right now, the Inn is the most attractive commercial property in what is coming to be a prosperous area."

"How much is the hemlock grove worth?"

"That's hard to say, too. But if I had to guess—it's three acres of prime real estate, and it's been zoned commercial—"

"I'm going to kill Carol Ann Spinoza!" Quill interrupted. She was mad all over again. "And I'm never ever going to bury anyone at Freddie's! I can see why Carol Ann did what she did, but Freddie? Freddie! I thought he was a friend of ours."

"It's business, Quill. And, hey! What happened to the cool calm collected manager? The one that quelled the Kitchen Riot? The balanced, focused leader of men and women who brought sweet reason to the revolutionaries?"

"I did all that, didn't I," Quill said, pleased. "I didn't feel like it, though. I felt like smacking Elmer Henry right up the side of the head. And Charlie Kluckenpacker, too." She sighed heavily. "What the heck. You were about to guess at the price of this little, out-of-the-way, three-acre plot that can't be of use to anyone."

"I wish. At a guess? Half a million."

"Half a *million?!*"

"Marge thought maybe four hundred. Of course with Marge, value depends on whether she's buying or selling. She said her asking price would be near seven hundred and fifty."

"Seven hundred and fifty *thousand!*" Quill believed it. Or rather, she believed John, who was very good at this sort of thing. "We can't even come close to affording that."

"Nope."

"You know, I even thought once that Meg and Andy could put up a little house there. And all those lovely trees . . ." Quill's eyes filled with tears.

"Hemlock trees aren't that attractive. Tell you what. We'll put up a hedge."

"Just what I was thinking." The tears were rolling down her cheeks now. "What do you think?" she sobbed.

"Yew," John said.

"What do I think? I don't care what kind of hedge it is. Just as long as we can't see the chicken beak!"

"No, Quill. A hedge of yew. Here." He took a handful of Kleenex from the box on her desk and held them out. Quill took them, mopped at her face, and stopped crying at once. "Hey!" she said. "Charlene!"

John shifted uneasily in his chair. "What about Charlene?"

Quill gazed at her handful of used Kleenex. "John, something very funny is going on here. Harry Holcomb chooses Hemlock Falls to put in a Holcomb's Wholesome. Plans for this start about eight months ago."

"We're growing, Quill. It was only a matter of time."

"Then Captain Cluck calls Elmer."

"He did?"

"He did. Elmer tries to sell him a parcel he owns out on 15. Elmer either refuses to sell out of hometown pride, or fear of Holcomb, or because Captain Cluck refuses to meet his price. Pick one."

"The last one, I should think."

"So Cluck recruits Doreen and Stoke to put up a franchise."

"That fell through," John said. "I talked with Stoke, and the deal was a bad one for them."

"Good. But Cluck's not giving up. Marge says we're not big enough to support two fried chicken places. Cluck *does* buy the hemlock grove and does meet Elmer's price."

"Elmer would have had to come up with twenty-five thousand; he probably needed the money."

"Yes. And Cluck owns the piece where Holcomb's contest is going to be held."

"And Banion O'Haggerty is murdered."

"Yes," Quill mused. "They all need to be investigated. But I can't believe Elmer would kill anybody, John."

Neither one of them said anything.

"Andy's mixed up in the middle of this." Quill rubbed her eyes. "Thank God Meg isn't. But, gee, this is a mess."

"There's bad blood between Charlie and Holcomb," John said. "But murder? Over fast food?"

"Where is she? Charlene."

"With her husband." John's coppery skin was tinged with dark red. "I hope."

"Poor John. Dina said this morning that she was trailing you. Did she back you into a corner?"

"Hm."

"Myles does that, too. Goes 'hm' rather than answer a direct question. It's something men do when they don't want to talk about it." Quill felt extremely wise. She would have to tell Dr. Benziger about this insight. "I'm going to do a little poking around. I'll start with Charlene. Do you know where she is? Is she with Harry?"

"Harry made reservations for dinner at nine. Reserved a table for four. Apparently he read Elmer the riot act in the bar and stormed off to take some action. He's called in a raft of lawyers. Right now, he's on the road with Mike to Syracuse to pick them up. Charlene's in the Lounge. In the corner booth, way in the back."

"This is pretty specific information. Oh! I see." She looked an apology. "I'm sorry, John. It's your own fault, you know. It's that devastating face of yours. It drives women mad. She wants you to meet her there, doesn't she?"

He grinned. "I'd planned on bringing Tricia."

"You and Tricia are relieved of duty," Quill said grandly. "I'll handle it."

"What is it we don't know?"

"You mean what do I want to find out? We have a murder, John. And Charlene may have been the last person to see Banion alive. And there's something else; I don't know how Charlie managed this, but there was a team of surveyors out in the hemlock grove last night, setting stakes."

John's eyebrows went up.

"You can see it yourself. And what's more . . ." Quill drew the Kleenex from the pocket of her skirt. "See this?"

"A used Kleenex?"

"What allergic blonde has been dropping balled-up Kleenex all over the Inn?"

"Charlene?"

"Guess where I found this?"

"At the site? You're kidding."

"I'm asking myself three questions: One: Where did Charlene go after Nate broke up the fight between Banion and Harry last night?"

"There was a fight between Banion and Harry last night?"

"You bet. Banion socked Harry in the nose. I wish he'd

socked Charlie in the nose. Anyway, the poor man's dead, so he can't sock anybody anymore." John closed his eyes briefly. "Okay, okay. I'll get back to the point. Banion obviously went down to the Croh Bar because his body was found by the dumpster. I found Charlene's used Kleenex at the hemlock grove. Did she go with him? Did they talk to the surveyors on their way down? What does Charlene know, and when did she know it?"

"When did she know what?"

"Exactly," Quill said, because she wasn't sure herself what she meant.

John put his head in his hands.

"When you check the tax map, it will say who surveyed the property, won't it?"

"If the plot's been filed." He interrupted himself. "Of course it's been filed. The zoning application was approved today."

"Can you find out who it is? I want to talk to them."

"Quill! You're not going to actually investigate this murder, are you? I thought you'd retired from the investigating business."

"Meg and I are a team again," Quill said proudly. "Don't look like that, John. Listen." She dropped her lighthearted tone and let some of her worry show through. "Andy's still a suspect, isn't he?"

"I'm afraid so."

"What's better—to have Meg worrying herself to death over him? Isn't it better to divert her with a great case?"

"Isn't it better if she just cooks, which is what she does best anyway?"

"Never mind," Quill said. "I know what I'm doing. I wish I had a hat."

"I'll bite, why do you wish you had a hat?"

"A fedora," Quill said wistfully. "Just like Lew Archer's."

•   •   •

Quill tossed the used Kleenex on the table in front of Charlene. She was, as John had said she would be, sitting in the small booth back by the doors to the flagstone terrace. She was drinking martinis. Used tissues littered the table.

Charlene poked at the Kleenex and sneezed. "Thanks. I've got some. Besides, that one looks used."

"I wasn't offering it to you. I found it." Quill paused for a meaningful silence.

Charlene blinked at her. She was an extremely pretty girl, despite the fact that her nose was red and her eyes were watering. Blonde hair spilled over her shoulders. She wore a low-cut red spandex top and hip hugger jeans. And a lot of expensive jewelry. Her wedding ring was a huge sapphire. Her Baume and Mercier watch was almost hidden under three platinum bracelets set with diamonds. Her cheekbones were terrific. "Okay. So you found a wadded up tissue. So what?"

"It's yours. And I found it by the hemlock grove. I want to know what you were doing up there last night."

Charlene's brow creased prettily. "Huh?"

Quill bit her lip. She'd read a lot of Raymond Chandler. All seven books, actually. Philip Marlowe's suspects always spilled their guts under his tough guy approach. Maybe you had to be built like Chandler's detective to get the same results. Quill wasn't a six-foot-tall, one-hundred-and-eighty-pound guy in fighting trim. She was five-seven and weighed one hundred and twenty-eight pounds, about the same size, as a matter of fact, as Charlene Holcomb. It was hard to loom menacingly over someone just your size.

Charlene sneezed again.

Sympathy. She was very good at sympathy. And tact, when she remembered to be tactful.

"I want another martini," Charlene said. "I stop sneezing when I've had enough martinis."

"I said do you want something, Quill?"

Jerked from her musings, Quill looked up to see Nate

patiently waiting for her order. "Um. Sure. The usual, Nate."

He winked at her and walked off.

"You have a usual, too, huh?" Charlene stubbed out her cigarette, drained the last of her drink, and ate the olive. She had a low, attractive voice, roughened by smoking.

"Excuse me?"

"My usual's a—"

"A martini, yes. I see that. I like a glass of red wine in the evening. It's supposed to be good for you."

"Martinis are supposed to be bad for you," Charlene said petulantly. "According to Harry. As if I cared what Harry thinks." Nate set the drinks down, and she gazed at hers. "John's stood me up, hasn't he?"

"He had a date with somebody else," Quill said tactfully.

Charlene's lower lip jutted out. "He works here, doesn't he? He's supposed to be nice to the guests, isn't he?" She blinked away easy tears. "What kind of hotel is this, anyway? Banny said it's one of the best in America. You don't even have any pool boys."

"We don't have a pool."

"Tuh! Some three star hotel—"

"It's one of the best of its kind," Quill said hastily. "We're an inn, after all. Not a hotel. Did you know Banion before yesterday?"

Charlene drained half the gin in her glass in one swallow. "Well, sure. He worked for Mummy and Charlie years ago." She frowned. "And we were married, of course. Not for long, though."

Quill's mouth opened. She closed it. She took a long sip of her wine—a shiraz, she noticed in some confusion—and not the Chateau-Neuf du Pap. She swallowed, choked, and said, "Oh."

"St. Tropez," Charlene said.

"I'm sorry, what?"

"We met while I was on a shoot in St. Tropez. You know, St. Tropez? In Europe?"

"You were a model?" Quill said cleverly.

"I was *Char*," Charlene said with an exasperated roll of her eyes. "I thought everybody knew I was Char."

"Of course!" Quill said effusively. "Char!"

Charlene smoothed her hair in an agitated way. "It's this blonde. I never should have let Harry talk me into blonde. My trademark was my long brunette mane. That's what they wrote, in *Vogue*."

"And Judith is your mother?"

"Well, *ye*-ah."

Like, duh, Quill thought. And I call myself an artist. She had a good eye. She was born with a good eye. And she hadn't caught the subtle line of cheek and jaw that would have told any artist worth her salt that these two were related?

"I'm adopted, of course." Charlene fished the olive from her glass with one long scarlet nail. "But I was adopted when Mummy was married to my father. She married Charlie later. I thought everyone knew that. Charlie," she added with a vicious twist of her mouth, "is a shit."

"I'm sorry," Quill said. "I didn't know."

"Well, when you live in the sticks, what do you expect? But Banny said you used to be somebody. Who was it?"

"I paint," Quill said. "I still paint."

Charlene chewed her olive, and then spit it out into a Kleenex. "Loaded with calories," she said. "It doesn't count if you don't swallow. So why are you here and not John?"

"I wanted to ask you about Banion."

"Now that was sad." Charlene shook her head. "Killed like that. I expected it, though."

"You expected it? You expected him to be murdered?"

"Everybody always said he was born to be hanged."

Quill did not believe Charlene was this stupid. She was, however, probably that drunk. "You both were here last night," Quill prompted.

"Yeah. We were like, flirting, you know? I was even thinking maybe I shouldn't have divorced him all those years ago." She sighed. "Who knew how famous he was going to be? Or how rich. Anyhow, Harry marched in and spoiled it. There was another fight."

"I heard about it. Did you go back to your room after Banion left?"

"Harry was pretty pissed off. He has this ownership thing. So he made me go back to the room and, y'know."

Quill held up her hand. "That's fine," she said quickly. "Never mind. I don't need to know that."

Her wide blue gaze shifted away to a point over Quill's left shoulder. "Afterwards I fell asleep."

"You didn't go out again? Was Harry with you?"

Charlene slid out of the booth and stood up. "It was nice talking to you," she said politely. "I have to go and get dressed now. Harry's lawyers are coming in for dinner and I have to look good." She wriggled her fingers. "Good bye, Quill."

Quill watched Charlene wobble across the room and out the door. She wondered what Dr. Benziger would make of this, because she was struck with sudden, violent pity.

Nate appeared silently and began to clear the table. He swept the used tissues into the capacious pockets of his bar apron and picked up the glasses.

"How many drinks did she have?"

"Four."

"Oh, my."

"Yeah. Beautiful woman, too. Takes 'em that sometimes. When they get older."

"She's not any older than I am, Nate!"

"Hm," Nate said.

"Do you have a minute?"

Nate glanced around the room. Very few tables were empty, and the seats at the bar were filled. "Convention at the Marriott," he said. "Sales guys, mostly. Heavy drinkers. If you want to talk, I'd better get someone from the dining room in here." Nate was short, thickset, and in recent years had adopted a thick beard. With his dark hair and small black eyes, he resembled an amiable bear. He was a good listener—a true virtue in a bartender. And as a good bartender, he made a lot in tips.

"That's okay," Quill said. "I just wanted to know what time you threw Banion and Harry out of here."

Nate scratched his head. " 'Bout eight, I think."

"Which way did Banion go?"

"Sheriff already asked me this, Quill. I didn't pay much attention to O'Haggerty." Nate's eyes twinkled. "Threw a good punch, I'll give him that. Guy was quick. Anyway, I thought about it after Myles went off and I think O'Haggerty left that way." He jerked a thick thumb in the direction of the French doors that led to the terrace. And from the terrace, it was a speedy jog down to the Croh Bar.

"And Charlene?"

"Now that one I did watch. That husband of hers dragged her off toward the rooms upstairs right at the same time."

"Thanks, Nate. I won't keep you any longer."

He slid out of the booth, the dirtied glasses in one hand. "She didn't come back for quite a while. Maybe an hour or so."

"She came back?!"

"Yeah. Had one drink. Looking for Banion, I guess, or maybe Holcomb. Who knows? Anyway, she must have a bottle up in the suite. You check with Doreen? Never mind, she's off on Tuesdays, isn't she? Mrs. Holcomb took off after just the one drink, which was fine, because I wouldn't have served her. She was pretty well-lit."

"And where did she go?"

"That I'm sure of, Watched her go myself. Right out the back doors and down toward the Gorge."

Nate gave her a cheery half-salute and headed back to the bar. Quill pulled her notebook out. If the fracas had ended about eight, and Charlene was gone for an hour, she would have headed off by nine o'clock.

Quill made a note.

But Nate wasn't sure of the time.

Quill made another note. VERIFY C. DEPARTURE TIME. WITNESS?? She pulled at her lower lip. It was unusual to have such a precise time of death established. She'd have to check with Nate to see who else was in the bar last night. It was a real problem having such a transient population at the Inn. The Tavern Lounge didn't really have regulars in the way that the Croh Bar did.

Her cell phone vibrated and she pulled it from her skirt pocket with an exclamation of annoyance. The damn things were an intrusion. Just when a person was settling down to think really hard the "breep-breep-breep" broke one's concentration. "Hi, it's Quill," she said into the receiver.

"It's me!"

Quill hated it when people did that. It was Dina, of course, but then maybe it wasn't. She knew Dina's voice. Dina knew that Quill knew Dina's voice. But it irritated her all the same.

"Who is this please?"

"Sorry, Quill. It's *me*. Are you cranky? I can't say as I blame you. Isn't the murder awful?"

Quill's agreement was heartfelt.

"And this stuff about the hemlock grove right on top of it. I mean, I heard about Captain Cluck, and I think it's just awful. Do you know those shacks have a neon beak—"

"Yes," Quill interrupted.

"Well! There's this great poly-sci professor I had a few semesters back. You know. At Cornell?"

"I know you go to Cornell, Dina."

"Anyhow, he's a wizard at civil liberties. I was thinking, maybe I could give him a call. We could like, pull a Henry David Thoreau."

Quill thought briefly of the advantages of living in a cabin on Walden Pond. There weren't any cell phones there. "We don't need any lessons in civil disobedience. In civility, maybe."

"Just a thought," Dina said meekly.

"Thanks for the idea. But our hands are tied here. We're

going to build a hedge, or something. There's nothing we can do, really. But I'm just as mad as you are." Quill thought about it. "Probably madder. Anyhow, thanks."

"*Wait!*"

Quill had been about to put the cell phone in her pocket. Dina's shriek sounded like a teeny fire alarm. Quill put the phone back to her ear. "Harry Holcomb wants to know if you would join him for dinner at nine."

"He does?"

"Yeah." Dina's voice dropped. "He just checked in a whole fleet of suits, Quill."

"Fleet? Of suits?"

"Well, two anyhow. And they have to be lawyers because who else wears three-piece pinstripes these days?"

"Bankers," Quill said. "Undertakers. Politicians." She stopped. She had a lot of unanswered questions. Poor Charlene. She'd let several cats out of the bag. But she had to talk to Harry, too. "Okay. I'll do it."

"Good!" Dina said in approval. "Maybe you can talk Mr. Holcomb into chasing Captain Cluck out of town. And you have time to change."

Quill looked at her skirt. "I've got a skirt on. I look respectable."

"That's not what I heard. I heard you look like a wild banshee. No offense. I mean, who wouldn't, given all that's happened today. Put on something really really glamorous. We'll impress these rich guys."

There was one advantage to cell phones. You could snap them shut with a very satisfying click and cut a rude person off in mid-insult. Quill did just that. Then she went up to change into something really really glamorous.

Quill arrived at the Holcomb table in a little black dress that had knocked two men into proposals of marriage. (She'd accepted the first, and divorced him. She was still thinking hard about Myles.)

"Black's the absolute best color for a person with red

hair," Charlene said. "That looks sensational." Charlene herself was in an eerily beautiful bronze slip dress worked in silver and turquoise beading. Quill, back in her Lew Archer mode, thought she glowed like a hundred-watt bulb in a room filled with candles. Then Lew Archer gave way to her Innkeeper mode, and she checked the table; everyone was drinking wine, except Charlene. The aperitif tonight was olives and small squares of Tuscan bread with shaved Parmesan. And the table was perfectly set.

"Gentlemen." Quill nodded to the men sitting on either side of Charlene as Holcomb helped her into her chair.

"This is Arthur Devlin and that's Chet Brewster," Holcomb said. "Devlin's the one in the blazer. This is Sarah Quilliam. She's a 36 percent shareholder here. Margaret Quilliam holds another thirty. The rest is divided among some of the staff. John Raintree has the bulk of the remainder at 20 percent."

"Not a particularly efficient way to divide it up, Miss Quilliam," Devlin said.

"Must have been split up according to the original investment?" Brewster asked.

No two faces were really anonymous or interchangeable, Quill thought. But these two came close. Both lawyers were of medium height, exceptionally fit, and affected semi-bald buzz cuts. Maybe one would be ruder than the other, and she'd be able to tell them apart that way.

Quill smiled and said pleasantly, "We're privately held. You must have gone to some trouble to get this information."

"We don't want to waste our time if you haven't got control," Devlin said. "Maybe we should get the sister out here, Harry."

"Would you mind?" Brewster asked.

Quill didn't respond immediately. She leaned back to let Peter Hairston place a glass of shiraz in front of her. "Have you all ordered?"

"Yeah!" Harry Holcomb said impatiently. "I ordered the lamb shanks. Why?"

"Because if you want to eat what you ordered, Meg needs to be in the kitchen." Quill, pleased with the delivery of this mendacious, but neat reply, put her napkin in her lap. "Why don't you tell me why you asked me to dinner, Harry? Then if we need Meg we can arrange a time when she's not so busy."

"She's not a pushover, is she, Devlin?" Brewster grinned at her. "Courteous and cute, too. Sorry if we came on a little strong, Miss Quilliam. But that's why we get the big bucks from Harry."

"Big bucks," Charlene said suddenly. "That's what it's all about, Quill. Big bucks." All three men waited politely to see if she had anything else to say. She beamed muzzily at Quill and took the last sip of her drink.

Harry snapped his fingers at Peter, pointed to Charlene's drink, and then smiled stiffly. "Actually, it's not about money at all. Charlie's screwed me over one too many times. I've had it."

"Harry believes Kluckenpacker's trying to usurp the Fry Away Home contest," Brewster (or maybe it was Devlin) said. "Been trying for years. Harry's pretty sure he sabotaged the New Orleans event—"

"Got the free-range chicken people to picket," Harry said. He took a large sip of wine. "And Dallas. Don't forget Dallas."

Harry waited while Peter put another martini in front of his wife.

"Dallas?" Quill prompted.

"Press releases to the local media. Said the event had been cancelled." Harry's expression hardened. "And there's more."

Brewster and Devlin exchanged the smallest of glances.

"Yes, there's more." Harry brooded into his wine glass. "We won't trouble you with the details. But now this."

"You mean Banion O'Haggerty's murder?" Quill said.

"You think Captain Cl . . . I mean Charlie killed him to disrupt the contest?"

"Murder?" Brewster said. He pulled at his tie. "You never said anything about a murder, Harry."

"Oh, that." Harry waved a hand in dismissal. "Yeah. Banion got himself strangled yesterday. Hasn't made the news yet?"

"We didn't see it," Devlin said carefully.

"Born to be hanged," Charlene said mournfully.

"Nothing to do with us," Harry said.

"But it does." Quill took a deep breath. "I'm sorry, Harry, but I know that Ch—"

Charlene sneezed. "Oops!" she said. Her glass tipped into her lap. "Oopsey doosey. Oh, dear."

"Here," Quill said. She moved swiftly, napkin in hand. Peter was at Charlene's side in seconds. "Let's get you up to your room, okay? Peter can help you. You don't want to spoil that wonderful dress. Just leave it outside the door and we'll take care of it."

Charlene struggled to her feet. She clutched Quill's arm painfully hard. "No! You come with me!" Charlene's large blue eyes looked pleadingly into Quill's.

Quill hesitated. She nodded once. "I understand. It's okay." She detached the distraught woman's fingers gently. "But I shouldn't leave our guests, Charlene. You know men, they'll just chatter away while I sit here not saying a word, but it would be rude of us both to leave, wouldn't it?"

"And you just have to sit there without saying a word?" She grinned crookedly. "I know men. They'll just blabber on. We don't need to say a word."

"That's right." She helped Charlene into Peter's capable arms.

The three men kept an awkward silence that lasted as long as it took Charlene to edge her way unsteadily out of sight. Quill took a minute to figure out what she was going to do next. Charlene had said that "everybody" knew she'd been married to Banion. But her desperation was clear. So she couldn't let that particular cat out of the bag . . . And Charlene's relationship to Judith? Was that a desperate topic, too? She'd have to wait until Charlene sobered up to ask her. So she'd glammed up for nothing. And she'd have to sit here listening to these bozos for hours. "Oh, bother," Quill said aloud.

"Her allergies are quite severe," Harry said angrily. "And the medication she takes for them is quite disorienting."

If this had been a defense of his wife, Quill would have heartily approved. But Harry had ordered her another martini. And Quill wouldn't forget for a long time how this man claimed ownership.

"Of course, they are," Quill said. "I was thinking of something else entirely. So, you were telling me about Charlie's plans to wreck the Fry Away Home contest."

"Not just the contest. I think the son of a bitch is after my business, this time."

Again that discreet exchange of glances between the two lawyers.

"Because he's going to put one of his restaurants next to my inn?"

"In a little podunk town like this? Who gives a rat's ass about that!"

Brewster cleared his throat. "Ah. We do, Harry. Remember?"

"Huh?"

Devlin said smoothly, "What Harry means, Miss Quilliam, is that we're distressed and dismayed by the events of the past few days. In a way, Harry feels responsible for what is going to happen to your inn." He looked out the windows to the Gorge. The moon was riding high, and silver light flooded the falls. "It *is* a beautiful place here. No question about that." He turned his attention back to Quill. "There's some merit to what Harry's saying. Mr. Kluckenpacker has made a point of being—obtrusive during contest week. And now, he seems to have talked your townspeople into moving the show onto this piece of property he just acquired. This whole situation isn't good for any of us, Miss Quilliam. We'd like you to join us in a lawsuit to prevent Charlie from acquiring the property."

Quill had learned a lot about litigation the hard way. They'd had their share of claims regarding food poisoning, dangerous stairs, wrongfully terminated employees. Once in a while the insurance company paid people to go away (a practice that made Quill tear her hair). Neither she nor Meg had ever sued anyone else. "You don't have a what's it called? cause of action without us, do you?" she asked tentatively. "I mean, it's my inn that would suffer from the proximity of the Captain Cluck's Chicken hut. You don't have any legal interest in this. I do."

"It's in your best interests as well as ours, Miss Quilliam"

Brewster had answered her question without answering it.

"As a matter of fact, I don't see that we have a cause of action either," she said. "I mean, the land was sold to Mr. Kluckenpacker. The Zoning Committee approved it for commercial use. We're zoned for commercial use. I can't interfere with Charlie's right to do business or Elmer's right to sell his own property."

"Quill, Quill, Quill." Devlin shook his head and chuckled in an offensively paternal way. "Oh, my dear. How little you know about the law."

Quill stood up. "I hate the idea of one of those stupid chicken shacks spoiling my view more than anybody! But Elmer's property is none of my business! No. I don't know a damn thing about the law. But! I know about justice!"

It was a perfect exit line.

So she left.

CHAPTER 8

"I didn't know whether to laugh or cry," she said to Dr. Benziger. It was Wednesday. She had a morning appointment. She had spent the rest of the evening in long discussions with John, then Meg, and finally Myles, who'd called from Syracuse to say goodnight. She had a list of potential suspects/witnesses to interview.

She was going to solve this case.

She'd been both passionate and eloquent with Dr. Benziger, too. He couldn't possibly be bored when the topic was murder. She felt . . . purposeful. That was it. And not at all confused.

"You have contradictory emotions because law and justice have little to do with one another? Or because no one seems to care about Banion O'Haggerty's death? Or because Charlene is a beautiful woman who has been used by men all her life?" Dr. Benziger's hands were clasped loosely in his lap. His gaze was kind.

"Everyone cares about murder!" she said indignantly.

He shrugged. What did that mean? Did he think she was naive?

Quill pressed on. "Of course, everyone has a different reason to care. Harry just *seemed* indifferent because he's a suspect. I figured this out, too. Charlene didn't want me to mention her marriage to Banion because Harry's put a gag order on her. If not," she added dispiritedly, "an actual gag. He's an awful human being. Now, Myles? Myles cares

about justice. He always has. It's one of the reasons..."
She trailed off. Dr. Benziger raised one eyebrow in an encouraging way and prompted, "One of the reasons? Yes?"

Quill veered like a squirrel in front of a pickup. "And Brewster and Devlin seem to care because their client might be implicated. Did I tell you that both of them collared me at breakfast and asked me at least five hundred pointed questions about the case? They care, all right."

"Yes, you did. And why do *you* care about the murder?"

"Why do you keep coming back to what I think?"

Dr. Benziger took a deep breath. Then he exhaled. Then he said, "Because that's why you're here," in such a mild way that Quill was abashed. Then she began to worry that Dr. Benziger would a. find her stupid, which was just as bad as b. boring, and worse than startling, distressing, or discomposing him.

Dr. Benziger re-crossed his legs. "Let's get back to Charlene. I think it's important to understand why Charlene has affected you so strongly. You defended her by keeping silent about her marriage to... I'm sorry. I'm getting a little confused. What was his name?"

"Banion O'Haggerty."

"Thank you. What's significant, Quill, is that you did not betray her. Why don't we talk about your decision to do that?"

"She's... vulnerable."

"Yes? And how does that make you feel?"

"It's unfair to take advantage of vulnerable people." Quill veered again. She knew she was doing it. She couldn't help it. "Now Harry, he's about as vulnerable as a granite cliff. Harry could have committed this murder out of jealousy. Charlie, out of spite, to wreck the contest. Poor Elmer, out of desperation. And Charlene? Well, I don't know about Charlene. There's at least three suspects here, Dr. Benziger. Four, if you count Charlene and I don't have any proof that one or the other did it. The only thing I do

know is that Charlene may have been there. I told you
about that Kleenex."

"Yes. Quite disturbing."

Dr. Benziger didn't sound disturbed. He sounded bored.

"Although I must say," she added broodingly, "that
having Charlie arrested for murder would make everybody
in Hemlock Falls happy. Except Elmer Henry, maybe."

Dr. Benziger had a face almost as anonymous as Brewster's and Devlin's. His body language was nonexistent.
Quill knew the therapeutic reasons for this: psychiatrists
were supposed to be reassuring, nonreactive sounding
boards. Not real people. But she got the impression (she
didn't know how) that he was grinding his teeth.

"You know you aren't responsible for Banion
O'Haggerty's murder."

"I really wish you'd stop that," Quill said crossly. "I
know. I know I'm not responsible for other people's tor-
ment. That doesn't mean I don't want to fix it!"

"Now that's very good."

"What?!"

"Your anger. You're standing up for yourself."

Quill didn't think she'd ever had a problem standing up
for herself. On the other hand, if Dr. Benziger thought so,
maybe she did. It was all very confusing.

"You've come quite a long way, you know." Dr. Benziger nodded his head in approval.

"I have?"

"You have, indeed." He tapped his fingers against his
chin. "Your problem is that you're inconsistently decisive.
Sometimes you take action. Sometimes you remain inac-
tive. Often, you are not sure where the boundaries are. Your
behavior with the kitchen staff—what did Mr. Raintree call
it? The incipient Kitchen Riot, yes. Your behavior was
quite appropriate. Decisive in the right way. You know
your boundaries as an innkeeper, Quill. Now what about
your boundaries as a woman?"

"What about my boundaries as a detective?" Quill said.

"Solving this case is a lot more important than my boundaries as a woman."

"Ah . . . when will the sheriff return?"

"Lunchtime."

"Well," Dr. Benziger said. "You might want to talk with him about that." He rubbed his eyes. "That's all for today."

"So," Quill said to Meg when she'd walked Max back to the Inn. "This therapy's working, bit by bit. I mean, he said so. That I was improving."

It was another mild spring day and they were sitting on one of the benches in the hemlock grove. Her Wednesday appointment was at eight o'clock, which was nice, because she had the whole day ahead of her, and Dr. Benziger always made her feel capable, confident, and focused.

It was nine-thirty, and the whole day lay before her. She slipped off her shoes and wiggled her toes in the grass.

"How are you improving?"

Meg had always been skeptical about therapists, but it was a good question. Quill thought for a moment, and then asked anxiously, "You haven't noticed any improvement?"

"You don't need improvement!"

This would have made Quill quite sentimental, except for Meg's tone of voice, which was exasperated. "I set aside an hour each day to paint or sketch," she said timidly.

Meg grabbed her by the arm and shook it. "I am a beast," she said. "Of course you do. And it's a huge improvement over the way you felt about your work before."

Quill wasn't sure about this. She missed the days when painting grabbed her by the back of the neck and didn't let go until she finished. When she would tumble exhausted into bed after days of frenzied work, knowing that she'd done it *right*. Of course, it was impossible to have another life when you worked like that. A life with people in it, for example. Well. Well. And the other improvements? "And I know I love Myles. I don't want to spend my life with anyone else."

"Have you told him that?"

Well, no. She hadn't. Because then he would want to get married. Quill slipped her shoes back on. "That's it, I guess. The sum total of my improvement. Oh! Wait! There's one more advance in the clarity of my vision."

"The what of your what?"

"That's why I went in the first place. I was so confused about what I wanted. Now I'm much less confused." Quill had been digging in her purse as she talked and she withdrew her investigative notebook with a flourish. "I make better notes!"

"The Chamber will be happy about that," Meg said dryly. "Let me see."

Quill proffered it. "I've made a list of questions, followed by the names of the people to be interviewed and actions to be taken. We can divide the items up." She read over Meg's shoulder with the complacency of those who view a job well done.

1. Who surveyed the hemlock grove? John R. Check County Clerk's office.

2. Who commissioned the surveying? (See #1.)

3. Did they see anything? (See #1.)

4. What time did Charlene leave the Tavern Lounge? (Ask Nate who might have seen her go.)

5. Did anyone see Banion around the Croh Bar?

Meg looked up. "Myles asked. Nobody saw him. I didn't see him."

"In the shape you were in I'm surprised you saw the bar stool to sit on," Quill said unsympathetically.

"I was not drunk. I was fizzy."

"I'll check on that, too."

Meg read on. "You're going to talk to Judith Kluckenpacker? And Charlie? Good luck with both of them. And who the heck are Skip and his evil twin Jeffy?"

"Brewster and Devlin. You can't tell them apart. They're Holcomb's attorneys."

Meg's eyebrows rose. "Why do you think they would

tell you anything, even if they knew it? They'll charge you two hundred and fifty bucks an hour and tell you absolutely nothing."

"I want to know if they really think that Charlie has been sabotaging the festivals. Something in the way they talked around him last night, if you know what I mean by that . . ."

Meg nodded. "Little nods and sideways glances and sneaky sniggers. Okay, go on."

"I received the impression that they think Harry might be a little loosely wrapped. At least on the subject of Charlie Kluckenpacker. It'd be interesting to know how loosely wrapped."

"You'd better talk to Dr. Benziger," Meg said.

"That's not a bad idea."

"I was joking."

"I don't know why it's a joke. Motive has everything to do with a killer's psychological state. Dr. B could be a terrific partner."

Meg looked a little miffed, but merely said, "Whatever." She bent over the paper. "The chicken farmer? You're going to visit the chicken farmer? Why, for heaven's sake!"

"Both Harry and Charlie wanted to see him. That's enough for me."

"I wouldn't, Quill. I really wouldn't."

"What if he's a hired killer masquerading as a chicken farmer?"

"Then he's been in disguise for a l-o-o-ng time. Derek Maloney's family has run that chicken farm for decades. He's close to sixty, and he has no teeth. You've never been to a chicken farm, Quill?"

"No."

Meg laughed, "Ha!" Then, "Wear your rubber boots."

"I will be fine," Quill said austerely. But she crossed the chicken farmer off the list.

"And Carol Ann Spinoza."

"She's not on the list, Meg. But she should be. And I

was thinking that you'd be the best person to inter—"

"No. I mean Carol Ann's coming across the lawn."

"Right now?"

Carol Ann was indeed mincing her way across the mown lawn to the hemlock grove. She was ironed from head to toe: crisp white blouse with a little Peter Pan collar; knife-edged navy blue pants; even her ponytail looked ironed. She carried a neat black purse in one hand.

Quill realized she was clutching Meg at the same time Meg realized she was clutching her. They let go at the same moment and sat up straight.

"Good morning, Carol Ann," Quill said pleasantly.

"Good morning, Quill and Meg." She stopped in front of the bench.

Carol Ann's voice was high pitched and sticky sweet. She bit her words off as if she were sinking her bright white teeth into the necks of baby pigeons. Her most annoying habit was using given names in almost every single sentence, a product, John had told Quill, of a self-improvement course called "How to Win Friends and Influence People."

"How can we help you?" Quill felt her sister move to get up and pinched her, hard. If Meg thought she was going to escape and leave her to Carol Ann's mercies, she was wrong.

"Where's that dog, Quill?"

"You mean Max?" Quill looked vaguely around. "I don't know."

"I'm sure he's off in some dumpster, Quill. You really ought to keep him under better control." There was patient reproof in her voice.

Meg asked, just as sweetly, "Have you moved on to the Municipal Utilities Board? Dumpster patrol?"

Carol Ann swiveled her bright blue gaze. "No, Meg. I haven't. I am here to make sure that there are no booby traps for the tents."

"No what for the what?" Quill was bewildered.

"Mr. Holcomb made a specific request, Quill. Of me. He

thinks someone may try to sabotage the contest. And the flatbed truck's due at eleven-thirty with the tent poles and the canvas and in my capacity as a member of the Zoning Committee, I must ask you to leave so that I may conduct a proper search."

"All you'll find out there is Max's . . ." Meg smiled. Carol Ann's tennis shoes were as squeaky-clean as the rest of her. "Go right ahead."

Carol Ann didn't move.

"Well?" Meg asked. "We're not keeping you, are we?"

"Actually," Quill said, "we'd be happy to help."

"We would?" Meg said. Then "Ow!" as Quill poked her.

"We would," Quill said. "Where would you like to start, Carol Ann? And what are we looking for?"

"I'm afraid that as a member of the Zoning Committee I must ask you to leave, Quill. And you too, Meg."

"Hogwash," Meg said. "The zoning board doesn't have the author—" She smacked her forehead with one hand. "I can't believe I'm even responding to this crap. *Who cares!*? Carol Ann? We're leaving. See? This is me, Meg, and my sister, Quill. Leaving." She grabbed Quill by the sleeve.

"I think we should help." Quill smiled brightly. "It's three acres, you know. That's a lot of ground to cover before eleven-thirty."

Carol Ann folded her arms and stuck out her chin. She looked like a Dresden shepherdess about to participate in devil worship.

Meg stamped her foot and growled, "Let's go, darn it. I've got shrimp to see to."

"All right. Fine." Quill turned to follow her sister. "Oh, Carol Ann?"

She still hadn't moved.

"Anything you find should be turned over to the sheriff's office."

"I have no idea what you mean."

"I think you do."

Meg waited until they were out of earshot and demanded, "What was that all about?"

"Holcomb sent her to search for anything Charlene might have left behind last night, obviously."

By now they'd reached the raised beds where Meg grew herbs and vegetables. Mike the groundskeeper had already turned the earth and raked it flat. Planting in upstate New York generally had to be held until Memorial Day, but Meg could never resist planting early peas, and she'd taken the time to put in several rows the day before. She stopped to pull some young weeds from the bed before she asked, in a long-suffering tone, "What sort of thing?"

"I don't know," Quill said. "But she's not going to get away with it. Where are the binoculars?"

Meg pulled the back door open with a bang. "It's nine forty-five. With all you have to do today, you're going to sit at the back window with a pair of binoculars for almost two hours in the hope that she's going to find what, a bomb? I don't think so."

"We'll see," Quill said.

Meg rolled her eyes but went off to find the binoculars. Quill wedged herself on the birch counter under the window that gave the best view of the hemlock grove. And for the first hour, Quill refused to admit to herself that Meg might be right. Carol Ann was methodical, there was no doubt about that. She walked up and down like a soldier on parade, arms clasped behind her back, eyes on the grass. Quill got tired. She got bored. Her eyes watered from staring through the binoculars. Her back hurt from her mashed up position on the counter. The normal activity of the kitchen swirled around her and she felt weirdly isolated. Invisible. A non-person.

"Quill is doing what?" she heard Bjarne ask. "Sur-what?"

Myles had told her surveillance was boring, and he was right. Meg brought her a cup of cappuccino. Meg brought her another cappuccino. Quill crossly refused a third.

At eleven-fifteen, Meg snuck up behind her and said, "Well?!"

"I was right." She was too excited to be smug. "She's stopped. She's bending over. *She's picking something up!*"

Meg grabbed at the binoculars. "What?"

"Cut it out, Meg. Ha! She's putting whatever it is into a Baggie. And into her purse."

Carol Ann did the single most suspicious thing she'd done all morning. She looked carefully from side to side before she stuck her chin in the air and minced down the meadow and out of sight.

"Ha-*ha!*" Quill put the binoculars back into the case. "If that doesn't prove *something* I don't know what does."

"Yeah, well," Meg said doubtfully. "What? What could it prove?"

"I'm not sure yet." Quill slid off the counter.

"Where are you going?"

"You mean where are *we* going? To my office. We have to make a time line. And we have to figure out when we can break into Carol Ann's house and look at that clue."

"Stop right there." Meg planted herself in front of Quill. "If you think for one minute I'm going to break into . . ." She broke off. Elizabeth and Bjarne were watching them both with fascinated intensity. Meg lowered her voice and hissed, "Into that woman's house you are crazy. Do you remember what you did to her last winter?"

Quill made a face. She'd tried to forget what she'd done to Carol Ann last winter, although to be absolutely fair about it, it was because of what Carol Ann had tried to do to her.

"I don't care," Quill said stubbornly. "If she's involved in a murder, we can't let personal considerations keep us from the truth. If Philip Marlowe had let personal considerations keep him from the truth—"

"He wouldn't have gotten beaten up so much," Meg pointed out. "Honestly, Quill. Carol Ann's mean, vindictive, boastful, and as slyly manipulative as someone as stupid as she is can be, but she's not a criminal."

"It was only a matter of time," Quill said darkly. "Are you coming with me?"

"To break into Carol Ann's house? Probably. I mean, sisters forever, and all that. Right now to make a time line? I can't. Louise Fisher's due for lunch."

Quill gasped. "Meg! I'm so sorry! I completely . . ." She broke off and said, "Hang on a second. The editor of *L'Aperitif* is coming to lunch and you aren't pitching a hissy fit? Are you okay? Are you dying of a dread disease?"

"A dread disease? No." Meg said this so calmly that Quill was certain her sister was dying of a dread disease. "I found a good shrimp recipe, that's all."

"That's all? Meg, that's terrific."

"Mm."

Quill looked at Bjarne, who shrugged and rolled his eyes. Elizabeth was prepping a large portion of fresh shrimp at the sink.

Meg ran her hands through her hair so that it stuck up in little points all over her head. "Louise is here to do an interview, so for once, this is going to be less about food and more about me."

"That's great."

"Maybe. I don't know. But I'm going with the stuff I already do well. Lamb in mint. Fresh peas from California. The breads. If I hadn't told her I had a new shrimp dish, it would have been fine." Meg sighed deeply. "So it's no big deal." Her eye fell on Elizabeth, who was putting the peeled shrimp into a large stainless steel bowl and she shrieked, *"Is that brine? I hope that's brine!"*

Quill patted her on the head and went off to do her time line. She managed to get through the dining room without being diverted by innkeeping duties and felt quite pleased with herself. On the other hand, Dina was in the foyer. And Dina always had some kind of innkeeping duty to bring to her attention.

Quill stopped in the archway. A tall man in late middle

age was slouched over the reception desk talking angrily to Dina. His suitcases were spread all over the floor. He wore a three-piece pinstriped suit, so he was either a lawyer, a banker, or an undertaker. Quill was willing to bet on lawyer.

Dina's face was pink, as if she had been crying.

"Hey!" Quill said. "Is there a problem here? Can I help you?" She crossed the foyer in three quick strides.

"Oh, hi, Quill," Dina said morosely. "This is Mr. Hauser."

"Has he been bothering you?" Quill asked firmly.

"Me? No. Why?"

"Ms. Quilliam?" Hauser had a courtroom presence: silver hair, heavy jaw, and a very loud speaking voice. Quill realized he'd been haranguing Dina in what for him was an undertone. "I understand that your guest list is proprietary. But your young receptionist here doesn't seem to understand that these men are in my employ. Or *were* in my employ. And I want to know where they are."

"Where who are?" Quill asked.

"Mr. Brewster and Mr. Devlin," Dina said. "You know what, Quill? They quit. Mr. Hauser is mad as anything." She perked up and looked at the angry lawyer admiringly. "He says when he finds them he's going to wring their scrawny necks."

"Well," Quill said. She was nonplussed.

"We've already had one murder here this week, Mr. Hauser, and Quill would have a screaming fit if we had two more. So," she switched her Bambi-like gaze to Quill. "I thought I'd better not tell him they're here."

"Thank you," Hauser boomed. "Where's the courtesy phone?"

"I don't believe they're in," Quill said.

"They aren't," Dina said. "They had this big huge fight with Mr. Holcomb. Mr. Brewster, or maybe it was Mr. Devlin, said he, Mr. Holcomb, was a lunatic. And they galloped off in all directions."

"A fight? With Holcomb?" Hauser's complexion lost some of its ruddy fury. "Hm. I might not be too late then. I'd like a room here, young lady."

"We're all booked up," Quill said, with little regret.

"No, we aren't. Mr. Brewster and Mr. Devlin checked out."

"They've gone!?" Hauser roared.

Quill resisted the temptation to put her fingers in her ears.

"Not out of Hemlock Falls," Dina said. "Just to the Marriott, which is cheaper than us. Mr. Holcomb said they could wait until the cows came home before he paid their bill here. So they left. Mr. Brewster put the room charges on his gold card."

"Was it a Hauser & Murphy corporate credit card?" Hauser demanded. "Because I'm not paying those bastards' bill either."

Dina gave him a long, level look. "I believe it was Mr. Brewster's personal credit card," she said primly. "Would you care to check in?"

"Holcomb's registered here?"

"Yes."

"Then I will. Thank you."

Hauser looked positively benign. Dina, on the other hand, had relapsed into melancholy.

Quill took her leave, and went into her office. As she closed the door, she heard Hauser ask, "You had a murder?"

We had a murder.

Quill retrieved a fresh yellow pad from her credenza and sat down at her desk. She made a chart and listed all the suspects in Banion's murder: Harry Holcomb, Charlie, Judith, and Charlene. She tapped her teeth with her pencil. She bit the end. She glanced involuntarily at the office door, which was closed. If the police were foolish enough to suspect Andy, the case against the real murderer had to be watertight. And Andy and Meg were suspects in the eyes of the cops. She added Meg and Andy to the suspects list. She felt incredibly guilty.

Everyone knew the murder had taken place between nine and ten o'clock. First, she had to establish the relevant travel times between where the suspects were at the time of the murder. Everyone had been at the Inn. That made the distance between suspects and corpse easy.

But how did the murderer get to the Croh Bar? Quill knew it took twenty minutes at a brisk walk if you cut through Peterson Park; she walked that way three times a week to see Dr. Benziger. It took five or ten minutes longer if you took the road. How long did it take in a car? How likely was it that the murderer had used a car?

Nobody had a car except Andy and Meg. And the van was locked up at night. What about a bicycle? There weren't any bicycles at the Inn, although Quill had thought about getting one for exercise. So the murderer had to get there on foot. Now all she had to do was establish who was where between eight-thirty and ten-thirty.

Quill contemplated her chart, pleased with herself. Yes. This would be a simple one to solve. She was surprised that Myles hadn't thought of it himself. All she had to do now was pin everyone down in artless, casual conversation. And she'd start with poor Charlene.

A tap at the door made her jump. Dina poked her head in. "There you are. I put Mr. Hauser in 218. Guess what?"

"What?"

"Those two guys did use the Hauser-Whosis gold card. But I didn't tell Mr. Hauser that. He might have called the credit card company, and we would have been out a thousand bucks. Pretty smart, huh?"

"Very smart," Quill agreed. "Dina, is something wrong? Are you okay? Did this murder upset you?"

"No more than usual. Hey. The sheriff's looking for you. He's back from Syracuse. And he's hungry, he says."

• • •

Myles leaned back in his chair and crossed his long legs. It was well after two o'clock. The dining room at the Inn was empty except for the two of them and Meg and Louise Fisher in earnest conversation in the corner. She had not told Myles about Carol Ann's odd behavior, or her suspect chart, or any of her plans to solve the case. He had started lunch by asking her to keep clear of the whole thing. They'd gotten to the middle of lunch and he still wanted her to stay out of it. He was concerned about Andy. And she was too close to Andy.

"You don't really think he killed Banion!"

Myles rubbed his eyes. "Of course I don't. But he's a friend of mine. And he's going to marry your sister. And the two of us are—involved. You can see how this might play out if an irresponsible reporter covers the story. Meg's well known. You're even better known. This is a high-profile case, Quill. And it's getting a lot of media attention already. O'Haggerty was both well known and popular. I've asked a friend of mine to come in from Syracuse and take over."

"You aren't serious!"

"Very."

"But—"

"But what?"

Is he as good as you are? But she didn't voice the thought. Instead she said, "I'm sure it's the right thing to do. What's his name? When is he coming? Shall we put him up here at the Inn? That might be a problem—we're totally booked for the contest—"

He put his hand on hers. "He'll stay at the Marriott. His name's Jordan Bellemarin."

"What a lovely name."

"He's from New Orleans originally. We've worked together in the past."

Myles rarely talked about his days with the NYPD. It had bothered Quill, this reticence. It still bothered her.

"Let's not talk about it. How was your day?"

"Um. Fine. I saw Dr. Benziger today."

He smiled at her.

"You know, Myles. This is dumb, but I keeping worrying that he thinks I'm stupid. Or boring."

"He may find you a little frustrating," Myles said. "But I doubt very much that he's bored." Then he asked, lightly, "Do you talk about why you don't want to marry me?"

Quill veered away from this. She gazed around the room. The trade had been light today. Louise and Meg had disappeared into the kitchen. No one from Hemlock Falls had come in for lunch. This was unusual. Quill had expected to see Marge, and certainly Miriam Doncaster and perhaps a brigade of sympathetic friends ready to protest the desecration of the hemlock grove with a Captain Cluck's Chicken Hut. And she hadn't seen Doreen at all. "They're helping set up the contest tents," she said suddenly. "I completely forgot. I'd better get over there, Myles." It would be a perfect time to engage each of the suspects in artless conversation, one by one. She became aware of Myles's steady, grave regard. "What? What is it?"

"Nothing at all," Myles said. "Tell Meg that this is a very good hamburger."

"She's a great chef." Quill's response was automatic. "Is that what's wrong? That it's a hamburger? I think she's having a reaction to dressy food."

"Dressy food?"

"You know, tarted-up stuff. Chocolate and salmon mousse, that kind of thing. There's such fierce competition among celebrity chefs these days that she claims the recipes are getting wilder and wilder." He'd left a bit on his plate and she'd reached over with her fork. "That is good! She's made a burgundy-based marinade for it. Maybe we should put it on the lunch menu permanently."

Myles folded his napkin and got to his feet.

"You're going already?"

"The coroner's report will be in. I want to go over the

hard evidence we gathered at the scene before Danny comes in this afternoon."

"That's what you call him? Danny?"

"And I'm going over to Roebuck & White in Ithaca."

"Aha! The surveyors. So I did provide you with some valuable information. And I told you about Charlene's Kleenex," Quill said. She could cross the visit with the surveyors off her investigative list. Myles couldn't object to telling her about that, and if he did, there was always Davey Kiddermeister.

"Yes, you did. If they did do the surveying job, one of them may have seen O'Haggerty leaving. Or Charlene."

"I know. I should have saved it. Nate threw it out, and I didn't even think about it."

"It wouldn't have mattered. You broke the chain of evidence. It wouldn't have been admissible." There was a glint in Myles's eye that told her she should stop talking about this right now.

"It would have helped place her there."

He bent down and kissed her. "Quill, I can't stop you from nosing around—"

"Hey! I've been very helpful on occasion. You said so yourself."

"But I can stop you from actively interfering in the case. And I will. We've been over this before."

They had. At length. In other cases. There were interesting penalties for civilians convicted of hindering the police in their inquiries. Some of them involved jail time.

"Will you be back early or late?" She was suddenly anxious. "You will be back, won't you? You aren't all that angry with me?"

"I'll be back. And no, I'm not angry with you." He paused in the archway, his face in shadow. "Remember, Quill. There's a reason for both of us to keep a low profile."

Andy. She waved as Myles went out the door. She had to talk with Andy, too, although it was merely to fill in the appropriate place in her chart.

Suddenly, she felt bleak.

CHAPTER 9

When Harry Holcomb put on a Fry Away Home contest, he did his company proud. In less than three hours, the hemlock grove had been transformed. Six huge blue and white striped tents were artfully grouped beneath the trees. A seventh, smaller tent was labeled "PRESS." White three-board fencing circled the meadow. Two charming white gazebos stood at the entrance to the whole, a banner stretched between them that read:

FRY AWAY HOME!
The Contest!

And in modest lettering beneath:

Brought to you by Holcomb's Wholesome Chicken.

Quill stood and looked at it. It was another lovely, warm May day. The sun was bright. The trees were that new spring green that made the heart ache. If you squinted so that the whole scene was blurry, it was reminiscent of the French Impressionists, Manet and his paintings of family celebrations by the Seine.

A few workmen pounded stakes into the ground. The flatbed trucks were leaving. Most of the Chamber of Commerce members seemed to be wandering through the area. Freddie Bellini avoided her. Howie and Miriam walked together under the trees. Harvey Bozzel trotted back and forth, a clipboard in his hand. Quill waved at Marge and went to meet her.

"What d'ya think? Kinda romantic, huh?" Marge had abandoned her blue bowling jacket for a red bowling jacket. Otherwise, she looked exactly the same.

"Very romantic," Quill agreed. "It looks terrific."

"Press'll be here in a bit, I expect. There's a press tent and everything." Marge looked around in satisfaction. "Had a promo on the morning talk shows this morning. See it?"

"No, I missed it."

"Gonna be good for the town."

"Do you think Captain Cluck's going to be good for the town?" Quill asked. She was almost sorry to see the hem-lock grove like this. It would make the asphalt parking lot and the neon chicken beak all the more painful.

"Well, no. Can't say as I do. I should have known that Elmer was up to something. I usually go to the zoning meetings. Learn a lot about the town that way. But that Carol Ann's just a pain in the butt, so I decided not to. That and they scheduled a daytime meeting. I should have known something was up just because of that. That damn Elmer knew I'd be down to the diner in the afternoon. I always am. You gonna do anything about it?"

"What can I do?" Quill expostulated. "Spend money on lawyers?"

"Wouldn't cost you a dime." Harry Holcomb strolled up. Quill regarded him for a long moment. He was a very barbered-looking man. That was the word. Groomed. His dark hair was clipped close to his narrow skull, and he had the kind of chin that always looked as if he'd just shaved.

"No thanks," Quill said. Then, politely, "It looks beau-tiful."

"It always looks beautiful," he said matter-of-factly. "God knows I pay enough for it." His narrow eyes flickered over the scene. Two men in orange coveralls wheeled a huge stainless steel deep-fat fryer into one of the tents. "It's a better spot than the school. I have no quarrel with it."

"One of those in every tent?" Marge asked alertly. "That fryer?"

"Yes. We have six expert chefs who specialize in deep-fat frying. Therefore the six tents." His tone was sarcastic.

"Mind if I take a look?"

"As a matter of fact, I do."

"We'll both take a look," Quill said firmly.. "Betty is going to be competing, you know."

"Whatever," Holcomb said.

She knew, in her bones, that poor Charlene had probably murdered Banion O'Haggerty. And she tried not to wish ill of anyone. But it wouldn't bother her much if this condescending jerk turned out to have done it instead.

"I've hired security guards, by the way," Holcomb snapped. "That ass Charlie's going to have a tough time getting through this year."

"Security guards," Marge snorted. "What the hell for?"

Holcomb's narrow black eyes darted from side to side.

"But he owns this land, now," Quill said. "How can you keep him off it?"

"I've got a case. Don't you worry about it."

Quill bit her lip. He had a case, but did he have a lawyer? Quill saw a tiny opening for her investigation. Holcomb clearly had some kind of obsessive fixation about his rival. His own lawyers, if they still were his own lawyers, thought him a lunatic on the subject. "What is it about Charlie Kluckenpacker?" she asked in as artless a way as possible. "How did all this feuding begin?"

"He's a spoiler," Holcomb said roughly. "But he's not going to spoil it this time. I'll kill him, first."

Marge stared.

"Has he interfered with the contest in the past?" Quill asked her question gently.

"Every year." Holcomb actually seemed to grind his teeth.

"That so?" Marge seemed unimpressed. "Thought you

two duked it out over market share. Didn't think you'd stoop to kid tricks."

"It's nothing less than sabotage," Holcomb snarled. "And what do you know about market share?"

Marge shrugged. She was quite good at being artless herself, Quill noted. She stood musing, trying to think of an artless and tactful way to find out where Holcomb had been at the time of the murder.

Marge shifted her weight. "How come you two are cozy enough to have lunch with each other?"

"What do you mean?"

"Well." Marge chewed on her lower lip for a bit. "There you were, the two of you. Eatin' at my diner."

"Yes. Well. Socially, you know. One has to cope."

"All under the surface, huh?"

"More or less." Holcomb's attention shifted. His lips drew back from his teeth. Quill turned to look in the same direction and saw Charlie and Judith coming through the gazebo entrance.

"It's closer than merely social, isn't it?" Quill asked. "I mean, Charlene is his stepdaughter, isn't she?"

"Is that a fact," Marge said. "Huh."

"It's a fact I prefer to forget," Holcomb said frostily. "I've managed to keep it out of the media lately, but somehow, some way, it gets back into the picture. Reporters are ruthless." He jerked his head in an abrupt nod as Charlie and Judith advanced on them.

"Want to register a complaint here, Harry." Charlie said. "Gotta teach the hired help a few manners."

"If you hadn't tried to interfere with the unloading, Charles, no one would have insulted you." Judith was unperturbed. "The tents look well this year, Harry."

Quill stood and watched the three of them. Charlie stood with his feet planted wide, a big grin on his face, obviously enjoying Holcomb's distaste. Judith said hello to both Quill and Marge in her gracious but cool way. She's remote from this particular struggle, Quill thought. She doesn't really care.

"What I want to know about," Marge said loudly, "is this Romeo and Juliet thing. I mean to say, how'd Harry here meet Charlene? Was it at one of these-here contests?"

"Romeo and Ju. . . . Oh!" Judith said. "I see. You mean how did Charlene happen to marry a man her stepfather hated? Charles and Harry knew each other long before the chicken business."

"Special Forces," Charlie offered with a grin. "We were in the army together. Just two good old boys, one from Missouri, that's me, the other from Boston, that's him."

"Trading secrets in those long nights together in the jungle, weren't we, Charlie?" Holcomb's grin was just as shark-like as Charlie's. Quill stood, fascinated. The case was shaping up nicely. There was history here. Dark history.

Charlie rocked back on his heels and looked around in an expansive way. "Looks pretty good, fella. Like the blue and white theme. Yes sir."

"Very nice," Judith agreed distantly. "I'd like to see the fryer setup, Harry."

"Fine. Fine." Holcomb snapped off the words in a very Carol-Annish way. "Everybody wants a look? Everybody gets a look. But I'll tell you up front, Charlie. The guards this year are damn good. Got them from a top notch firm in Syracuse."

"Global Investigations?" Quill said before she could stop herself. Myles's firm. She bit her lip.

"What about it?"

"Just that I've heard they're very good."

Holcomb looked at his watch. "They're due in at four o'clock for the first shift. Come on, then, if you insist. I'll show you around. But don't go poking your nose in, Charlie. How long have you been here, anyway?"

"Long enough, pally. Long enough."

Quill trailed the group, still turning over ways to coax

where-were-you information from Harry, Judith, and Charlie. This opportunity was a good one, if she could just introduce a topic of conversation that would get them all to casually discuss their whereabouts last night.

"The tents are all set up like this," Holcomb said as they entered the tent closest to the gate. "The fryer's at the rear, as you see, with the prep tables and sinks right next to it."

"Huh!" Marge barreled over to the fryer, trailed by the others. One of the orange-suited maintenance men was busy setting it up.

"That's a beauty, that is," she said. "What's the gallonage?"

"Dunno," the maintenance man said. The embroidered name over his breast pocket read "Burt." "I'm just wiring her up. She's a heavy sucker, though. They didn't warn me about that."

"It's sixty-gallon capacity," Holcomb said. "There's a central heating core to keep the fat at an even temperature. I can do a hundred and twenty pounds of chicken in that."

"Open 'er up," Marge demanded.

"There's nothing to see," Holcomb said. "What do you care, anyway?"

"She starts deep-fat frying her own chicken we both got problems, Harry." Charlie stuck a toothpick in his mouth and rolled it from side to side. "You taste that stuff in her diner yesterday? Better than the recipe I got, that's for damn sure."

"Boots boiled in cow manure are better than the recipe you got, Charlie," Marge said cheerfully. "Tell you what, Burt. Soon as you get 'er hooked up, you give me a holler."

"Will do."

Marge put her hands on her hips and looked around the tent. Her lips pursed in approval. "Not a bad setup. Not a bad setup at all. Might learn something from this."

"Good God," Holcomb said disgustedly. "If you're through poking around, I'd like to get going. I've got a press conference here in half an hour."

"Hang on to your shorts, Harry. You've got some time, don't you? Not a lot of tables and chairs," Marge observed. "What you got, seating for a hundred and fifty?"

"The tickets are quite expensive," Judith said. "Harry did that deliberately, didn't you, Harry. And I must say I approve. You don't want to turn this into a rout with just anyone getting in."

"Sure you do," Charlie said. "The more the merrier."

"Where's the judge sit?" Marge stumped over to a small table with an elaborate armchair behind it. It was set well away from the rest of the activity. "This is it?"

Holcomb nodded. "Need room for the TV feed." His hands were in his pockets. He jingled the change angrily. "Seen enough?"

"Meg Quilliam going to judge, now that O'Haggerty's toes?" Marge asked.

"Toes?" Judith's eyebrows rose.

"Y'know. Dead."

"Yes," Quill said. "Meg's going to judge. She's very pleased to be asked." Now, this was the perfect opportunity to slip into detective mode. She'd start with innocuous questions. She cleared her throat. "By the way, how did you all like Meg's food last night? I saw you were all in the dining room?"

"Heck with that," Marge said. "What I want to know is which one of you knocked off Banion O'Haggerty."

"I beg your pardon." Judith looked as if she had stepped barefoot on a snail.

"Stands to reason it was one of you."

"I fail to see—" Judith began.

"Fail to see what? Nobody here knew him but Meg. And she was at my bar all night long. Got an alibi as watertight as one of Freddie Bellini's coffins. So it must have been one of you."

"I understand that young doctor is under suspicion," Judith said. "I understand that he has no alibi, either."

Marge narrowed her eyes. "Oh, yeah? Small town like

this. Everybody knows the doc. Everybody likes him. The sheriff? He's got a close relationship with the family. Kinda like you and Charlene, Charlie. Even if Andy done it, you think he's going to be arrested for it? No way. No way at all. We don't like outsiders, here in Hemlock Falls." Marge's steely gaze moved slowly from Charlie to Holcomb to Judith. When it reached Quill, she winked.

Quill blinked in admiration. Blackmail! Why hadn't she thought of that?

"O'Haggerty was killed between nine and ten o'clock. In *my* parking lot." Marge's lower lip protruded a little further. "I don't like that at all. So, where were you all at?"

"This is ridiculous," Holcomb said angrily.

"You expecting a big crowd on Friday?" Marge asked. "Want those TV cameras to pan out over all the folks that are waiting to get into this contest?"

Quill saw at once that this was a misstep in an otherwise admirable campaign of intimidation. These people dealt in power, real or perceived, and they had no idea of the economic might residing in the stocky little woman before them. "Excuse me," she said. "Perhaps you don't know that Marge owns most of the Hemlock Savings and Loan. If she doesn't want people to show up—"

"The bank?" Marge waved a pudgy hand. "The bank's nothin'. You want to know what I got? 22 percent of FoodOil. That's what I got."

Holcomb stopped jingling his coins. Charlie's grin disappeared.

"You own a controlling share of our solid fat supplier?" Judith asked.

"Same company that's got you both tied into ten-year contracts for your canola oil, Harry. And your shortening, Charlie." Marge's gaze didn't waver. "Lotta those semis are due for some pretty heavy maintenance checks. Might have to take a good few off the road."

Semis? Quill thought. Oh, delivery trucks. She bit her lip.

"We were with your mayor," Judith said stiffly. "Dinner. At his house. With that dreadful wife of his. And unless you think the four of us conspired to dispatch that unfortunate Irishman, we are in the clear."

"Wondered how far Elmer was in bed with you two," Marge said bluntly. "But I can't see as it'd go beyond business. You never know about people, though. Now you, Holcomb. What about you?"

"I retired with my wife about eight o'clock," Holcomb said. "I was asleep by nine. I believe housekeeping opened the door to check the room about nine-thirty." His black eyes darted to Quill. "Of course, the housekeeping staff is in her employ, so I suppose I can't count on the truth, can I?"

"Maybe." Marge snapped her gum. "Courts don't take the testimony of a wife, far as I know. You know about that, Quill?"

"My wife," Holcomb snarled, "was not with me."

"She wasn't?" Judith said. "You mean she was out murdering the Irish chef? Even dogs take care of their own." Her lip curled. "What a common little man you are, Harry."

"Know where she is now?" Marge asked.

Holcomb shook his head. "I haven't seen her all day. She went . . . out."

"Starting her up, Marge!" Burt the maintenance man plugged a thick yellow extension cord into a cable. The lights on the deep-fat fryer began to glow. Then they went out.

"Shoot!" Burt disconnected the cable.

Charlie spat his toothpick onto the canvas floor. "Let me see that, Burt. Used to maintain these babies myself."

Holcomb's face reddened. "Leave it alone, Charlie! Keep your hands off!"

"Open her up, Burt," Charlie called. "You might have a loose wire in the core."

"Oh, God," Burt said.

"What? Somebody leave something in there?" Charlie

rolled forward, his face set in a humorless smile. "You got some trash in there, Burt?"

"Oh, God. Oh, God." Burt was pale. His hands shook. He backed away from the fryer and stumbled heavily.

"It's Mrs. Holcomb."

CHAPTER 10

"The press conference was delayed, of course," Quill said glumly.

"I still can't believe Holcomb *held* it." Meg set her glass of wine on the old oak trunk Quill used as a coffee table. Doreen sat in the Eames chair to the right of the French doors that led to Quill's balcony. "Tsk," she said, and put a coaster under the wine glass.

"Oh he held it, all right. Said Charlene would have been 'fully supportive' of his decision to go on with the competition. And a lot of other blabber. He posted a reward for whoever finds the killer."

Meg made a derisive noise in her throat.

Outside, the night wind whipped around Quill's balcony.

"Comin' up for rain," Doreen observed. She wasn't wearing the chicken outfit. She had, she'd said, decided not to go into the chicken business. Too many jerkolas in it. She was dressed in blue cotton trousers, a blouse printed with pink roses, and a baggy navy cardigan.

" 'And the sky wept rain,' " Quill said. "Isn't that from some poem?"

"If it is, it's a horrible one." Meg clasped her hands behind her head and leaned back with a sigh. "It's a pathetic fallacy, to boot. Very pathetic, if you ask me."

Quill didn't rise to the bait. She rose from the couch and paced restlessly up and down her small living room. "This is awful. This is just awful."

"Quit that," Doreen said. "You're makin' me nervous."
Quill sat down again.

"Didja see the body?" Doreen asked into the silence.

"Do-*reen!*" Meg ruffled her hair. She looked at Quill. "Well, did you?"

Quill coughed to avoid crying again. "Yes. I saw the body."

"Well?" Doreen asked alertly.

"Well, what? The poor woman had been strangled. It was obvious."

"What with?" Doreen demanded.

Quill shuddered. "I didn't look very closely," she admitted. "Everybody's first thought was to get her out of that damn machine in case she . . . well, it was pretty obvious that she was dead. And she'd been so beautiful." Unbidden and unwelcome, the memory of Charlene's distorted face came to Quill. She began to cry again, and wiped the tears away with the back of her hand. She took a deep breath. "Just a second. There. Okay. Let me think. There was a . . . cord . . . buried in her . . ." She drew her hand across her own throat.

"Just like Banion O'Haggerty," Doreen said in satisfaction.

"Perhaps," Quill said. Another memory intruded on her. Bound by a horrified silence, they had tipped the fryer on its side and tried to pull Charlene out. The body had been limp and heavy. And warm.

"How much is that Holcomb offering for the reward?" Doreen asked bluntly.

Quill recalled all of Dr. Benziger's advice about understanding feelings. She made a conscious effort to relax. She made an even more conscious effort to look at Doreen's wholly inappropriate comment with Dr. Benziger's detached and kindly insight.

Then she regarded her housekeeper. Doreen was in her seventies, as vital and vigorous as ever. Quill was convinced that a large part of her physical vitality was due to her practical, hard-headed approach to life. "You know what, Doreen? You don't believe in crises, not emotional ones, at least. If you can't fix it, you accept it and go on. It isn't that you don't grieve. You do. But it's a purposeful grief, and when the time for mourning is over, you march on straight ahead. It's hard to imagine you flattened by anything. So I am *not* upset by your seeming disregard for this . . . this tragedy."

Doreen opened her mouth, shut it, and looked baffled. Then she said, "You with us, missy? I said, just like Banion O'Haggerty. And then I ast you how much—"

"We don't know that it was just like Banion O'Haggerty," Meg intervened. "She could have been strangled after she was shot or poisoned."

Quill turned to her sister. "Now, Meg. You become very linear in a crisis. For someone as volcanic as you are, it's odd. You focus on detail; you just trust that if the smaller facts are in order, the larger picture will emerge."

"Well, lah-di-dah," Doreen said, astonished.

"How much longer are you seeing the rat therapist?" Meg asked. "I mean, your insurance benefits must be running out. I hope."

"Was I rude?" Quill asked anxiously.

"Very." Meg glared at her.

"I didn't mean to be rude. But I'm just beginning to realize that the therapeutic process can be very freeing. I mean, suddenly, I understand almost everything. Dr. Benziger said so himself. I'm improving. I'm gaining insight. And I want to share it, of course."

"You do, huh." Doreen's skepticism was obvious. "How come?"

"How come?" Meg asked. "I'll tell you how come. This is just like the time you had a dread disease, Quill. Remember? First it was amytrophic lateral whatsis—"

"Sclerosis," Quill said stiffly.

"And then it was a brain tumor, and god knows what all after that. And it was all because you bought that used copy of the *Merck Manual which* I might add was twenty-two years out of date! And now. And *now!* You're going to walk around psychoanalyzing everybody."

"She's seeing a shrink," Doreen confirmed. "Bound to take 'er this way."

"A rat therapist," Meg corrected her. "And if you are going to spend the rest of the week psychoanalyzing everybody, Quill, I am going to quit and cook for Charlie Kluckenpacker."

Quill was insulted. "He probably wouldn't hire you."

"Oh, yeah?!"

"Yeah!"

"Cut it out," Doreen said. "We got a murder to solve here."

Meg subsided. "We sure do. Only it's two murders."

Quill, who was still mad that her helpful insights into Doreen and Meg's behavior had been so summarily rejected, rather pointedly sipped her wine and said nothing.

"Biggest question is, who could've done it and why?" Doreen looked hopefully at Meg. "You got any ideas?"

"From what Quill says about him, it has to be Harry Holcomb."

"You think Holcomb kilt O'Haggerty, too?"

"Probably. From what Quill says—"

"I'm sitting *right here*," Quill shouted.

"Glad you decided to rejoin the conversation," Doreen said cordially. "So, you think that Holcomb did 'em both in?"

"Holcomb says he has an alibi for the first murder." Quill got up and retrieved her time line from the kitchen counter. "But it's a shaky one. We have a terrific advantage as far as the first murder is concerned. We know *when*, almost to the minute. Or to the half hour, anyway."

"And that was when?" Doreen asked.

"Between nine-thirty and ten." Quill spread her time line on the coffee table and regarded it thoughtfully. "I called the garbage disposal company. The computer clocked the pickup at nine-twenty-two." She pulled her lower lip. She was just beginning to see it. There was a problem here. Who was where at what time wasn't going to solve this murder.

"Couldn't have been Holcomb," Doreen said decisively. "He was in his room at nine-thirty or thereabouts. Seen him myself."

"You did?" Quill frowned. "Did you see him or a lump in the bed?" She sat back against her goose down cushions. She was right. She had to be. Timing wouldn't solve this murder. Motive would solve this murder. Understand the psychology of the killer, and you understand the case.

Doreen squinted with the effort of recollection. "I didn't actually see him, as such," she acknowledged. "But I heard 'im. I hollered 'housekeeping' like you ast me to do all the time, and I opened the door with the master key and he," here Doreen lapsed inexplicably into quasi police-ese, "confirmed his presence."

"How did he confirm his presence?" Quill asked in a prosecutorial way. Her brain was racing with detectival possibilities. Forget forensics (which they weren't equipped to do anyway). Forget alibis, which almost always had holes in them. The *mind* of the killer was the key. Look at Hannibal Lecter.

"Hollered 'get out of here'."

Quill blinked. "I beg your pardon?"

"You ast me what Holcomb hollered. He hollered—"

"Right. Could it have been anybody?"

"Anybody? It was Harry Holcomb!"

"How did you know, if you didn't actually see him?"

"I heard 'em, didn't I? And he was in the room he was supposed to be in. The Provencal suite. Number—"

Meg interrupted. "But it could have been someone else, couldn't it? Someone pretending to be Harry Holcomb?"

"Who in tarnation would want to pretend to be Harry Holcomb?"

"Charlene," Quill said absently. She was thinking furiously. "Charlene, of course. And it might not have been on purpose. She is—was—a smoker. Her voice was low. Harry's is rather high-pitched. And she'd been drinking heavily that night—"

"Drank heavy all the time," Doreen said. "Bottle of vodka a day, far as I could tell."

There were no secrets from housekeeping staff, Quill thought ruefully, not for the first time. All guests beware. "It's amazing, isn't it? But if she'd sort of semi-wakened from a sound sleep, Doreen, you might have mistaken her for Harry. Don't you think?"

"Maybe."

"I thought Nate told you she went out that night, Quill," Meg said.

"He did. But he thought it was about eight o'clock or so. What if Harry woke up? Found she was gone. Went out to find her. Brought her back, put her to bed, then went out and killed O'Haggerty?"

"That's a lot of what if's," Meg said dubiously. "There's no evidence."

"Not direct evidence, no." Quill got up and again began to walk around the room. "Listen, guys. I've stumbled onto something. And with all due modesty—it's brilliant."

"You want to solve this murder based on incisive psychological insights into Harry Holcomb," Meg said in a bored tone.

It was Quill's turn to be astonished. "How did you know that?"

"Oh, just a wild guess." Meg jumped up and went to the bookcase that divided the ktichen from the living room. "This copy of the *DSMS*. It's new." She flipped the cover and checked the copyright page. "At least it's current. And these copies of *Psychology Today* on top of all your art magazines. And—"

"What's the *DSMS*?" Doreen asked.

"It's a listing of all the psychiatric pathologies accepted by the American Psychiatric Association." Meg flipped through the volume, stopped, read for a moment, and said "Ugh."

"Here! Lemme see that." Doreen advanced on the book. Quill grabbed it out of Meg's hands and put it on top of her refrigerator. She put her hands on her hips. "Criminal profiling is accepted by every police department in the United States. Meg! Stay out of my bookcase. What are you looking for now?"

"Thought you might be hiding your Ph.D. in clinical psychiatry," Meg said. "Nope. That's not it. Nope, that's not it, either. Whoa. What's this? This month's copy of *Cosmopolitan*. Hmm. How to please your . . ."

"All right. Enough!" Quill grabbed the offending magazine and threw it into the kitchen sink. "One of the guests left it lying around."

"Right." Meg stamped to the couch and sat down. Quill flopped next to her, scowling.

"You two through?" Doreen asked. "You know," she added, diffidently, "might be better to talk about this in the morning. Give yourself time to get over it, Quill. Sleep on it, like. You had a bit of a shock."

"Yes. It was a shock." Quill clenched her fists. "I just wish we could do something. I hate not being able to do something."

"Yuh," Doreen said. Then after a moment, "Plus there's that reward."

"Forget the reward," Meg said. "Let's approach this logically. What can we do that the police can't do? Because that's it, isn't it? The police have all these rules and regulations about gathering evidence—"

"Based on civil liberties," Quill added dryly.

"Civil liberties," Meg agreed, "Yes. But criminals are, well, criminals. What about Charlene's civil liberties?"

"I'm following you so far," Quill said.

"And we aren't the police, right? We don't have a duty to protect Harry Holcomb's civil liberties because we aren't supposed to be detectives!"

The logic of this was a bit convoluted, but Quill nodded agreement anyway. "So?"

"So if we're going to solve this we have to apply logic. You're right, Quill, the Tompkins County Sheriff's Department can do the forensics, so that's out. And they have profilers and other experts and we don't. What they can't do is surmise."

"Sur-what?" Doreen asked. "You mean guess, like? Like we were doin' before you two went all hissy."

"We weren't guessing," Quill protested.

"Yes, we were," Meg said. "But we were making educated guesses. And the other thing we can do is think outside the box. Because we are not," Meg said triumphantly, "cluttered up with tons of facts."

"That's for sure," Doreen agreed. "So where are we at, now?"

"We are 'at' being pretty sure that Harry Holcomb committed these murders," Quill said. "Let's take the first one. The death of Banion O'Haggerty." She held up one finger. "One. Harry Holcomb had motive: his wife was flirting with her ex-husband right in front of his nose."

"Charlene was married to Banion?" Meg said. "Hm. I didn't know that."

"It was a short marriage, she said."

"All Banion's marriages were short," Meg said wryly. "He was impulsive. He even asked me to marry him, and I only slept with him once."

Quill ignored this. She held up a second finger. "Two. Harry had opportunity. As a matter of fact, he may have created the opportunity. Who knows how long he's been planning this murder?"

"What do you mean?" Meg asked.

"Think about it. From the beginning, he insisted on Banion as the person to judge this contest."

"He what?" Meg's face reddened. Quill, in pursuit of this theory, didn't really notice.

"Yes. He made a big deal, at first, of choosing Hemlock

Falls for the Fry Away Home contest this year. Every year in the past, the Fry Away Home contest has been where— San Francisco, New Orleans, Atlanta—places where a high-profile chef—several high-profile chefs—have been right at hand. But here—"

"Is that so?" Meg said in a dangerous way.

"Here, he made a big deal about importing out of town talent. Now, admittedly, he let Elmer ask you first, Meg, but I'll bet you five dollars that if you'd accepted, he would have found some reason to get Banion here and not you. Not famous enough, or whatever."

"You bet that, do you?"

"I'm sure of it," Quill mused. "He dismissed the whole idea of you as judge out of hand, Meggie. And he only backed off when it became obvious—"

"Don't you throw that wineglass at your sister, missy!" Doreen shouted.

Meg, startled, drew her hand back just in time. "Can't get red wine out of this carpet," Doreen grumbled. "You two just stop!"

Quill clapped her hand over her mouth and withdrew it, slowly. "I am really really sorry, Meg. All I meant was that Holcomb was so intent on getting Banion here that he ignored you as the best possible choice. Don't you agree that it's highly suspicious?"

"Yes," Meg said shortly. "I do."

Quill breathed a sigh of relief. "Well, then. As far as opportunity on the night of Banion's murder. It's highly possible that you disturbed Charlene, Doreen. And that would give Harry a motive for the second murder, too. Charlene could have broken his alibi."

"And three?" Meg said. "We have motive, opportunity. What about the means?"

"Holcomb was a Special Forces soldier," Quill said.

Meg's eyes widened. "No kidding."

"Good old Charlie let that drop today."

"Special Forces?" Doreen asked. "You mean the Green Berets, like?"

"All those Arnold Schwarzenegger movies you drag me to," Meg said. "They've finally paid off. Special Forces soldiers, Doreen, are trained to kill with the garrote."

"That so?" Clearly, Doreen was impressed. "So you tell the sheriff this?"

"Not yet," Quill said. She looked at her watch. "Myles didn't say what time he'd be in, but it's only nine-thirty. I'll tell him, though." She settled back, took a long drink of wine, and said suddenly, "I don't buy it."

"You mean he didn't do it?" Meg shrieked. "You just spent five minutes convincing us he did!"

"It doesn't fit . . ." Quill hesitated, "psychologically."

"Oh, Quill!" Meg tossed a pillow at her. Quill ducked and said, "I'm serious. Think about it. Holcomb's a successful businessman. CEO of the largest chicken franchise in North America. He built the business himself. That takes a lot of planning, a lot of brains. If a man like that is going to commit murder, it's going to be a foolproof one."

"This one is," Doreen said.

"How can it be? A six-year-old could have figured out that he did it."

"How ya gonna prove it?" Doreen asked. "You want to talk psychological? How's this for psychological. Guy's so smart he commits a murder where everyone knows he done it, *but they can't prove it.*"

"That would fit," Quill said after a stunned moment. "By God, that would fit. He's arrogant. Power mad. Vindictive."

"And Charlene?" Meg said. "What do we know about Charlene's murder?"

"Harry borrowed the van to go out to the chicken grower this morning after he had the fight with Brewster and Devlin," Quill said slowly. "It's a good forty-minute drive there and back. That's easily checked. Mike keeps a mileage record for the billing. And of course, the chicken guy himself—"

"Maloney," Meg said impatiently. "I keep telling you! But we don't know what time Charlene was killed, do we?"

"The body was warm," Quill said reluctantly. "So rigor had either passed off, which means she'd been dead at least twelve hours, or she'd been killed very recently. I don't know which."

"Sure you do," Doreen said bluntly. "You've seen dead bodies before. She look new dead or long dead?"

Quill tugged on her hair. Doreen was right. Blood settled to the ground side of a corpse very quickly. The eyes sank in the sockets. The skin had a distinctive, blue-white pallor. And if Charlene had been in the fryer for longer than half an hour, there would have been a slight odor of decay. Quill was very sensitive to smells. "It was recent," she said. "I mean, we'll have to pump Kathleen, because Myles told me in no uncertain terms to stay out of this case, but I'd guess she hadn't been dead long. As a matter of fact, I'd bet on it. She looked too . . . lifelike."

"There you are then," Meg said.

"Do you think he really could have been that cold-blooded?" Quill wondered. "He was as cool as you please talking to Marge and to me just before the body was discovered. And he had to have been quick. So quick. The place was crawling with people."

"Trucks were backed up against the big woods, weren't they?" Meg asked. "It's possible, I guess."

"It's scary, is what it is," Quill said. "But it fits him. Yes, it fits him."

Doreen yawned. "Where does that leave us, then? I gotta go soon. Stoke's waiting. Jeepers. It's after ten."

"We have to find some evidence." Quill picked restlessly at her skirt. "There has to be something."

"No there don't," Doreen said. "Guy could get away with it. Lots of 'em do."

"Lots of them do," Quill agreed tiredly. "I'm going to sleep on it."

There was a tap at her front door. It opened. Myles stood

there, looking as tired as she felt, and she went to greet him with a kiss.

Their meeting was over.

Quill went down to breakfast early in a depressed frame of mind. There was a lot to do today. She had, for courtesy's sake, to stop in and speak to Judith. She had collapsed at the sight of Charlene's body, like a tree toppling, Quill had thought at the time, and Andy Bishop had given her a tranquilizer. Meg had sent dinner up to the Kluckenpacker's suite.

Myles had been restless all night, and by five o'clock he was up and out. He'd answered her most pressing question: Charlene had been killed about an hour before her body was discovered, perhaps two. The fryer was vacuum-sealed, which made a closer approximation of the time difficult. But with a kiss he'd brushed off her inquiries into where the trucks had been parked before they'd arrived at the Inn.

When he left at five-thirty, Quill found herself at loose ends. The kitchen opened at six. Meg usually arrived at six-thirty to supervise setup. At the moment, everyone was asleep. (Could Judith sleep? Could Charlie?) She could take Max out for a walk, if she could find him. Ever since John had put in the dog door in the kitchen, Max pretty much roamed when and where he wanted.

But dawn was breaking, and if they walked in the hemlock grove, perhaps she could find something, anything, that would help bring Harry Holcomb to justice.

She took Max's leash and started downstairs.

Harry Holcomb stood in the foyer, his back to her. He was on his cell phone. He turned at the light sound of her step, said, *"Danke schön"* into the phone, and clicked it off. "Good morning."

"Good morning." Quill searched his face. There was a slight darkening of the skin under his eyes. His hair was brushed flat. He had shaved. His clothes looked as if they had just come from the press. "You're up early," she began, and bit down on her lip, hard. She was not going to babble. She was going to be cool, calm, and collected.

"Yes. I had to make a call to Germany. The reception in the rooms is pretty spotty, so I came down here."

Was that accusation in his voice? Quill bridled. The man's wife was dead, and he was complaining about cell phone reception? "The Inn's very old. Most of the walls are the original plaster, not sheetrock, and the roof is copper. I imagine that makes the difference in reception. Sorry."

"I'd like some coffee, please. I'll be working in the conference room this morning."

"The kitchen doesn't . . ." Quill stopped. Have coffee with a murderer? Why not. If she could find Max, she'd take him with her. Max wasn't much as a guard dog, but he was so ugly people assumed that he was fierce.

"We're set up for coffee in the Lounge." She pointed down the hall. "That way. Past the conference room."

"I'm aware of the way to the Lounge. After you."

Was that mockery in his voice? *You* mean that lounge? The lounge where I found my wife two nights ago? Where I tried to beat up her lover? And will you be afraid if I walk behind you? Quill shook her head to clear it. She walked ahead of Holcomb at a deliberately casual pace.

The Lounge was dark and smelled faintly of the floor polish Nate used to clean up at night. A faint triangle of gray light came in from the doors to the terrace. Quill snapped the switches up, and the tin chandeliers glowed. She crossed to the bar, pulled the coffee tray from under the counter, and began to grind the beans.

Holcomb settled at the bar stool across from her. "Quite a production."

"I like good coffee." She switched the kettle on and tapped the filter into the funnel.

"What do you think about putting a Starbucks in the franchise?"

"Me?" Quill said, startled.

"Nobody settles for BUN anymore. Or so the marketing people tell me."

Quill made a face. "It's fast, that's true."

"You don't like Starbucks, either?"

"I like coffee," Quill said. "They add flavoring to it."

"Charlene lived on Starbucks."

"And she died on what?" The words were out before she realized it. The kettle was just under the boil. Quill switched it off and poured the water slowly into the cone. She could throw the kettle at him if he came across the bar top. There wasn't anything specific in the innkeeping rules about throwing hot kettles at the guests.

"I wish I knew." Holcomb's eyes were on his hands. Quill couldn't see the expression on his face. She set a coffee cup in front of him.

"That cop, McHale?"

"Yes," Quill said.

"The boys did some checking. He's got quite a reputation."

"The boys? Oh. You mean Skip and his evil twin Jeffy."

The smile on Holcomb's face was savage. "Hey. They were the best guns for hire around."

"They were?"

"Bastards quit on me. Yesterday." He looked up at her. "But they'd done the research on McHale first. McHale's as straight as they come. And he's good. Nobody less likely to cripple a case, from what they tell me. There's also more to your Marge Schmidt than meets the eye. She had me going, there. Thought the town would string me up by the thumbs."

"Marge is terrific," Quill said. "Tell me, Mr. Holcomb. What was Charlene really like?"

"Really like?" He shifted uneasily on the bar stool. "What kind of question is that? What business is it of yours?"

Quill thought about a response that would satisfy him. That Charlene was vulnerable, and lost, and a victim of her own beauty—that truth might not mean a thing to him. That Quill wanted her avenged—well, justice had little place in this man's world, made up as it was of profit and loss. "I feel sad," she said. "It doesn't seem fair. And why would anyone want to kill her?"

"Yes, Harry. Why would someone want Charlene dead?" Judith Kluckenpacker threaded her measured way through the tables and walked up to the bar. She stood erect, and when she sat down, her back was straight. She wore a knit dress this morning. Black. And the ever-present strand of pearls. She had light gray eyes, and they stared coldly into Harry Holcomb's face.

"Would you like some coffee, Judith?"

"Tea. If you would."

Quill plugged the kettle in again. There was an awkward silence, broken only by the hissing of the kettle. "I'm so sorry," she said. "I'm so sorry."

"Charlene was lost to us years ago, when she married you."

"Charlene was a drunk," Holcomb said. "Drunks aren't at home to anyone, Judith."

Judith's arm jerked sharply against her side. It was a strange, involuntary gesture. This woman was rigid with grief. "First the modeling career. They're all on drugs, you know. The pressure of that kind of career forces it on them."

"She didn't take drugs," Holcomb said harshly. "She was a drunk. And if she was a drunk, it didn't start with me."

"She drank after she married you," Judith insisted, in a flat, even voice. "You want to destroy all of us. Me. Charles. And you've started with Charlene. Am I next? Is Charles? She didn't care about her looks anymore. She didn't care about anything anymore. She told me so. First it was the modeling. Then you. Then the liquor." Her arm jerked again. She set her purse on the counter and opened it with a deliberate snap and pulled out a gun.

Quill didn't know much about guns. This one was small,

with an oily sheen to it. It looked like a small and dirty sin.

Judith stood up slowly, as if her back and legs hurt. She leveled the gun at Holcomb's chest and steadied it with both hands. "You killed her," Judith said. "You are going to kill me. And Charles. And now I am going to kill you before you hurt us anymore."

Quill threw the kettle at Judith. Her aim was good. Holcomb rolled off the stool and under the nearest table. The gun went off. A light exploded in the tin chandelier directly overhead. Holcomb sprang. The table went flying. Quill ducked down behind the counter and then forced herself to stand up again. Holcomb had Judith in a choke hold. His left arm was tight against her throat, the right held her wrist in a painful grip.

Judith's expression hadn't changed a bit.

Quill took deep, gasping breaths. In the hall beyond the Lounge, she heard shouts and the thud of running feet. She leaned her head against the counter and fought off dark-red waves of dizziness.

John burst into the lounge and came to a skidding halt. He held both arms wide, away from his sides. "Hold it!" he said. The tremor in his voice was well-controlled. "Just hold it. Everyone just calm down. Quill? Get down behind the counter. *Get down!*"

"It's okay, it's okay, it's okay." Quill bit her lip hard to stop from babbling. She tasted blood. "He's got her. It's all right. It's okay."

Holcomb shook Judith's wrist and the gun dropped to the floor. John moved so quickly that he had the gun in his hand before Quill had time to blink. He smacked the butt end and removed the cartridge. Then he said flatly, "What happened?"

Holcomb released Judith slowly, reluctantly, as if leaving a lover he would never see again.

"Not a thing, Raintree. Not a goddam thing."

CHAPTER 11

"If she had plugged 'im, it woulda saved us a lot of trouble."

"Do-*reen!*" Meg shook her head in exasperation. She gave the brioche dough a couple of hard smacks and expertly twisted it into an elegant mound. The kitchen staff worked quietly, for once. Perhaps too quietly. Meg gave them a glower, yelled *"Stop listening in!"* and lowered her voice. "That's vigilante justice you're suggesting. The worst kind."

"Wasn't that what we was talking about last night?"

"Not exactly." Quill finished her second croissant and started on a third. She was ravenous. "We were talking about working outside the constraints of the police process but within civilian law."

Meg rolled her eyes. "Phuut! If you hadn't just escaped death by a hairsbreadth, I'd sock you one." Then she began to sing (to the tune of "Tradition"—a fine tune, which didn't deserve it) "Pre-*tention!* Pre-*tent*-ion. La la la la."

"Oh, shut up," Quill said amiably. It was very good to see her sister back to her old obstreperous self.

"I don't need to shut up, do I?" Meg said heartlessly. "It's my kitchen." She cleaned dough off her engagement ring with a fair degree of concentration.

"Heat's off Andy," Doreen said shrewdly. "Gotta be, with that second murder and all."

"Andy was in the operating room all morning yesterday,"

Meg said. "With about a million witnesses plus the patient. So yes, he's in the clear. And Myles said he could go to the cardiology convention next week and present his paper. I just may go with him." She darted a glance at Quill. "If this is all settled, that is."

"Holcomb's not pressing charges," Quill said.

"Yeah. You told us." Meg cocked her eyebrow. "You have some trouble with that, obviously."

"More than some. I mean, the woman's carrying a gun. In her purse. She threatened him. She might have killed him."

"Sullivan Act," said Doreen, who occasionally surprised them with odd bits and pieces of knowledge. "Can't carry a concealed weapon in New York." She picked up the other half of Quill's croissant and stuffed it in her mouth. "You can in Texas, though. She a Texan?"

"I don't know. And it doesn't matter." Quill put the last of her croissant down. She wasn't hungry anymore. "I have to tell Myles. Now, why do I feel like a prissy little kid because I have to tell Myles?"

"Maybe because you're acting like one. Let it go, Quill. Holcomb's offered to replace the chandelier. He's not dead. He doesn't want to make a big deal about it. Leave Judith alone with her grief. Quill? Are you listening to me?"

"Yes."

Doreen leaned over and peered in her face. "Maybe she's got that what dy'a call it. Post-traumatic stress syndrome. You keep playin' that scene over and over in your head?" She grabbed Meg's eight-inch sauté pan and smacked it against the birch work top. "Noise like that make you jump?"

"Of course a noise like that makes me jump. It'd make anybody jump. I'm not suffering from anything but worry. There's something about that whole scene with Judith that bothers me."

"No kidding? Because you might have been shot yourself?" Meg bit her lip and shuddered. "Honestly. I could have lost my only sister. Bleah."

"She wasn't aiming at me. I'm upset, sure. But I wish I could put my finger on it. Something doesn't fit."

"What should bother you is that we're no closer to finding evidence to convict that Holcomb," Doreen said. "I say we horse something up."

"Horse some . . . you mean plant fake evidence?" Quill said. "Are you crazy?"

"Well, what else we gonna do? That durn festival is tomorrow. Holcomb'll be leaving the day after, if he's not arrested first."

"I need to talk to Elmer," Quill said suddenly. "He's been working with Holcomb and with Charlie for months. There has to be some weird connection between all of this."

"*That* goofball." Doreen made a small, precise spitting motion. "If he thinks he's gonna get reelected next time around, he's goofier than I think he is."

Quill rubbed her forehead hard, in the hope it would stimulate blood flow to the relevant parts of her brain. "The relationship between the four of them—the five of them, if you count Banion—just doesn't make sense to me. They all hate each other, right? But they seem to have this fatal attraction. They manage to show up in the same place at the same time *all* the time." She nodded wisely. "You know what it is, it's pathological. I told Dr. Benziger all about it and he agrees. And maybe that's all it is—the pathology of a sick, dysfunctional fam—"

Meg grabbed the sauté pan and threw it at the refrigerator. Quill stared at her. Meg stared sweetly back. "If you don't drop the psycho-babble right this minute, I am going to tie you to the rocking chair and sing the complete libretto from *HMS Pinafore* into your ear."

"I'll help ya," Doreen grunted.

Quill found herself getting huffy. "But the motive for these murders is clearly rooted in—"

Meg's face got very red. "It doesn't *matter* how dysfunctional that damn family is. What matters is that *Hol-comb stops knocking them off*!"

"He'll stop knocking them off if we can establish the psy—"

" 'Ne-e-ver *mind* the why and wherefore, love can level rank and there—' " Meg sang.

"Okay," Quill grumbled.

" 'In my set could scarcely pass. Tho' you oc-u-py a *Sta*-tion in the lo-wer mid-dle class!' "

"Help!" Elizabeth Chu said. "Help."

"She will not stop now," Bjarne said glumly. He tore off a bit of paper towel and stuffed both ears. "Although it is a good sign. She has made up with her lover. That song is about happily married people."

"Okay!" Quill threw her hands up. "I give up. I quit."

Meg, caught by melody, reduced her yowl to a hum, which if not as loud, was just as painful to hear.

"Okay," Quill said briskly. "We are going to apply cold logic here. Right?"

"Right," Doreen said. Meg, who'd gotten to the "ring the merry bells on-board-ship, rend the air with warbling wild" part of "Never Mind the Why and Wherefore" ignored them both.

"We haven't seriously considered any other suspect than Holcomb, right?"

"He did it," Doreen said flatly. "We just can't prove it."

"Maybe that's because he didn't do it," Quill said. "Now, Charlie is widely known as a dirty trickster in business, right? A rat among rats. He and Judith were supposed to be at Elmer's for dinner at the time Banion was killed?"

"I dunno, were they?"

"Yes. We went over this last night, Doreen. I checked with Kathleen who checked with Davey. They were there. From seven-thirty on. But were they both there all night? And would Elmer lie for them? I have to talk to Elmer to see if Charlie was there all night. He might have stepped out for a while. He might have gone out for cigarettes or something, leaving Judith to the social niceties. Think about it. Charlie was right in the grove yesterday at the time Charlene must have been killed. And you know what I discovered this morning? Holcomb may not have had time to kill Charlene. I checked the van records after the fracas. There's a time out and time in on the sheet. Holcomb got back fifteen minutes before he met Marge and me at the grove, and Mike's initials are on the sheet."

"Why would Charlie kill his own stepdaughter?"

Quill rubbed her eyes. "Charlene and Charlie hated each other. They had that big scene in the foyer, you remember?"

Meg stopped in mid-hum. "Charlie and Holcomb were socking each other. I'd probably yell at the other guy, too."

"There was a lot more behind it than that. Charlene was very bitter about him when I interviewed her in the Lounge. And the day of Charlene's murder, Charlie was bouncing around the grove all morning. Judith said the truck drivers were complaining about it. And what if . . ." Quill trailed off and subsided into thought. "What if Judith tried to kill Harry to save Charlie?"

"Tinkers to Evers to Chance," Meg said. "I can sort of see it. What I can't see is why Charlie killed Banion."

Quill shook her head. "Maybe we'll never know. I'll tell you this, though. I can see why the police look at motive last. It's facts that will solve this case, ladies. Not speculation."

Meg and Doreen looked at each other. Then they looked at Quill. "You just flat-out contradicted yourself from last night," Meg accused.

"It's just not as simple as I'd hoped, that's all. So I'm going to track down Elmer and talk to him today." She looked at her watch. "It's only eight o'clock. Will he be in his office?"

"Either that or in the hemlock grove fussin' around the tents," Doreen said. "There's a lot of folks checking in today, Quill. You think you ought to go ramming around with them bigwigs showing up?"

"What bigwigs?" Quill asked, nettled. She hated the expression "bigwigs" almost as much as she hated the expression "big boys."

"Two of the six contestants are stayin' here. The writer from *Gourmet* is stayin' here. A whole passel of folks who bought them thousand-dollar tickets'll be here. You don't think there'll be ructions? Especially with that Dina in the state's she's in?"

"What's wrong with Dina?" Quill asked.

"Beats me. But if her lower lip stuck out any further, she'd trip over it. She's been a-cryin and a-cryin all week. Any fool can see that."

"I hadn't noticed," Quill said. She recalled Dina's woeful behavior when Mr. Hauser checked in. "She would have said something to me, wouldn't she?"

"You been pretty busy," Doreen grumbled.

"I'll have to be busy today, too." Quill sighed. "First thing is to talk to Elmer to discover just what's going on, business-wise with the Holcombs and the Kluckenpackers. And Doreen, let's keep this morning's—well, you know, the attempted shooting—to ourselves if we can. Poor Judith has had grief enough for a lifetime."

"Mum's the word."

Kathleen pushed the swinging doors from the dining room open and came in, a stack of orders in her hand. She handed them to Meg, who scanned them and went off to nudge the staff into action.

"Busy out there," Kathleen said. She pushed the hair off her brow and leaned on the prep table.

"Do you need extra help?" Quill asked. "I can call one or two of the backup workers."

"Did it already. We've got a lull, now. The tables are full, and all the orders are in."

Elizabeth handed Kathleen a large tray with juices and

coffee on it. Kathleen wedged it onto one hip. "What are you going to do about Dina?"

"Dina?"

"Called in sick. Didn't Doreen tell you?"

"Me?!" Doreen said. "I din't know she called in sick. But," she added with a satisfied air, "I ain't surprised."

"I left a note on your bulletin board," Kathleen said. "Quill was so busy with the you-know I didn't think she'd want to handle small stuff like that."

"The you-know?" Quill asked, although she was afraid she knew already. "Hang on a minute, Kath." She turned to Doreen. "Could you please give Dina a call and see what's wrong? We really need her today. And if she can't get in—aaagh, I don't know. Who have we on call for backup?

"You," Doreen said. "I'll call 'er and be right back."

Quill turned to Kathleen. "Okay. What's with the you-know?"

"Well, everybody's talking about it! Mr. Holcomb tried to shoot Mrs. Kluckenpacker." Kathleen leaned forward and whispered, "They say you threw yourself right in front of the gun, Quill!"

"Who says? And it was the other way around." Quill corrected herself in midstream. "Never mind." She could solve the disappearance of Amelia Earhart faster than trying to pin down who spilled the beans. It wasn't John, that was certain. Mike the groundskeeper, maybe. He was always up and around early. Or one of the cleaners.

"Gotta go!" Kathleen whirled out the doors before Quill could stop her and ask if Davey knew. Because if Davey knew, Myles would know. And if everyone was talking about it, then she'd have to talk to Myles. Now. Before he got really mad.

"Dina wants to talk to you!" Doreen shouted. She leaned halfway out of her little housekeeping office. It was nothing more than a small cupboard next to the staples room, but Doreen was quite proud of it.

Quill went into the office and picked up the phone. "Hey, Dina."

"Hey, Quill." Her voice was sad and miserable.

"Do you have the flu?" Quill wondered where they could put her if she had the flu. Dina shared a small house with four other graduate students, two dogs, and a collection of birds, courtesy of the budding ornithologist. It was no place for a sick person. Then she wondered when she'd have time to go get her. How did other amateur detectives have *time* to detect?

"Quill?"

"Sorry, Dina. I was thinking about something else."

"You're always thinking about something else," Dina pointed out in a helpful way. Her voice sounded a lot better. "It's really interesting, Quill, the way you kind of float off in the middle of a conversation. A person could be like, totally devastated in front of you and you'd never notice."

"You don't sound like you have the flu."

"Who said I had the flu?"

"Dina! Why aren't you coming in this morning?"

"I don't know. I just feel . . . lousy." Her voice got sadder. "It's David." Her voice thickened. "He's seeing somebody else. I just know it."

Quill counted to five, slowly. "We need you here. If you can come in, please come in."

Doreen leaned over her shoulder and shouted into the phone. "That Judith Kluckenpacker tried to shoot Harry Holcomb. You don't come in now, you're going to miss stuff."

"No kidding? Well, I guess I can make it."

Quill hung up the phone. "Doreen, I thought we'd agreed to keep this quiet."

"It's out already."

"Then I should call Myles. You said I shouldn't call Myles because it was too much like ratting on poor Judith."

"You asked if you'd be rattin' on Judith to tell the sheriff if nobody else knew about it. The answer to that is, yeah, you would. But if he hears about it the regular way, it's different."

"What regular way?"

"Gossip," Doreen said.

Meg appeared at the door. "Myles is here," she said briefly. "He's heard about it. And if you're going to have a fight would you *please* not have it in my kitchen? I like things peaceful."

"You like as much uproar as possible," Quill said as she followed Meg out. "I can't believe . . . Oh! Hi, Myles."

Myles was in his civvies. So was the slight black man with him. "Why don't we go to your office, Quill? Jordan's got a few questions." His gray eyes glinted at her. "And so do I."

At least her office was neat. Someone from the cleaning staff must have set things to rights after her temper tantrum the night before. Jordan Bellemarin and Myles both sat at her small cherry conference table. After a moment's hesitation, Quill sat down, too.

"I'm Sarah Quilliam," she said, extending her hand.

"So I hear." Jordan had an engaging smile. "I've seen your work at MOMA. I must say I'm a fan."

Quill felt herself relax. "Thank you. Do you live in New York City?"

"I do now. After Myles left the force, they needed someone to come in and keep 'em all straight." He gave Myles a friendly punch in the arm. "So I packed up and left New Orleans." He had a soft, Creole accent that Quill found very appealing.

"Would you like some coffee, Jordan? I can give the kitchen a call."

"No, ma'am. Thank you all the same, but I'm all coffeed out."

Quill bit her lip. She glanced at Myles under her eyelashes. He looked grim. Not angry, but grim. "Myles, I'm sorry I didn't call you right away." She turned to Jordan.

"I mean, I assume that you're both here because of what happened this morning."

"That's right, ma'am." Jordan said. The smile had hardened a bit.

"But Holcomb doesn't want to press charges. And I know it may be hard to tell because of her general . . ." Quill struggled to find the right word, "demeanor. She doesn't look like a grieving mother, but I'm sure she is terribly unhappy. I thought we'd just let it blow over."

"A firearm was discharged in a public place. The shooter—sorry—alleged shooter was carrying a concealed weapon. And you just want it to blow over? And the three people involved in this situation are also tied to two murders?" Jordan's smile was completely gone. His face wasn't cold, but it was hard. A cop look. Detached, acute, and tough.

"Three?" Quill faltered. "Oh, you mean me."

"Tell us what happened, Quill." Myles's eyes softened, just a little. "Back off on the editorializing."

"If I do that," Quill said wryly, "there's not a whole lot to tell. I was up early. So was Mr. Holcomb. When I came downstairs he was just wrapping up a call to Germany, he said. He wanted coffee, so I took him into the Tavern Lounge. About fifteen minutes into the conversation, Judith showed up."

Quill described how Judith had accused Holcomb of trying to kill her, too, and then how she pulled the gun and how Holcomb had rolled into a ball and under the table. "It was such a quick reaction," she marveled, "but of course," she looked at Myles out of the corner of her eye, "he was in the Special Forces, you know."

"We know." Jordan had been making an occasional note in a pad he'd taken from his pocket. He flipped back through the pages and read: "Harry Pierce Holcomb, born da da da. Yes. Here it is, Armed Forces Special Force—eight-year hitch."

"They teach those guys how to use a garrote, don't they? Quill said innocently.

Jordan tucked the pad in his pocket, never once taking his eyes from her face. "So I hear."

"Listen," Quill said. "Jordan . . ." She'd been about to say that he seemed like a nice guy, but he didn't. A tough guy, yes. A fair guy, that, too. But nice? "Let me be perfectly frank."

"Please do."

"Isn't Holcomb your prime suspect for these murders?" Jordan looked at her politely.

"It seems obvious to everybody that he had means, motive, and opportunity. Poor Judith. Charlene was her daughter, for heaven's sake. This whole tragedy seems to have driven Judith . . ." Quill paused. "Around the bend" was not really psychologically accurate. "Delusional with grief. She thinks Holcomb is going to kill her next! And there have been two murders, not just one. As if one weren't enough. Charlene was her daughter."

"Adopted as a two-week-old baby." Jordan agreed. "You're saying have a heart?"

"Yes. I am."

Jordan patted her arm. "Cops don't have hearts. We can't afford them. I've some more questions for you."

He took her through her meeting with Harry Holcomb in the grove the day before. He didn't take notes; just listened intently. Then he switched back to that morning. Quill went through it all again. Then he said, "Where's Judith Kluckenpacker now, Ms. Quilliam?"

Quill couldn't keep the dismay from her voice. "Up in her room. I took her up there after the . . . umm . . . incident. She wanted a tranquilizer, so I gave her one. Dr. Bishop had left them, you see, last night. Surely you're not going to question her now?"

Myles shifted in his seat. "We've already tried her room, Quill. She isn't there."

"She isn't?" Quill said, bewildered. "But where could she have gone?"

"We were hoping you could tell us that."

Quill shook her head. "Have you asked her husband? Charlie?"

"When did you last see him?" Jordan's voice was soft, insistent.

"I don't know."

"Hang on." Jordan dug into his sports coat pocket and pulled out a cell phone. Quill hadn't heard it ring. He just said, "Yeah," listened for a short time, then clicked the cell phone off and said to Myles, "They got them. At the Ithaca airport." His expressionless gaze rested on Quill. "Your driver took them there. You give those orders?"

"No," Quill said tightly. "Mike's in charge of the van scheduling, and he probably didn't know anything about this. He lives in town and wouldn't have talked to anyone this morning. Judith and her husband just could have called him and ordered the van. Any of our guests can do that."

She hated talking to the police. She hated it. It was like talking to lawyers. You were forced into defensive positions and betraying people and it was humiliating. She set her jaw. "Can't you just let the poor woman be alone with her grief? She's not responsible right now. These tightly wound personalities are very, very fragile. It's a psychological fact that some very repressed personalities are simply unable to handle major life crises. Like the death of a beloved daughter. And she was afraid for her own life, too. Let's not forget that."

"You in therapy?" Jordan asked.

Myles's lips twitched.

"I suppose you're going to arrest her?" Quill demanded.

"I suppose we have to."

Jordan rose to his feet. Quill noticed for the first time that he had a gun strapped to his chest, underneath the sports coat. He put a friendly hand on her shoulder. "Just to set your mind at ease, Ms. Quilliam, she said she had to make a stockholder's meeting in Detroit City tomorrow. I don't think she was grieving too much."

"As if the man had the slightest idea of what Judith felt!" Quill stormed. After Myles and Jordan left her office, John had come in with the monthly financials, and Quill had let loose. "So you know what they've dragged her in for?"

"Carrying a concealed weapon? Threatening to commit grievous bodily harm?"

"Yes," Quill said. "How did you know that?"

"Seemed like the most likely charges."

"Honestly, John. Holcomb is running around committing murder right and left. But are Jordan and Myles arresting him? No."

"There is the evidence problem," John said. "And you know, if Judith feels her life's in danger, maybe it is. Maybe they pulled her in to protect her?"

"Why would her life be in danger?" Quill pulled her time line out of the top drawer. "She and Charlie were at dinner with Elmer and Adela the night Banion was killed. So she couldn't have seen anything she wasn't supposed to see. Now she and Charlie were in the hemlock grove the morning of Charlene's murder. And if she'd seen anything suspicious, you can bet your stock portfolio she would have said something by now." Quill stopped and stared into the distance.

"Quill?" John rapped her desk top. "You there?"

"She said she had to make a stockholder's meeting. She was trying to get a flight to Detroit." She looked at John. "Cui bono."

"If you mean, 'who benefits,' I totally agree. The motive behind many a murder."

"She said that Holcomb was trying to take them over. John, how can we get copies of Holcomb's Wholesome annual report? And the Captain Cluck's Crispy Chicken annual report?"

"Current copies? Charlie might have one. Maybe Holcomb does too. Why?"

"Charlene said Banion started out working for Charlie. Back when the business began. And she and Banion were married. And then she and Holcomb were married."

"Stock?" John said. "By god, Quill. You might be right. A number of these privately held businesses give stock to relatives and key employees. You think Holcomb might be trying to get control of the company by killing off shareholders?"

"Don't you?"

"It's a theory. But you know enough not to—"

"Theorize in front of the facts." Quill finished the quote for him. "How do we find out who owns stock in a company?"

"They're both publicly traded," John said. "But it can be really difficult. If we can get a copy of the annual reports, we can at least start to try. We need the name of the transfer agent, and that's always listed on the back page." He smiled a little at her blank expression. "There's only five or six transfer agents. Each of them has a detailed record of who owns stock. Once we have that . . . well, it gets a little tricky. They aren't keen on public exposure, those guys. But if we're lucky . . . well, we'll see."

"I know who might tell us. Skip and his evil twin Jeffy. Let's ask Dina where they are. She usually knows everything about where the guests are. Even the ones who've left the Inn. It's spooky, really."

Quill and John came through her office door and into the foyer at almost the same time. Dina looked at them dolefully.

"You're here," Quill said.

Dina nodded. Her eyes were pink behind her big round glasses.

"Thank you for coming in."

"It's okay. We're going to get really busy in about an hour. Mike's bringing back a bunch of guests from the airport, and the train from New York gets in at ten. So I'm just sitting here, thinking. Quill, why are men such *jerks!*"

"John's not a jerk," Quill said, "and Myles isn't either and I don't have *time* for this now. Do you know where Mr. Brewster and Mr. Devlin are?"

"Nope. Wait. Maybe. I think they went down to the courthouse to see if they could get an injunction for Captain Cluck. I mean Charlie. They're trying to see if they can stop Mr. Holcomb from having his contest."

"They what!?" In all the years that John had worked with her, Quill had never seen him so taken aback. "Brewster and Devlin have taken on Charlie Kluckenpacker as a client?"

"Yeah. I guess they quit and opened up their own business."

Quill sighed. "How do you know these things, Dina?"

"Well, I know about the injunction because Lillian Saxon works at the courthouse on Wednesday and Thursday and we were just chatting on the phone a while ago—"

"Don't ask," Quill said. "I think Lillian's the ornithologist roommate. You look disturbed, John."

"I'm not disturbed, exactly." He shook his head a little. "If those two don't get disbarred for this, I'll be disturbed. No wonder Hauser came racing down here yesterday. Well, well."

"Maybe they know for sure what we're guessing. That Holcomb committed both those murders. Dina, what about Holcomb? Do you know where he is?"

"Oh. Him. Myles and that really cute black guy had him taken in for questioning, like minutes after what happened this morning."

They could have told me that! Quill thought. "You weren't even here," Quill said aloud. "How do you know that?"

"Well, maybe not minutes. But David said he came and picked Mr. Holcomb up right after Kathleen called him and told him what happened." Dina nibbled at a pencil. The mention of David seemed to make her weepy. She sniffed. Then her face brightened. "Did you really throw yourself in front of Mr. Holcomb to save his miserable life?"

"Of course not," Quill said. She turned to John. "Wouldn't *somebody* be trying to get Holcomb out of jail? If Brewster and Devlin are now working for the other side, who's helping him? Howie?"

"Mr. Hauser's doing that, or he will when he gets back. He went off to Ithaca early this morning," Dina said. "I have a phone message here from him for Mr. Holcomb." She looked at Quill and John over the rims of her glasses. "Do you think I should let David know? I mean, I could call him, and he can get word to Mr. Holcomb. The man should know if his own attorney isn't going to show up to bail him out for another couple of hours—"

"For all of me," Quill said tightly. "You can lose that message for a couple of days, Dina. The man doesn't deserve to be bailed out."

"But I should call David, right?"

"Yes. You can call David."

"And I'll like, make it clear that I'm not calling to find out why he broke our date Monday night. It'll be strictly business."

"He broke your date because he was on duty Monday night," Quill said. "Remember? He reported finding Banion's body."

Dina's eyes filled with tears. "He didn't go on duty until nine o'clock! We had a date for six, for dinner at the Fork in the Road. He never showed up!"

"Oh, Dina!" Torn between exasperation and affection, Quill grabbed a handful of tissue from the box on the reception desk and rather clumsily patted her receptionist's face dry. "There. Now call David. And give me the keys to 308 and 314."

John said, "Quill," in a warning way.

"I don't care. This is one of those times when we have

to suspend the civil liberties of criminals. And besides, it's our Inn."

"You're going to break into Holcomb's room? And Judith's too?" Dina said.

"We're not breaking in, Dina, we're . . . um . . . conducting a citizen's search. And if you tell David, I'll personally break your neck."

"I am *not* speaking to that jerk," Dina said. "Except on official business." She handed over the keys. John followed Quill up the stairs.

The Holcombs had booked the Provencal suite, which was one of Quill's favorite rooms. There was a lovely stone mantel on the fireplace, and the French doors led to a balcony that jutted out over the waterfall. The drapes and the upholstery were a heavy damask in peacock blue and yellow.

The cleaning staff hadn't been in Holcomb's room yet. The bed wasn't made, and there were damp towels in the bathroom, but his clothes were hung neatly in the large armoire. A large green plastic garbage bag was stuffed in the back. Quill pulled it out and opened it up.

Charlene's clothes and cosmetics were stuffed all in a jumble. Quill dumped the contents on the floor and went through them quickly. Small scraps of lace underwear. The bronze evening gown, crumpled in a sad heap. Cosmetics of every kind. Quill wanted to fold them carefully and put them back. But it would be obvious she'd been snooping.

The bed looked as if someone had been fighting with the sheets. Quill went over to the nightstand and picked two of the pillows off the floor. A balled up handkerchief lay beneath them. Quill picked it up. It was soaking wet.

Tear soaked?

She shoved aside her pity and put the pillow back on the bed.

"Here it is," John said. He stood at the French Provincial desk, a four-color magazine in his hand. He turned it over and said softly, "We're in luck."

"We are?"

"Delaware Transfer. The transfer agent."

"And that's lucky?"

"Maybe."

"John. That's his briefcase." Quill brushed past him. "Don't make that face at me, John Raintree. The police have probably already been through it."

"I doubt it," John said dryly. "But go ahead."

Quill covered her finger with the edge of her skirt and tried to snap it open. "It's locked."

"They usually are."

"Can we . . . ?"

"Open it? Without being discovered?" John bent forward and examined it. "It's a combination tumbler. The kind where you have to know the numbers."

Quill scratched her nose. "What about using a credit card?"

"That works on hotel doors, Quill. With very old locks."

"A penknife?"

John shook his head. "This is a good briefcase, Quill. You'd have to bomb it. And then all the evidence would be destroyed anyway."

"Very funny."

"Hey, we have the transfer agent. It's a start."

"I *hate* leaving a perfectly good piece of evidence out like this."

"You can steal it," John said. "Do you want to steal it?"

"Of course not," Quill said.

John let his breath out. "Good. I wouldn't want to have to turn you in. Okay, let's roll."

The Kluckenpackers had the Shaker suite—Judith's choice, Quill guessed. The simple lines of the furniture were warm, yet austere. The bed linens were ecru, the drapes a heavy cream. Handwoven rugs in soft colors covered the plank floors.

This bed hadn't been made, either, but the covers had been pulled up, and the pillows were neatly plumped. The room was bare of clothes and personal items, and the suit-cases of course, were gone. Quill imagined Judith moving like an automaton through her packing, her mind on her dead daughter.

John set the wastebasket by the desk down with a thump. "No luck here. They must have taken everything with them. But you could stop by the library and see if Miriam has some kind of access to annual reports. She may be able to go online and check for you."

"What about the mayor?"

"Elmer?" John grinned. He almost never grinned. "A faster, better idea. If you can keep from punching him, Quill."

"I'll try. He's probably got three file drawers thick with Captain Cluck background material. Although," Quill added crossly, "Adela must have to read it to him."

"I wouldn't be too hard on him," John said kindly. "Good luck."

"You're not coming with me?"

"We've got a business to run, Quill. And it's a busy day."

"Oh, lord," Quill said ruefully. "I should be helping you."

"I think this is helping all of us. The sooner this case is solved, the better. The reporters are already swarming over the hemlock grove."

"With Holcomb hauled in for questioning, they can't possibly run the contest now, can they?"

John gave his faint, ironic grin. "I checked this morning. Elmer's in charge."

"Oh, dear!"

"Listen. If you can get that information on Captain Cluck from Elmer, take it and go straight to Marge."

"Marge?"

"Absolutely. She's the only person I know with the right kind of muscle to get that stock information from those guys."

"Do you think she'll help us?"

"You know, I think she might."

CHAPTER 12

Quill drove the Honda past the activity in the hemlock grove and braked hard. The mayor's bright-red Escalade was parked next to the gazebo entrance. The morning was beginning well. She pulled in behind it and parked. For some reason, she'd expected that the grove would be teeming with people. A fair number of cars were parked along the edge of the driveway, but the only person in sight was a young kid in a gray guard uniform standing under the shelter provided by the gazebo.

Quill hadn't paid too much attention to the weather in her rush to find Elmer; she realized now that it was raining and cold. She was dressed in jeans and a light sweater. There was no umbrella in the car, and her raincoat was back at the Inn. She opened the driver's door and shivered at the rush of damp air.

The guard wedged a clipboard under his arm, opened a black umbrella, and came up to her.

He touched his hat. "Can I help you, miss?" A badge clipped to his shirt pocket read "Global Security," and below a four-color photo of him, the name "Allan Sherman" was lettered in red. "I'm afraid that this area's closed to visitors at the moment."

"Mr. Sherman?" Quill said brightly. "I'm Sarah Quilliam. I'm here to see the mayor on—um—village business."

"Miss Quilliam?" He frowned and consulted the clipboard. "Sorry, miss. Mr. Henry gave me a list of people to watch out for—the press, mostly. You're on it. I'm afraid I'm going to have to ask you to leave."

"Oh," Quill said. She considered her options. Option one was to grab the guard's umbrella, whack him over the head with it, storm the tent, grab Elmer by what hair was left on his balding head, and shake him until he turned blue.

"Miss? I said I'm afraid . . ."

Option two was to retreat.

A Quilliam never retreated.

Option three was to bluff, and to heck with the consequences.

"Allan Sherman, isn't it?" She gave him The Smile. Quill and Meg had developed and perfected The Smile after years of practice.

"Yes, miss. But I don't think I've—"

"Oh, the two of us haven't met. Myles has mentioned you, though. Allan Sherman, isn't it?"

"Yes, miss. Mr. McHale? Mentioned me? You know Mr. McHale?"

Quill lowered her eyelashes in a becomingly shy manner. "Oh, yes," she said softly.

"The guys at Global . . . we think a lot of Mr. McHale. And he's talked about me?"

"He doesn't talk about his work much, you understand," Quill said. "Not the, you know, high security parts. But he is keeping his eye out for good men. You know. For the team."

There *was* a team, apparently. Allan squared his shoulders and blushed.

"Actually, I fibbed a little about village business. Myles thinks he may have left his good leather jacket in the press tent. I thought I'd just sneak in and get it for him."

"Oh! You want to wait right here Miss—"

"Call me Quill."

"If you want to wait right here I'll just go in and find it for you. Do you know where he might have left it?"

"I should probably check for it myself." She peered around him and squinted at the press tent. "There seem to be quite a few people in there, and I wouldn't want you to grab the wrong jacket. Myles always says one of the important things for a guard is to keep a low profile. If they don't notice you, you can keep your eye on them."

"He does?"

Quill bit down on her lip. Meg maintained she couldn't quit while she was ahead. Maybe Meg was right.

"Well, I suppose. But don't take too long, okay? They're having some kind of meeting in there. Here, you can duck under my umbrella."

Quill accepted the offer with a smile and stepped out of the Honda with studied grace, which would have worked beautifully except that she stepped into a puddle. She sloshed over to the small tent with a big PRESS sign stuck to the outside. She left Allan Sherman at the entrance with another, larger smile, and stepped into the tent.

"Here! Who let you in?" Elmer bolted to his feet in alarm.

Four or five people were seated at a folding conference table. There was Elmer, of course. With him were Harvey Bozzel (president and sole employee of Bozzel Advertising), two men with hard hats in their laps, and Charlie Kluckenpacker. Quill was familiar with the long rolls of paper littering the table top: architectural plans. She was even more familiar with the company logo at the top of each sheet: Roebuck & White. Surveyors.

"It's Miss Quill," Charlie said with a genial curl of his lip. His chinos were wrinkled and stained with mud. Damp patched his striped dress shirt. He'd been tramping around outside, Quill noted. She narrowed her eyes at him suspiciously. "Hello, Charlie. I didn't expect to see you here."

"I didn't expect to be here. Thought the old ball and chain and I'd be on our way to Detroit now. But no. Thanks to that tall boyfriend of yours, Judith's locked up in the Tompkins County clink."

"Now, Charlie," Elmer said hastily. "I'm sure the sheriff is going to let her out just as soon as this little misunderstanding is cleared up."

"You know how these small town sheriffs are," Harvey said. "Just a hick misunderstanding." He quailed under Quill's fierce glare. "The sheriff, of course has his reasons, I'm sure."

"You have *your* reasons, Quill?" Charlie asked with false geniality. "Come to take a gander at the Chicken Hut plans, maybe? Here." He grabbed her shoulder. His grip was stronger than it needed to be. "Come and take a look."

Quill shook herself free. She was suddenly absolutely furious. "I need a word with the mayor. Then you gentlemen can go back to work. Elmer?"

"I don't know, Quill. I'm a pretty important part of this meeting. Maybe I can talk to you later, hah? Down to the Inn."

"She's come to ream you out, pally!" Charlie shouted. "Might as well step outside and take it like a man. Go on Elmer, beat it. As for you boys, let's get to it. Time's money."

"Out here, Elmer," Quill said grimly. She stepped outside. The rain was coming down harder now, but she was so mad she didn't care. Elmer followed her out like a whipped dog. He began blustering as soon as the tent flap closed behind them and they were out of sight.

"Now look here, Quill. You got every right to be mad at me. Every right. But I can explain everything. This land's just been sittin' up here, see? And Adela's been on me about expenses. And I had to come up with that money to pay Mr. O'Haggerty." He came to a full stop. "I don't get it," he said in a sad little voice. "How come everybody can make money but me?"

"Oh, Elmer." Quill's anger ebbed like water down a pipe. "You *were* going to pay Banion yourself. I thought you told the Chamber the village had the money in the discretionary fund."

"It was my fault," Elmer said. "I did it. It was on'y fair that I paid for it. I don't know why I get folks mad at me, Quill, but I do. But I sure pis—I mean annoyed the heck out of that chef. I was going to announce twenty-five gees as a gift, see, at one of the press conferences. Then I thought maybe I could get elected again. I thought I was fixed good for sure when Mr. Kluckenpacker came along and made an offer on that piece I got by Route 15. But then he found out about this one. It comes from Adela's side of the family, see, and he put the screws to me really hard."

The rain dripped off Quill's hair and onto her nose. She dabbed at it with the back of her sleeve. Then she said gently, "Elmer, does it really matter so much? Money, that is? You? Why you're the mayor of Hemlock Falls! That's an important position. You don't have to be rich, too. The chief thing is, you have to accept yourself. You have to like yourself. That's what's important."

"I heard you been seein' that shrink down to Andy's clinic," Elmer said irritably. "For goodness' sake, Quill." He heaved a deep sigh. "Oh, well. I got a packet for this land, so it's not all bad. So, there it is. I'm sorry you're gonna have this chicken hut right to the side of your pretty Inn. But we can put up a hedge." He squinted up at the sky and seemed to notice it was raining. "If that's all, I guess I better get back inside. Although it don't seem right somehow, using this tent of Harry's for Charlie's business."

"It isn't right," Quill said. "It's not illegal, but it isn't right. It's . . ." Quill searched for the right simile, but all she could think of was how dogs marked their territory to keep other dogs away, and how they would do it over and over again. "Men," she concluded. "It's just . . . men."

"I'm glad you're not mad at me, Quill," Elmer said humbly.

"Who says I'm not mad at you? I'm furious! You've got to learn to stand up for yourself, Elmer. You can't let these—these—" She tried to think of a word bad enough to describe the greed and carelessness of the Charlie Kluck-enpackers of this world, but couldn't. "Men! You can't let men like this trample all over your dignity. Now look. I want something from you and I want it right this minute. Do you hear me? No excuses. No questions. Just go back in there and get it. If you have it, that is."

"If I have what? What is it you want?!"

Quill noticed that the whites of Elmer's eyes showed when he was alarmed. His expression would make an interesting charcoal sketch, if she ever got back to her painting. "This year's annual report for Captain Cluck's Crispy Chicken. That's what I want."

"The . . . what the heck? Sure I got it. It's in my briefcase."

"No questions." Quill held her hand out. "Get it."

Elmer got it.

Quill flipped it over and checked the back. There it was. Delaware Trust, Trust Agents. Good. It would make Marge's job easier.

"That it?" Elmer asked hopefully. "You want anything more?"

"No. That's it. And Elmer?"

"Huh?"

"Just . . . oh, never mind. But think about this. Who are your real friends?" Guys punched each other in a friendly way to express fond emotion. Quill had noticed that a lot lately. She gave Elmer a friendly punch in the arm.

"Ow!" Elmer said. "Guess I deserved that. See you around." He disappeared inside.

Quill sloshed back to the Honda. Allan Sherman stepped out from the shelter of the gazebo, umbrella at the ready. "Did you find it?"

"Yes," Quill said.

"Do you have it?" He scanned her anxiously.

"Oh! The jacket. No, it wasn't there. Myles must have left it somewhere else."

"Sorry about that. I'll keep an eye out."

"Thanks for your help, Allan."

"So, you've known Mr. McHale for a while? Did you know him when he was in New York? We hear stuff about him all the time. Is he on to these murders they been having here?"

"I'm sorry, Allan. I've got an important errand to run. I'll be back for the contest tomorrow, though. Maybe we can talk then."

"Sure. If there's anything else I can do to help him just let me know. Hey, you want a towel? You're pretty wet."

Quill's hair was a soggy mass at the back of her neck. Her feet were freezing from her wet shoes. And her jeans felt as if they weighed a hundred pounds. She couldn't slosh into Marge's diner like this; Marge would throw her out.

"I'll go dry off at the Inn, Allan. Thanks, though."

She turned the Honda around and drove the short distance back to the circular drive at the Inn's front door. The van was there; Mike was unloading suitcases from the airport run. There'd be a ton of people in the lobby and she looked like a drowned rat. Quill backed up and bumped across the lawn to the vegetable gardens. Meg hated it when she parked in the brussels sprouts, but it was the least obtrusive way to get inside.

She parked and squished up to the kitchen door wishing, not for the first time, that she had a little fireman's ladder attached to her balcony, which was immediately overhead. Max met her, as wet and muddy as she was.

"There you are."

Max panted happily. He'd been down at the Gorge; last year's leaves were stuck to his coat. "I hope you've had a better day than I have."

Max barked.

"I take it that's a yes."

Max stuck his head in the dog door flap and wriggled inside, tail wagging furiously. Quill opened the door and followed him in.

The kitchen was in its between-meal lull. Meg sat at the prep table absorbed in a sheaf of papers. Doreen was scrubbing the sink.

"Hey," Meg said absently.

"Hey," Quill returned. "Doreen? Why are you scrubbing the sink?"

"She says we have to fire Richie Peterson. Either that or Doreen's going to teach him to clean herself. I'll give him the option." She looked up. "Have you been napping under the waterfall?"

"It's raining out."

"I guess so." Meg looked down at Max, who was nosing around her feet. "You're a damp, damp dog," she scolded. "Go away."

"He's fine," Quill protested. "Just don't let him in the dining room."

"I didn't mean him. I meant you. Go change."

"I *have* changed. My mind, that is. About these murders."

Meg looked up. "You learn something?"

"Maybe. I hope to learn more today, after I see Marge."

"So, did you find evidence to put that sum-a-bitch away for a good twenty years?" Doreen draped her damp dish towel over the faucet and sat down next to Meg.

"It depends on which sum-a-bitch we're talking about." Quill settled cautiously on a prep stool. "Right now, it's even money between Charlie and Holcomb. We don't have any *proof* that it's either one. The sheriff's office doesn't have any *proof*. But the *proof* is out there."

"Thank you, Muldar," Meg said,

"I'm Scully. My hair's red, so I'm Scully. Listen to me, guys."

Quill summarized her discussion with John, and described the meeting going on in the press tent. "The thing is, I'm pretty sure that Charlie has been searching those grounds, too. Just like Carol Ann was. I don't think he knows she's found it."

"You said he was meeting with the surveyors," Meg protested. "It's only natural that they all would have been out stomping around the grounds."

"Charlie," Quill said, "was the only one who was wet. Why would he be out walking around in the rain alone?"

"It's thin," Meg said after a moment. "Very thin."

Quill tapped her forefinger insistently on the table top. "All of the evidence here is thin. We have guesses. We have surmises. We have a murderer who's ruthless, competitive, and smart. Psychologically speaking—"

"Don't go there," Meg said. "I'm telling you."

"This is just common sense. Forget therapy. There's a clue in that field. Carol Ann found it. Now, we've taken a few wrong turns in this case—"

"A few!" Meg snorted. "It's more than a few!"

"But we were right about one thing. There is something that we can do, that we *should* do that the sheriff's office can't."

"Oh, *no*!" Meg groaned. "I'd hoped you'd forgotten all about that!"

"About what?" Doreen asked. "What is it?"

Quill told her about Carol Ann and the mysterious piece of evidence.

"You're goin' to break into Carol Ann Spinoza's house and find out what she took from that-there field?" Doreen chewed this over very slowly.

"Either that or steal her purse," Quill said. "It might be easier to steal her purse."

"Huh," Doreen said. Then, "Huh-huh-huh."

"I think she's laughing," Meg said anxiously.

"It'd be a lot easier to steal her purse, now that I think about it. And Doreen, we need your help."

"Nope."

"Nope? What do you mean, nope?"

"That woman's as mean as a pit bull with a skin rash. And she's got the memory of a elephant. A raging bull elephant. You want to mix it up with Carol Ann, you get somebody else."

"Okay," Quill said: "I will."

"You want to what?" Marge Schmidt folded her arms under her considerable bosom and leaned over her lunch counter.

"She comes in here for lunch, doesn't she?" Quill asked.

"Everybody comes in here for lunch." Marge sucked her teeth. "You know why?"

"Why?"

"Cause the food you serve up *there* is too fancy for regular folk."

"You are absolutely right, Marge," Quill said meekly.

Marge cocked her head to one side. "You must really want that Carol Ann's purse. You didn't turn a hair."

"Oh I did, I did," Quill reassured her. "I'm nettled, Marge, if that's what you're after. I'm just keeping it in. So, does she come in here for lunch everyday?"

"Carol Ann comes in at twelve-fifteen on the dot. She's got some exercise class she goes to ends at noon."

"So I could be seated next to her. Or maybe I could be seated somewhere else and get up and go to the ladies room and pass by her table. I could just sort of bump into her and trip or something."

"You need a diversion," Marge said. "Leave that to me. But you better go through that purse pretty dam' fast."

"I know what I'm looking for," Quill said with assurance.

"Hm. You want something else, too?"

"Yes. So it's two big favors, actually."

Marge sighed deeply. Quill could tell she was pleased. "You better come on back to the office, then. Be more private. We don't want every Tom, Dick, and Harry buttin' in our business." She gave poor Betty Hall a severe look.

"Beef stew today, for the special, Quill," she said. "Can I bring you some?"

Quill glanced around. The diner was about half full,

mostly with the local farmers, so it was about eleven-thirty or so. People who got up to milk cows at four o'clock in the morning wanted lunch early, too. "As a matter of fact, *I* got up early and I haven't had breakfast. I'd love some of the stew. When Marge and I are finished with this business we have."

She followed Marge back to the small cubicle where she did her business. It always amazed Quill that Marge's empire was run from offices like this one. She had a desk reclaimed from some bankruptcy sale, a lot of file cabinets, and a phone. That, and a patched linoleum floor, seemed to be all that she required to be worth millions.

"Elmer's been in here, hasn't he?" she asked as she sat down.

"Mor'n once," Marge agreed. "So what?"

"Nothing. Well, actually, Marge, I don't think any of this would have happened if Elmer hadn't been desperate to be like the big boys."

Marge considered this awhile. "You don't mean he killed O'Haggerty and that. You mean if he hadn't been so all-fired anxious to make himself important with this Fry Away Home thing, none of it would've happened here."

"Perhaps. What if he'd just put the phone down the minute Charlie Kluckenpacker started nosing around? What if he'd just said no? Turned away from all the glamour he seems to think the big boys possess?"

"Lotta what-ifs," Marge said. "But if Holcomb is behind the killing, like we all think he is, he just would have killed them somewhere else."

"Maybe. Anyway, John said to tell you he thought you had the muscle to find out who the stockholders are in both Holcomb's Wholesome and Captain Cluck."

"Need the trust agent's name to do that."

"Delaware Trust."

"Hm." Marge popped a piece of gum in her mouth and chewed it vigorously. She caught Quill's glance and blushed. "Tryin' to lose a little weight, is all. Keep my mouth busy with this, I don't eat."

Harland Peterson hadn't been one of the early lunchers. As far as Quill knew, he'd eaten lunch at Marge's diner everyday since his wife had died four years before. "You know what Marge?" Quill said warmly. "You don't need to lose an ounce. Not an ounce. The thing is to accept yourself as you are. Which is wonderful."

Marge snapped her gum. "I'm gonna buy you a T-shirt, kiddo. One that says "I DIGRESS." You can wear that one Tuesday, Thursday, and Saturday. Then I'm going to buy you another that says "I'M IN THERAPY. DON'T ASK." You can wear *that* one Mondays, Wednesdays, and Fridays. When you go see that shrink."

"Very funny," Quill grumbled. "Does the whole *town* know when I go to see that guy?"

"Sure. Everybody sees you trot down from Peterson Park with that damn dog Monday, Wednesday, and Friday and trot back up after an hour. Doesn't take a detective to figure that one out. Getting back to the point here, what is it you're detecting now?"

"I want to know how much of Holcomb's is owned by Captain Cluck. Or vice versa."

"It's tough to get that kind of info out of the Delaware boys. I'll have to call in a few favors." Marge flexed her arms. "We'll see. Now, about the other thing. Why'n the heck do you want to steal Carol Ann Spinoza's purse?"

"I'll put it back," Quill said nervously. "She . . . um . . . took something from the Inn. I think. I just want to check, that's all."

"You're a bad liar, Quill."

Quill knew when to keep quiet. She kept quiet.

"Okay," Marge said. "I'll give you a hand. When d'ya want to do it?"

"If I don't do it right now, I'll chicken out."

"Well she's not tax assessor anymore, so you're safe

there. You plannin' on doin' any more remodeling at the Inn?"

"Who knows? But I have to take the chance."

"It's your funeral."

"Well, if it is," Quill said, "*don't* send my body to Freddie Bellini. That jerk was in on the zoning scam, too."

"We got one advantage," Marge whispered loudly when they went back into the restaurant proper. "She's such a pinhead, she sits at the same table all the time. That one, in the corner. So I'll put you next to her, okay? But I'm gonna have to fix it so it's the only place open when you come in, got it? Otherwise it'll look funny. Here!" she roared. "You, Petey! Get outa there! Sit at the counter why doncha." She threw Quill a glance over her shoulder. "Come back about quarter after twelve. Betty'll keep that stew warm for you."

Quill had about thirty minutes to kill, and it was still raining. She'd showered and changed into a creamy turtleneck and a long russet skirt and her second-best boots. She'd also brought her umbrella and a raincoat. It would take about ten minutes to walk all the way to the beginning of Hemlock Drive, if she didn't walk too fast. From there, she could see up the hill to the Inn.

The rain kept people indoors, so the sidewalk was free of anything but puddles. She passed Esther's dress shop, and Adela's gift shop and the Croh Bar, where Meg and Howie had sung their way through Sondheim. She came to the intersection of Main and Hemlock Drive and turned to look up the hill.

There it sat, looking so romantic that Quill wanted to cry. A silvery mist curled around the mellow stone. The copper roof was dawn-lit with damp. And the green of the trees and the rolling lawn was gently brushed with rain so light it might have been gauze.

Quill mentally constructed a yellow hut shaped like a squatting hen with a neon beak on the roof, and put it smack down in the middle of the hemlock grove.

Ugh. Damn that Charlie Kluckenpacker anyway.

Well, if she'd needed courage to take her first step into actively criminal behavior, she had it now. The vital clue was in Carol Ann's purse. She would untangle the intricacies of the fried chicken business and put Harry Holcomb in jail. She might have a neon chicken beak in her backyard, but she'd achieve success as a detective.

She spun on her heel and marched back to Marge's.

The diner was crowded, and seemed even smaller than it was because umbrellas and raincoats were everywhere. Quill walked in to a chorus of sympathetic greetings. "*I* think it's just awful, that Captain Cluck's going up next to your beautiful Inn," Esther West said indignantly. She sat with Miriam Doncaster. Miriam nodded agreement. "My petition to revoke the order has twenty-two signatures on it. I grab everyone who comes into the library."

"Thanks, guys," Quill said.

Miriam widened her big blue eyes. "Are you here for lunch? Here, sit down. We can make room. Scooch over a bit, Esther."

"She's scooching into me," Nadine the hairdresser said from the next table. "Sit here, Quill, with me."

"Room for ya over here," Marge shouted. "Don't sit there, dammit. It's a fire hazard. Innit, Denny?"

Denny, his mouth full of beef stew, turned on his stool at the lunch counter and nodded uncertainly. Davey Kiddermeister, in uniform, was sitting next to him. Quill swallowed. Maybe this was a really dumb idea. On the other hand, the place was so crowded and so noisy, it should be really easy to quietly snatch Carol Ann's purse.

"Here you go, Quill." Marge gave a chair filled with one of the larger Petersons a hefty shove, and opened a path to a table.

It was a small, postage stamp-sized table. Despite the crowded room, there was a little space around the equally small table next to it. Carol Ann Spinoza sat there, eating an egg salad sandwich.

"Marge!" Nadine Nickerson (Nickerson's Hardware and Farm Implements) spoke in a shocked whisper. "You can't put Quill *there*."

A silence fell over the restaurant. Quill almost patted her hips to see if her six shooters were in place. Instead, she draped her raincoat over the pile hanging precariously from a hook on the wall. Clutching her umbrella, she edged her way toward Marge and Carol Ann.

"Whaddya want to eat?" Marge demanded as Quill settled into her seat. She sat sideways, facing the wall. Carol Ann was at her left. She stared straight ahead toward the lunch counter.

She was a slow chewer.

"Quill? You want to eat?"

"Yes. Um. The special, please."

Marge leaned over her and hissed, *"When the stew comes!"* She rolled off, and Quill was alone with Carol Ann in an oasis of quiet.

"Hi," Quill said. "Wet out today."

Carol Ann lowered her bright blue gaze, looked directly at Quill, and smiled complacently. "You didn't order the chicken?"

"Nope."

Carol Ann's grin widened. There was no egg salad stuck between her teeth. It wasn't fair. "I suppose," she said sweetly, "that you'll be able to get fried chicken any time you want pretty soon. Just walk out your backdoor." She walked her fingers over the table top. "Just like that."

Quill leaned forward a little. "Gosh, Carol Ann? Is that the start of a nail fungus?"

She examined her nails with a frown. Quill took the opportunity to put her umbrella under her table. Yes! There was Carol Ann's neat black purse. Neatly placed on the chair at her side. Exactly in the center of the seat.

"One beef stew coming up!" Marge bellowed, and

promptly dumped the bowl upside down on the table. Quill ducked, reached for the purse, and felt a small, stew-covered hand grip her wrist.

"Gotcha!" Carol Ann said.

CHAPTER 13

"I've been in jail before, you know," Quill said reassuringly. "I don't want you to think I've been traumatized or anything."

Dr. Benziger crossed his left knee over his right leg and used one forefinger to push his glasses up his nose. So she had definitely startled him. Distressed him, too.

"That might be a good topic to discuss this session," Dr. Benziger said. "I wasn't aware that you had spent time in jail before Ms. Spinoza had you arrested for stealing her purse."

"I didn't do anything, that time." Quill said. "I'd been accused, falsely, of running a red light."

"They put you in jail for running a red light in Hemlock Falls?"

Now she'd done all three of the things she'd been worried about in therapy because he was definitely discomposed. And she'd just started the session, too.

"Well, they don't do it to everybody of course."

"I'm glad to hear that. We'll discuss why you feel singled-out for these things in a moment. But let's get back to why you felt the need to steal Ms. Spinoza's purse."

This was the same question Myles had asked. In a much more exasperated tone, of course. And he'd confiscated the evidence, as well. Really, if her therapist was going to ask her the same kind of questions that the police did, she preferred the police. The police didn't bill her at one hundred and fifty dollars per hour.

"Quill?"

"Because I thought there might be a clue in a Baggie. To Charlene and Banion's murders."

"And was there?"

Oh. Now that was mockery, or something very close to it.

"I don't know."

"You feel a strong need to continue this investigation, don't you?"

"Harry Holcomb has to be stopped."

"I'm curious. You seem to have fixated on Holcomb. Do you have evidence?"

"He's the only suspect who has a clear, unambiguous reason to want both Banion and Charlene dead," Quill said flatly. "Even his own lawyers don't want anything to do with him anymore."

"Oh?"

"Yes. They quit his account, can you believe it? There must have been huge fees involved, too. That's pretty significant, isn't it? When his own lawyers are fed up with him?"

"I suppose it is. But that isn't evidence, Quill. I am concerned about this concentration on Holcomb. I am concerned that you seem compelled to pursue this case."

"I am." Quill made herself calm. She'd had a hectic afternoon yesterday. And after Howie Murchison had released her on her own recognizance, she'd had quite a testy exchange with Myles. So she hadn't slept well. And because she had this appointment, she hadn't had time to call Marge to see if she'd managed to shake any stockholder information out of Delaware Trust. She sat up in the leather chair and folded her hands in her lap. "Somebody took a length of wire, added two handles to it, and wrapped it around Banion O'Haggerty's neck. And then the murderer jerked it. One powerful jerk. And everything that made

Banion who he was ran out of him and disappeared. Gone.
Like that. Then the murderer did it again. To Charlene.
Who had the bones of a kitten. And everything that made
Charlene who she was disappeared." She was looking in-
ward, now, talking more to herself than to Dr. Benziger. "I
paint to capture that force. That vitality. That whatever it
is that transforms cold flesh into life. That something that
drives the world. And this guy stamps it out. Who is he to
stamp it out? Who is he to steal it? People like me paint,
and sculpt, and write to save it, even if it's in a small way.

"I don't understand any more than that about why I need
to see him caught. Just that it makes me angry. Just that
it's not fair. And I can't just sit. I have to do something
about it."

"You believe in justice."

"I do. Of course. Don't you?"

Well, she'd funked it there. It wasn't appropriate for a
therapist to respond with a personal opinion.

But he said, "We have a philosophical difference of opinion, Quill. Personal justice is my job. Which is fine. So yes,
I believe in justice. But of quite a different kind than
yours."

She looked up at him. "Hey. I live in a small town. I run
a very nice inn. I love my sister and Myles in the profound-
est possible way. I like what I do. I like who I'm with. I
can't sit on my hands when someone else tries to destroy it."

Dr. Benziger took his glasses off and tucked them into
his pocket.

"Well, Quill. Well. I think we've achieved our letter of
agreement."

"We have? You mean that I've listened with an honest
heart and changed in a way that's good for me?"

"I don't know that you've changed, Quill. I do know that
the confusion has cleared up. And that you see, more
clearly than you may know at this moment, what it is you
want to do with your life. I don't think you need to see me
anymore."

"I don't?"

"No."

Quill wondered if she felt disappointed. She wasn't sure. Regretful, perhaps. She would miss talking to Dr. Benziger.

He smiled a little. "It's been—"

"Interesting?" Quill said. "You weren't bored?"

"Not at all. Thank you, Quill." He uncrossed his legs and put both feet on the floor. "Our time together is up."

"So that's it?" Meg said. "You're cured?"

"I guess so." Quill looked doubtfully at her breakfast. She'd come back to the Inn at ten, and she and Meg had decided to have a huge breakfast at the best table in the dining room.

The sky was a clear blue, the rain a memory, and the falls ran sparkling in the sunlight. Quill took her fork and looked at her plate again. It was the good china, with the exquisite painting of the rose-breasted grosbeak. "What are we having here?"

"Bacon and eggs."

"Just bacon? Just eggs?"

"Fried to a crisp and sunny-side up."

"It's delicious. A nice change from Eggs a la Quilliam and Eggs Florentine."

"I thought so."

Quill dunked her toast in the eggs. It was Meg's sourdough toast, and it was fabulous. "So, I've graduated from therapy, I guess."

"You can go back to see him anytime, can't you?"

"Oh! Sure! He said all the usual stuff. Anytime I'm feeling depressed, or confused, just give his office a call. I was a very rewarding patient, et cetera, et cetera."

"I think you're miffed," Meg said shrewdly.

"Miffed?" Quill drew her brows together.

"Miffed like you were when you discovered you really didn't have a dread disease. Miffed that you didn't have a more interesting psychiatric condition. Quill, it would be a terrible burden on you if you had an interesting psychiatric condition. I'm so glad you don't."

"Hey!" Doreen slammed the swinging doors to the kitchen open and marched through. "Dina's looking for you. Where you bin?"

"Right here," Quill said. "And before I was right here, I was at Dr. Benziger's, which," she added with a slight edge to her voice, "everybody in town should know since it's Friday. And that includes Dina."

"You know what they say down to the diner." Doreen dropped into the extra chair at the table and poked her head forward. "That you were found not guilty of stealing Carol Ann Spinoza's purse by reason of mental defect."

"I'll just bet that 'they' is Carol Ann herself," Meg said. "And Quill hasn't got a mental defect anymore. It's official. She's graduated. No more visits to the psychiatrist."

"Huh," Doreen said. "So he's got some extra appointment time, probably. Thing is, we were all thinking maybe Elmer might drop in to chat with him. Poor guy's in a awful state."

"Is he?" Quill asked. "Has something happened? I saw him yesterday and he was," she stopped to think, "a little subdued. But no more than that."

"He's more than that this morning," Doreen said. "He's snatching his hair out, and he ain't got that much to lose. Nobody's seen hide nor hair of Holcomb, and that contest starts at one o'clock sharp. Got all the press here. Those six deep-fat frying experts are here. Elmer's fit to be tied."

"Holcomb's got to be somewhere," Quill said. "Myles had him brought in for questioning, but he came back here in the afternoon. Spent most of it with Hauser having a huge argument. It was about Skip and his evil twin Jeffy, of course! Brewster and Devlin are around. I saw them this morning, and they were headed back to the conference room. I'll bet Holcomb's there, too, and they're all yelling at each other. Why don't you tell Elmer where to find them?"

"Maybe you could go down and tell him," Doreen suggested. "I got a lot of stuff to git done this morning. The Inn's full."

"All right." Quill sighed. "But first let me see if I can find Holcomb. It's his job to take care of the Fry Away Home contest, after all." She folded her napkin and got up from the table. "Okay. I'm off. First to the conference room and then to see Marge."

"I'm right here," Marge grumbled. She stumped through the archway. Dina was right behind her.

"There you are, Quill," Dina said. "Didn't Doreen tell you I was looking for you?"

"You've found me," Quill said cheerfully. "Hi, Marge! I was just going to give you a call."

"Woulda saved me a trip up here." Marge sat down next to Meg and exhaled loudly. "Betty's all excited. She's been breading chicken all morning. I shouldn't have left her."

"It's not *my* fault," Dina said. "I tried to give Quill the message. But that's not the only thing—"

"Can't it wait a bit, Dina?" Quill said. She really wanted to hear what Marge had to say.

"Not really."

"Ten minutes," Quill promised. "Just give me ten minutes."

"All right. Fine!" She spun on her heel and walked out.

"Oh, dear." Quill moved forward to follow her. Marge grasped her arm. "Siddown a second, kiddo."

"But she's been upset lately. I've been neglecting her."

"Man trouble," Doreen said. "Usual at that age."

"It's very *important* at that age." Quill tugged at her hair. "Dina's twenty-two but in many ways, she still is an adolescent. And the most recent studies on the neurology of the brain—"

Somebody went "Phuut!" It might have been Meg. Somebody else groaned. She glared at Marge.

Marge grinned. "Trouble with you, Quill, you think everything has to be done right this minute or the world'll fall in. It's like what you might call fix-it fixation or whatever."

"It's EBD," Meg suggested. "Excessive Bossiness Disorder."

"Nah," Doreen said. "It's a mother complex. You're not responsible for how Dina feels. *Dina's* responsible for how Dina feels."

Quill narrowed her eyes at all three of them. She was right. Marge was chuckling. Doreen was smirking. Meg whistled in a meaningful way—but so tunelessly she couldn't tell what the message was, except that the intent was to aggravate her. "Stop," Quill ordered. "Stop right there. You see this? This is me, taking the pledge. I solemnly swear not to dispense psychiatric advice without a license ever again."

"Do you promise not to *get* a psychiatric license?" Meg asked sweetly. "You're running out of hotel management courses to take at Cornell. And if I'm not mistaken, I saw a Cornell catalogue for the School of Clinical Psychiatry in the mail."

"Gawd help us," Doreen cackled.

"He'd better, because I won't," Quill said in an extremely dignified way. "It's all very funny, I'm sure."

Marge rapped her knuckles on the table. "Come on, ladies. I got work to do."

"You started it," Quill said.

"Yeah, well, I couldn't pass up an opening like that, could I? Here, I shook something interesting out of the trees for you." She dug into the pocket of her bowling jacket and took out a scrap of paper. She dug a pair of drugstore reading glasses out of the other pocket and fitted them carefully over her nose. "Got hold of a buddy of mine at Delaware Trust. Been a lot of activity at Captain Cluck's this week. First, Banion O'Haggerty owned 13 percent of Charlie's company. Got it when he signed on with the company when Charlie was no mor'n two franchises in Ann Arbor. The boy made a considerable amount," Marge mused.

"Considerable. Anyhow, one of the conditions of his termination was that the stock be left to his wife, Charlene Kluckenpacker O'Haggerty. Some funny business there. Seems that the company was growin' big time, and if Banion had forced Charlie to cash him out, Charlie woulda had a bad case of the cash shorts. Now where I get a little flummoxed is with the how-come of this deal." She peered over her glasses at Quill. "Maybe we need some of that psychological insight here. Anyhow, I ast my pal at Delaware why Banion just didn't force Charlie to cough up the cash, and he said he was pretty crazy about his wife and didn't have the financial sense of a wet puppy. I mean to say, she ups and leaves the poor slob for Harry about a year after Banion quits, and she musta got an agreement that she be Banion's legatee as part of the divorce." Marge shook her head and heaved a deep sigh. "Durn fools. Big chunks of stock outa the control of the rightful owners.

"Anyhow, here's where it gets interesting."

"I was hoping it was going to get interesting," Meg muttered.

"Charlene owned 13 percent of Captain Cluck's Crispy Chicken, right? Well she also owned 30 percent of Holcomb's Wholesome. All by her ownself. Now *that's* enough to swing control."

"So Harry owns a part of Charlie's business now?"

"A good part," Marge said.

"But it's not enough to control the company, is it?" Quill asked. She knew, in a vague way, that with very large corporations, a relatively small amount of stock in one individual's hands could wield enormous power.

"Nah. Judith and Charlie own 51 percent. But the important thing is, Harry has control of his company now. You flew right by that one, Quill, and it's the most important part. He sold off to investors early on, see. He kept 60 percent, but like a fool he gives 30 percent to his little wifie."

"I think it's sweet," Meg said.

"It is very bad business," Marge said. "No fool like a guy led around by his pecker."

"So Harry has two strong motives to kill," Quill said. "He was jealous of his wife and her attraction to her ex-husband. And his business would have been gone like that," she snapped her fingers, "if Charlene left him to run off with Banion again."

"You got it."

"Wow," Meg said. "What do we do now?"

"We find Harry Holcomb," Quill said grimly. "And we ask him what's going on."

"Shouldn't we call the p'lice?" Doreen said.

"What good will it do to call the police? We don't have any more evidence than we've had before. But I want him to know that we know. If he knows that we know, he could slip up, couldn't he? And if he's innocent, why should he care that we know all this stock stuff?"

"We've certainly invaded his privacy," Meg said. "That's not nice."

"It's not nice," Quill agreed. "But there's a lot about solving a murder case that's not nice. You think we should back off because we won't look nice? Two people are dead, Meg."

"Well," Meg looked worried, "this guy may be a trained killer."

"What if he's a trained killer who's going to get away with it?" Quill asked. "And if he isn't the murderer, all he can do is be really pissed off that we know things about his stock situation that we shouldn't."

"I knew there was a reason why I stayed outa this de-tectin' business," Doreen muttered. "We're pokin' our noses in with a guy who could kill us all."

"Gotta agree with you there," Marge said. "Wouldn't like it myself. Maybe you should butt out, Quill."

"I can't." Quill had been striding up and down the dining room. She came to a halt. "I keep thinking of Anne Bol-eyn."

"Anne Boleyn?" Meg said. "What in the world do you mean?"

"Her last words to the executioner, when she was on the scaffold. That it should be easy for him, because she had such a little neck."

Quill blinked away tears. "Charlene had such a little neck."

Nobody said anything. Then Meg stood up. "He's in the conference room, right?"

"He should be. He booked it for every morning between eight and ten for the length of his stay. Are you going with me to talk to him?"

"Sure. If he's the killer, he might have time to kill one of us, but not both. I nominate you for the corpse. I'll run for help. After I judge this stupid contest, of course. So bleed slowly, okay?"

"Ha ha." Quill took a deep breath. Her stomach felt fluttery. "We can always end on a positive note. Tell him that Elmer needs him in the hemlock grove."

"That's a positive note?"

But there was no need to confront Holcomb after all. When Meg and Quill arrived at the conference room, Harry was slumped over the table.

Strangled with a third garrote.

CHAPTER 14

"I'm telling you, the Bar Association Canon of Ethics forbids us to have any contact at all with that son of a . . . I mean our former client. *We didn't see him this morning! And God knows we didn't kill him!*"

Devlin stood at the head of the conference table. Brewster stood behind him. Both were scowling. Neither looked neat, well-groomed, or professionally competent anymore.

Harry Holcomb's body was gone. It was late in the afternoon. Myles and Jordan sat at the conference table. Hauser stood by the door with his thumbs hitched in his belt. Quill leaned against the wall in the corner as inconspicuously as possible. She didn't want anyone to throw her out.

"The Canon of Ethics wasn't on your mind when you two quit my firm to set up your own shop," Hauser said angrily. "I'm going to have both of you up for censure."

"We haven't done a goddamned thing," Brewster snarled. "We don't represent the bastard anymore."

"And you didn't come down here to start a solo firm with Holcomb as your principal client?" Hauser threw a bitter glance at Myles. "Bastard's worth three million in billings on his liability business alone. You tell me that's not a motive."

"It'd be a motive to keep him alive, wouldn't it?" Devlin sneered.

"Not if I got him to disbar you two," Hauser said. "And I damn well had him convinced, yesterday afternoon. He had no intention of going solo with you two. And you damn well had it out with him, right here, in this room." He jerked his thumb at Quill. "Miss Quilliam can testify to that, if need be. She's a credible witness."

Quill tried to look properly stern and credible.

"You've got it all wrong." Brewster threw himself into a chair. "We didn't want Holcomb. The guy was as crazy as an outhouse rat. We've got another client."

"I don't think we should talk about that right now," Devlin said smoothly. "The point is, gentlemen, that we had no motive at all to kill Holcomb. And if I'm not mistaken, whoever killed Holcomb killed his wife and that chef, O'Haggerty. I'd like to remind you all that we have the best possible alibi for those murders. We weren't here."

"Not for Banion's," Quill said. "But you were here when Charlene was strangled."

Brewster threw her a look of cold dislike.

Jordan Bellemarin tapped a manila folder on the table. "You served in the Gulf War, Brewster. Special Forces. Learned a lot of ways to kill efficiently there."

"So what?"

"Just pointing out that these murders have the hallmarks of a professional."

"We were at the Marriott this morning with Judith and Charlie," Devlin said. "We've told you and told you. They verified it. The manager of the Marriott verified it. For God's sake, what is this? Some kind of police harassment?"

Myles had been sitting with his feet propped on the table. He swung them to the floor and remarked, casually, "I take it this was a meeting with your new clients?"

"Jesus!" Hauser screamed. "That's six million a year in billings!" His face was so red that Quill really worried he was going to fall over from high blood pressure. Then he screamed, "Is that right? You moved from representing Holcomb for five years to his bitterest rival? Not good, Brewster. Not good at all. I'll have you up before the Ethics Committee if it's the last thing I do."

Jordan slapped the table. "That's it. Take it outside, gentlemen."

"It's about bloody time," Devlin snarled. He and Brewster picked up their briefcases.

Hauser smiled like a shark. "I'll follow you out. As a matter of fact, I'm going to be following you two for quite a while. Get used to it."

Quill waited until the sound of their footsteps in the hall had faded. Then she sat down next to Myles.

"Now what?" she asked anxiously

Jordan ran his hands over his head, pounded his fist on the table and yelled, "Crap!"

"What does that mean?" Quill said. "You can't give up!"

Jordan looked at her, then at Myles. "We're fresh out of leads, baby." He pounded his fist on the table again. "Damn! It was Holcomb for sure! It had to be! Means! Motive! Opportunity!"

"Evidence," Myles reminded him dryly.

"We've nailed perps on no evidence before," Jordan said. "There's always evidence. Something always turns up. Holcomb killed his wife and O'Haggerty. I'd stake my reputation on it. But who the hell killed Holcomb?"

"What if you're dealing with two killers?" Quill asked slowly. "What if the second killer copied the first two murders?"

"Yeah? Who? Where's the motive?"

Quill thought of Hauser's powerful hands. His explosive anger.

"We just have Hauser's word for it—that Holcomb had agreed to stay on as his client. But now Holcomb's dead. And Hauser just shouted it out. Holcomb's will leaves the firm as executor. Probating that will has to mean a lot of billings, doesn't it? And Hauser's firm has more than just probate at stake. Harry and Charlene didn't have any children. He left his money and shares to the company. If Hauser's firm serves as corporate counsel—"

"That's big bucks," Jordan said. He smiled at Myles.

"This woman of yours, McHale. She want a job on the force?"

Myles closed his eyes briefly and growled, "Cut me some slack."

Jordan leaned back. "It's a start, anyway. It's a good start. I'm going to dog this one."

"That's it?" Quill said. "You aren't going to arrest anybody?"

"The mills of God grind slowly, but they grind exceedingly small," Jordan said. "Which is to say, you done good, girl, but sometimes you gotta be in it for the long haul. Hey!" He shook her elbow gently. "You look disappointed. Not every case gets wrapped up nice and neat."

"Justice," Quill said. "Charlene deserves justice. Even Holcomb deserves justice."

"There's all kinds of justice, baby. All kinds. Some just take longer than others."

The two men gathered their files and prepared to leave. Myles dropped a kiss on her hair, and said, "As usual, Quill—"

"You'll be late. That's okay. You take as long as it takes." Then, just as he was leaving, she called out, "Myles? It'd be nice to know just one thing about this miserable case. What *did* Carol Ann Spinoza pick up in the hemlock grove, and why was she making such a big secret about it?"

Jordan gave a shout of laughter. Myles gave Quill a look compounded equally of humor and mild distaste.

And he told her.

"You're kidding!" Quill gasped. "Oh no!"

Quill wandered into the foyer in a broody mood. The Inn was quiet, the big oak front door open to the mild spring air. Outside, she could hear faint music and the chattering brook sound of a large crowd.

The Fry Away Home contest. She wondered how Elmer was coping. She wondered if Meg had pitched a fit. The door to her office opened, and Dina came out with a stack of mail in her hand. "There you are!" she exclaimed. "Finally!"

"Hey!" Quill said. "You should be out having fun at the contest."

Dina's cheeks reddened. "I'm waiting for David."

"He'll be awhile, I expect."

"Yeah." Dina's expression sobered. "Another awful day for you, huh?"

"For all of us," Quill agreed. "I'm so glad everything's okay with Davey, I mean David."

"Yeah." Dina stacked the mail in a neat pile on the reception desk. "You know who he was out with that night?"

Quill raised her eyebrows in an interrogative look.

"Carol Ann. They were up in the hemlock grove." Dina waved her arms in emphatic disgust. "Isn't that the most revolting thing you've heard today?"

It was the second most revolting thing Quill had heard today. She had taken a blood oath never to tell Dina the first, which she'd heard just twenty minutes ago.

"Anyway, David confessed all. And I forgave him. That woman is a menace to society. And she went and had you put in jail, too. What a jerk."

Quill bit her lip, hard, and thumbed through the mail to distract herself. The mail was usually bills, which generally had quite a depressing effect on her sense of humor, even though these days they could pay them all.

"I almost forgot. Well, I didn't forget. If you'd come and talked to me this morning like I said you should I could have given it to you sooner."

"Given me what?"

Dina proffered an envelope. "Dr. Benziger's bill. He brought it up himself, wasn't that sweet?"

"I would have paid him," Quill said indignantly. "Did he want a check right away, too?"

"No. He can wait for payment, he said."

Quill tore open the envelope. There was a little yellow

sticky note attached to a letter on heavy bond, which was
headed:

LETTER OF AGREEMENT

The handwriting on the sticky note was bold and clear:

*My dear Quill: Judith Kluckenpacker is waiting for
this. I held it as security until the job was complete.*
                                                    —B.

"My gosh," Dina said. "The bill can't be that bad."

"Do you know what this is?" Quill was dizzy. She sat
down. The floor was comfortingly solid.

"This is a letter from Harry Holcomb. It's to Charlie. It's
dated thirty-five years ago. It promises Charlie all of the
stock in his company. In the event of Harry's death."

CHAPTER 15

The four of them sat in the gazebo in the hemlock grove. A light, gauzy rain was falling. The tents had been taken down and hauled away. The gazebo had been left behind. The hemlock grove was smooth and unspoiled under the silver-gray skies.

And Meg had awarded Betty Hall "Best Fried Chicken in Show." She and Marge were negotiating with Swanson for the sale of the recipe. Brewster and Devlin had sued Elmer to get Charlie Kluckenpacker's money back. Charlie was in the middle of negotiations to sell Captain Cluck's to Kentucky Fried, and Kentucky Fried had no interest in Hemlock Falls.

So the hemlock grove was safe.

It had been a hectic two weeks since Judith Kluckenpacker had been arrested on three counts of conspiracy to commit felony murder.

"Myles? What was the deal with that letter of agreement?" Meg asked.

Myles paused, then said, "Judith's not talking. But Charlie is. When he learned that she'd hired Benziger to get rid of all the stockholders one by one, he told us everything.

"He and Harry met in the army. You already knew that. The recipe for the fried chicken was Harry's; it's what he used to open his restaurant, and as you know, it's a large reason for the chain's success. But Charlie's the one with the business vision. The brains to make it big. So on those long, slow nights they planned a partnership. To cement the bond, they gave each other letters of agreement. Had them drawn up by the JAG officer. When they got back to the states, they realized right away that their friendship wasn't going to survive peacetime. So they went their separate ways. My guess is that Holcomb forgot all about the letter. Put it down to youthful exuberance. Charlie says they both agreed to rip the letters up. I don't know about that. At any rate, Judith got hold of it." Myles thought for a moment. "To tell you the truth, I think Charlie would have been next to go. But she needed him to verify the contract's authenticity."

"So she had three people killed," Quill said.

There was a death sentence attached to those crimes in New York.

Quill unwound her hair and let it fall down her back. Meg and Andy sat comfortably close together on the bench. Myles stood with his arm draped across Quill's shoulders.

"Is there enough evidence to convict Judith?" Meg asked.

Myles removed his arm from Quill's shoulders and put it around her waist. "Jordan had enough to indict. A conviction's more difficult."

"You're worse than a lawyer for equivocation, McHale," Andy said.

"It's hard to tell what a jury's going to do. There's one thing you learn early on in law enforcement. You bring them in and go on to the next one. After we do our job, we let the justice system do theirs."

"I know what I'd do if I were on that jury," Meg said fiercely. "She hired that man to kill her own daughter."

"She denied it all," Myles said. "And the only evidence we have is Charlie's testimony. That, and the note to Quill."

"Phuut!" Meg managed to sound both indignant and disbelieving at the same time.

"Each time Jordan hammered Judith about the death of her daughter, her response was the same. A very cool correction. 'Adopted daughter, Lieutenant. The girl was adopted.' That's not going to sit well with a jury. Nor is the large amount of cash that disappeared from her personal account. At regular intervals. On the Monday, the Wednesday, the Friday of each death. She had the funds transferred through Mark Anthony Jefferson at the Hemlock Savings and Loan. Your Dr. Benziger must have insisted on payment after each murder."

"He's not *my* Dr. Benziger," Quill said in some dudgeon. "He wasn't even a real psychiatrist."

"The real Dr. Benziger's pretty upset," Andy said ruefully. "Can't say as I blame him. It was a pretty neat trick, pulling that off. You know, Myles, I never even thought to question him. He gave me his cell phone number so I could call him anytime, and of course it didn't have any connection to the actual Benziger's office in Rochester. And his rent check cleared the bank, of course."

Meg hugged him. "How were you to know he was a hired assassin?"

"I feel as if I should have known. I should have had him checked out."

"He counted on professional courtesy," Myles said. "It worked. It didn't have to work very long, of course. Just a few weeks."

"But why?!" Meg demanded. "Why such an elaborate game? I mean, he could have checked into that dive motel on 96 like any other respectable hired assassin. He would have been anonymous enough there."

"He liked the game," Myles said flatly.

"He had some elaborate idea of personal justice going on," Quill said. "If we could find him and ask him, I think he'd say that he did what he was hired to do. He sent me the letter of agreement so that I could choose to do what I had to. Don't you see? He doesn't believe in the fundamental good. He doesn't believe in rights that belong to every human being. He believes in himself. He's a terrorist. He's a sociopath. But he's a consistent sociopath."

"You're going to catch him, aren't you, Myles?" Meg asked.

"I hope so," Myles said.

RECIPE

Meg refuses to deep-fry chicken, and Betty Hall sold her winning recipe to a huge conglomerate for a lot of money—and she is sworn to secrecy. So you won't find a recipe for fried chicken here! But Doreen likes this version of deep-fried apples a lot, and she hopes you do, as well.

There are two important points about deep-frying: the composition of the oil that's used, and the temperature. Look for a highly-refined, pale-gold, combination vegetable oil; these oils have a high smoking point and can withstand the necessary minimum 350-degree temperature. If you enjoy deep-frying, it is probably a good idea to invest in a deep-fryer—just make sure that the appliance will reach the proper degree of heat. In a pinch, a cast iron skillet will do.

BATTER:
Pour 12 ounces of beer into one-and-one-half cups of flour. Whisk until smooth. Refrigerate for at least an hour.

FRITTERS:
Peel six to eight tart firm apples such as Granny Smiths. Cut into quarter-inch strips. Mix with batter. Slip fritters a spoonful at a time into oil heated to 350 degrees. Fry until golden brown. Remove, drain, and sprinkle with confectioner's sugar.

DATE DUE

Demco

Claudia Bi
teries. She
editor of t
has writter
adult nove
Claudia
New York
readers, an